SEVENTH DECIMATE

Also by Stephen Donaldson from Gollancz:

THE CHRONICLES OF THOMAS COVENANT THE UNBELIEVER
Lord Foul's Bane
The Illearth War
The Power that Preserves

THE SECOND CHRONICLES OF THOMAS COVENANT
The Wounded Land
The One Tree
White Gold Wielder

THE LAST CHRONICLES OF THOMAS COVENANT
The Runes of the Earth
Fatal Revenant
Against All Things Ending
The Last Dark

Daughter of Regals and Other Tales

Mordant's Need
(*The Mirror of Her Dreams* and *A Man Rides Through*)

THE GAP CYCLE
The Gap into Conflict: The Real Story
The Gap into Vision: Forbidden Knowledge
The Gap into Power: A Dark and Hungry God Arises
The Gap into Madness: Chaos and Order
The Gap into Ruin: This Day All Gods Die

The King's Justice
The Augur's Gambit

SEVENTH DECIMATE

BOOK ONE OF THE GREAT GOD'S WAR

Stephen Donaldson

GOLLANCZ

LONDON

First published in Great Britain in 2017 by Gollancz
an imprint of the Orion Publishing Group Ltd
Carmelite House, 50 Victoria Embankment
London EC4Y 0DZ

An Hachette UK Company

1 3 5 7 9 10 8 6 4 2

ISBN (Cased) 978 1 473 22166 6
ISBN (Export Trade Paperback) 978 1 473 22167 3

Printed and bound by CPI Group (UK) Ltd, Croydon, CR0 4YY

www.stephenrdonaldson.com
www.gollancz.co.uk

CONTENTS

PROLOGUE

Under the paling stars before dawn, Prince Bifalt and the squad in which he served gathered on an escarpment overlooking the valley where the battle would take place. There they settled themselves to wait for their captain's final instructions. A few years ago, they had been uncomfortable around the Prince; but he was a veteran now, one of them. Resting while they could, they sat or squatted some distance from the rest of the Bellegerin cavalry and the pickets of waiting horses. Elgart tossed a stone from hand to hand, apparently studying how it rose and fell. Klamath wiped his palms in the dirt to rub away sweat. Camwish, the squad's horse-master, who fancied himself its entertainer as well, had nothing to say. In the night's chill, the breathing of the clustered men made faint plumes that gathered around their heads like the dimmest of halos.

Whetting his saber, the Prince considered the task ahead of

them. This squad was essential to Belleger's tactics now, and to their homeland's hopes for survival. If they succeeded, they might enable an eventual victory. They would ride with the rest of the King's army, yes, and throw themselves headlong against Amika's forces; but their purpose was their own. They had been chosen for it in secret, trained in secret, equipped in secret: twenty-one men including their captain and the Prince, King Abbator's eldest son. In the battle, they would learn whether they were the last desperation of their people or the first bright promise.

Prince Bifalt intended to be an instrument of promise, if he could. The idea filled him with a fierceness like joy. He had lost too many comrades, too many friends; seen too much misery. Belleger had become a wretched land. His father's grief and pain at what had been done to the realm's people were a burden the Prince carried constantly. He wanted to end it.

It had to end, in victory or extinction. Belleger and Amika had been at war for so long that even their grandfathers had forgotten the two realms might once have been at peace. Now they only met when their forces were strong enough to inflict more slaughter. The men of Belleger called those struggles "hells." No one knew what the Amikans called them.

Below the ramparts along the far side of the valley, the enemy cavalry waited. That army was as ready as Belleger's. No doubt the Amikan sorcerers had chosen their stations above the battlefield, coverts from which they could watch and kill without danger to themselves. Certainly, Belleger's Magisters had done so. But the fighting would not begin until daylight emptied the lowland of dusk and dawn; until the armies and their precious theurgists could see. At present, Prince Bifalt and his comrades had nothing to do except wait for Captain Swalish to return from his last meeting with the King's lead commanders, and for light.

Most of the men remained still, conserving their stamina. Some kept their hands busy. The rest hardly turned their heads: Camwish and Nowel, Elgart and Gret, even Klamath. But the Prince was not surprised to see Flisk squirming with anxiety. Flisk was the youngest soldier among them, new to fighting, untested before his first ride into hell. He had been chosen for his quickness and accuracy, despite his lack of experience. Although his comrades and captain had prepared him as well as they could, he had no real understanding of what it would be like to face gusts of arrows and flurries of blades, howling Amikans and raving sorcery. Prince Bifalt knew this about him. All the veterans knew it. For that reason, they were patient with Flisk's restless questions. They did not snap or sneer when he asked the darkness, "How many battles have you seen?"—a question he had asked before, and had been answered often.

The other men deferred to the Prince for his father's sake. "Two," he replied curtly. He had the scars to prove it.

"Three," said Jeck, one of the men who would ride shoulder to shoulder with the King's son. The other was Gret, who never spoke, even when he was addressed directly.

"Captain Swalish," rasped Elgart, "claims five." He was the squad's cynic, a man who questioned everything despite his obvious alacrity and courage. The stroke of an Amikan sword had scored him from hairline to jaw, but he had killed two more men before his comrades had rallied around him.

———

Flisk's voice cracked as he asked, "Do you doubt him?"

Before Elgart could retort, Bartin pronounced harshly, "Seven. I have come through hell seven times." Then his tone softened. "If I thought a wife would spare me an eighth, I would marry."

This was a jest. Bartin, the oldest of the veterans, was an inveterate misogynist. To say he would not touch a woman to save his life was an understatement. He might not have touched one to save his closest comrades. They suspected that he had been beaten unmercifully by his mother when he was a boy, usually for no reason he knew.

Camwish chuckled dutifully, and a few other men joined him. But their hearts were not in it.

After more squirming, Flisk breathed, "Seven? *Seven* hells? How many have there been?"

Another familiar question. Flisk knew the answer as well as anyone. But to ease him, or perhaps simply to fill the silence, Nowel replied, "My father survived three." The squad's stitcher and bone-setter, Nowel had learned kindness from gushing wounds and crushed limbs. "Not the fourth." His tone suggested a shrug. "The war was old when he was conscripted."

Flisk's silhouette nodded against the pearling sky. After a moment, he ventured, "They say we have fought Amika forever. But they do not say why. What is it *for*?"

"For us?" muttered Elgart. "Survival. For Amika? Who knows?"

Elgart may have been the only man there who wanted to know what the enemy gained in this war. For the rest, it was enough that Amika hungered to destroy Belleger. It was enough for Prince Bifalt. However, he was the King's son. He had more education than his comrades. He had been tutored—and had studied on his own as well. Until now, however, he had kept what he knew to himself. He had bided his time, saving what he had learned for this moment: the hour before Belleger's fate turned toward life or death; toward future victory or final defeat.

"There is a tale," he said as if the subject held only casual interest. "It is preserved in the records of the Fist." The *Fist* was the high citadel of the land's kings. When it was first raised, it was known as *Belleger's Fist*, brandished against the unrelenting heavens, but over generations it became simply the Fist. "It claims there was a time, decades or more before the reign of my grandfather's grandfather, when Belleger and Amika were one realm."

His comrades were little more than outlines under the waning stars, vague shadows of themselves. Still Prince Bifalt felt their attention, their held breath.

"One realm," he repeated. "It must have been a prosperous land, blessed with fertile fields and ripe forests and mines rich in metals. But it changed because the King in those days had two sons, twins. Their names were Fastule and Brigin, and they grew to be mighty men, equal in strength, ambition, and desire for dominance. They were their father's pride, admired everywhere. Yet when they grew to manhood, they discovered they were in opposition. Although they loved each other, and did all things with easy excellence, they could not resolve their one conflict. Which of them should rule when their father passed? Which should stand aside?

"Being stubborn as well as ambitious, when their father did pass they chose the only imaginable course to keep peace between them. They divided the realm into two parts so they could both rule.

———

Fastule chose the northern region. He named it Amika and made himself its monarch. Brigin took the southern land—Belleger—and became its king.

"They intended peace, and might have achieved it. But they were doomed by their alikeness. They both fell in love with the same woman. Her name was Malorie, said to be the embodiment of every womanly perfection, and the brothers strove extravagantly to win her.

"Sadly for them—and for us—they were not *entirely* alike. There was a strain of savagery in Fastule that Brigin did not share. Even in matters of sport and training, Fastule often fought to the death, while Brigin knew when to hold back. For that reason, Malorie chose Brigin to be her lord.

"From that moment, there was no true peace. Grinding his teeth, Fastule appeared to concede defeat. While all Belleger prepared to celebrate King Brigin's wedding, Fastule withdrew to the fortress he had built to house his ambitions. There he waited, readying himself, until the time for the ceremony came. Then he marched into Belleger with a small squad of soldiers, a large retinue of royal adherents—and two Magisters disguised as courtiers. Grinning like a beast, he presented himself and his court to attend the wedding. His soldiers he left to share the festivities at the city gates."

To the rapt curiosity of his comrades, Prince Bifalt explained, "The records do not describe what followed in any detail. A host of armed Amikans approached the Hand in secret." The *Open Hand* was the fortified city surrounding Belleger's Fist. "The guards at the gates were killed so the host could enter. At the same time, when King Brigin bent to kiss his new bride, sealing their marriage, there was a clap of thunder in the hall. In an instant, Queen Mal-orie's loveliness became a mask of boils oozing pus, of rashes squirming like worms under her skin, of bruises like sudden can-kers." Prince Bifalt heard hoarse surprise from his comrades, but he did not pause. "Fouled blood gushed from her eyes, her nose, her ears. She had been struck by the Decimate of pestilence. In her finery, she resembled an embodiment of plague. And while she shrieked her last, Fastule rushed to kill his brother.

"Fortunately for us, there were brave men in King Brigin's court. They saved his life. Many of his own Magisters were in attendance. They struck down the Amikan sorcerers with fire and lightning. And Fastule had not risked enough of his forces to ensure his victory over the Hand. There was terrible carnage in every quarter, terrible suffering. The city had not been taught to defend itself. But King Brigin's Magisters were able to drive out the Ami-kan host. When Fastule fled, he fled in bitterness. His brother still lived. And Belleger knew its enemy.

"From that time to this, we have been at war, fighting again and again to defend ourselves. That is the tale. The heritage of Fastule's bitterness and savagery still rules Amika."

Every veteran knew he rode into hell in self-defense. Belleger was losing. Every battle took place on Bellegerin land—although the border, the Line River, was less than a league away. But among his comrades, only Prince Bifalt knew that several times during the long war, various kings had sent emissaries to talk peace with Amika. On each occasion, the emissaries had been killed as soon as they revealed their purpose.

The Prince's audience fidgeted, uncertain what to make of his story. Bartin swore under his breath. "All for a woman." But Elgart surged to his feet. Flinging away his stone, he asked, almost demanded, "Do you believe it?"

Prince Bifalt shrugged. "It is one version of the tale." He had a different idea. "There is another.

"It says Fastule had no sorcerers with him. Rather, he was gifted himself, born with the talent for pestilence. That was the savagery in his nature, the strain of viciousness he could not restrain. With his own theurgy, he made a ruin of the one woman who had spurned him. But he could not kill his brother by the same means because he had expended too much of himself—and because Belleger's Magisters acted too quickly. He needed all of his host to help him escape the city."

Then Prince Bifalt declared, "*That* version I believe. It explains the killing strain in Fastule, a *gift* Brigin lacked. It explains the power of his heritage in Amika."

And, thought the Prince, it was typical of sorcerers. Some of them acted like amiable men. All of them had savagery in their hearts.

Abruptly, Nowel spoke. Harsh as acid, he said, "I have seen the truth. After every battle, Amikan Magisters kill their wounded. They do not allow prisoners or hostages. While we struggle to retrieve every fallen comrade who still breathes, *they* lash theirs with fire, or swallow them in cracks in the earth, or drain the life from their lungs. And ours they kill as well, as many as they can."

Every veteran knew this. Prince Bifalt knew it. He had been burned more than once, and slashed with stones, and almost suffocated while he tried to help hurt Bellegerins. Some of them had been his friends.

Flisk had been forewarned, of course. Only the Prince's tale was new to him. But now Prince Bifalt saw a more vivid horror on the young man's face.

The Prince approved. Flisk would fight harder because he felt more horror. The whole company would fight harder.

After a long silence, Klamath concluded sadly, "Tales change nothing." He was a brave soldier with a notoriously soft heart. Sooner or later, he wept after every battle. The Prince had seen him. "We fight because we are attacked. What else can we do?"

Retreating to familiar ground, Flisk asked—an implicit plea for reassurance—"Then why have they not overwhelmed us? Why does the war go on?"

Again, the squad deferred to Prince Bifalt. Unlike his comrades—unlike even Captain Swalish—he was present when King Abbator debated with his counselors and lead commanders.

"Our sorcerers are as great as theirs," answered the Prince. "The proof is that Belleger endures. Our Magisters hold when we cannot." His tone was sour. Many of his comrades saw theurgists as protectors, even saviors. Prince Bifalt did not. Amikan sorcery had caused the war. Amikan and Bellegerin sorcerers sustained it. "But we cannot hold without them. Amika has more men. This war is less ruinous there, or Amika is more populous. Or they have allies while we do not." Belleger was isolated along all its borders, unable to look for aid in any direction. For all he knew, Amika was less constricted. "In every battle, they outnumber us more.

"Perhaps it was not always so. It is so now. You know this." The truth was terrible, but it could not be denied. "We only remain to fight again because the carnage of each hell is so great." Most of it wrought by theurgy. "Two years pass, or three, or even four, before they grow strong enough to strike again. Without that respite, we would not have enough men to face them. Even our Magisters would be overrun eventually. They are too few."

He did not add, And their gifts have too many limitations. Instead, he concluded grimly, "That is why *we* are here. Today we will test our fate. We will learn if we can accomplish what sorcery cannot. If there is hope for Belleger, it rides with us."

Every man in the squad knew what he meant. They had spent a year training for it. Still, the weight of Prince Bifalt's assertion silenced even Flisk. Abruptly, most of them stirred, unable to rest longer. As dawn spread down from the opposing heights into the lowland of the battlefield, the soldiers began to re-count the arrows in their quivers, or test their bowstrings, or sharpen their sabers one more time, or check the contents of their satchels.

Soon they would be able to see their enemy clearly.

Then a muffled voice warned them Captain Swalish was coming.

After all their training together, the Prince knew his Captain well. Scarred and burly, with the shoulders of a wrestler and the legs of a man who stood his ground, Swalish was not a man who tolerated disrespect. He obeyed orders himself, and expected his to be obeyed. At the same time, he knew what his soldiers were about to face better than any of them except Bartin. Experience had taught him when to tighten discipline and when to relax it. In addition, he was not a tactician. He understood what his squad had been commanded to do, but he was not entirely sure it was reasonable—or even possible. And—a further difficulty—his habit of submission to Belleger's ruling family ran deep. Prince Bifalt's presence in the squad made Captain Swalish uncomfortable.

As he approached his men, the Captain glared as if he meant to lash them for not leaping to attention. But when he reached them, he hesitated until he caught Prince Bifalt's eye; until he saw the Prince's slight nod.

By that time, the soldiers were on their feet.

"Listen well," began Swalish. "Even you, Bartin." The effort of compensating for his doubts made him harsh. "Soon we will ride into hell, where better men than you have died between one heartbeat and the next. I will have the hide of any man who ignores our orders.

"You know why we are here. You know why you were chosen. You know why we have done everything in secret. You know what we must do. I will tell you again.

"For the first time, we will let Amika see our rifles. We will let them see what rifles can do. You were chosen for this duty because you are skilled riflemen. But you—*we*—are too few to turn the battle. We do not have enough guns to turn any battle. What we will attempt is a test. We must know whether rifles can kill Amikan sorcerers.

"*Hear* me," insisted the Captain fiercely, although he kept his voice low. "Our task is not to *fight*. It is to *win through*. That is why we ride in threes," twenty men and Swalish himself. "To make a way for each other. We must survive Amikan sorcery, Amikan tactics, Amikan cavalry. We must breach their lines. And we must do it without revealing our guns. We must keep our purpose hidden until we are in range of the ramparts where the Amikan sorcerers stand.

"*Then* we will shoot. We will do what we can to drop those theurgists. If we can kill enough of them—hells, if we can kill *any* of them—in the next battle we will be able to repay generations of Bellegerin blood."

Like his comrades, Prince Bifalt held his rifle in front of him, hardwood stock under his elbow, barrel pointed safely at the sky, showing Captain Swalish he was ready. His pulse beat a fighting rhythm. He was not afraid to die. He was not a man who flinched or shirked. His courage was proven. But he could admit to himself that he was afraid to fail. If his homeland could not be saved with rifles, it could not be saved at all.

"Do I need to add," rasped the squad's commander, "that the enemy must not be allowed to capture any of our guns?" Camwish, Nowel, and others shook their heads. Unnecessarily, Captain Swalish explained, "That is the only exception to our orders. We are allowed to shoot if that is the only way to keep our rifles out of Amikan hands.

"More than that, I have only this to say. Any man whose rifle misfires because it has not been properly cleaned and tested will *not* be punished. He will already be dead."

His soldiers had trained hard. They knew a veiled order when they heard it. In the sun's rising light, they removed the loaded clips from their weapons, confirmed the pressure of the springs that advanced the cartridges, then unlocked the breeches, checked the action of the triggers and bolts, squinted down the long barrels. With practiced precision, they relocked the breeches, replaced the clips. Then they went through their satchels, counting their spare clips, assuring Captain Swalish more than themselves that the clips were loaded.

"Right," said the Captain. That was as close as he ever came to expressing approval. "You know your threes. You know your place in our lines. It is time to mount. Protect each other. Protect your guns. Succeed if you can. If you cannot, return alive. I will not be amused if you compel me to train more men."

Only Elgart laughed, a humorless sound quickly stifled. Around him, the squad formed its teams. Captain Swalish and a big man named Malder, a natural brawler, took Flisk between them, protecting the young man's inexperience. With Gret and Jeck, Prince Bifalt followed the horse-master Camwish toward the pickets where the mounts waited.

As the Prince walked, blood beat like music in his veins. He did not relish killing his enemies, but their deaths were necessary. Belleger's extremity justified him. Amika's attack justified him. What his heart craved, however, what he burned for, was to shoot sorcerers.

In every generation, they were few. Most men were born without the gift to wield incomprehensible powers. Nevertheless, they were mighty. Their sorceries were enough to start the war—and to block both Belleger and Amika from victory. Without the aid of theurgy, Belleger would have been erased as a separate realm long ago. Its remaining people would have been forced to live their lives under the dominion of Amika.

Prince Bifalt believed all sorcery was dishonorable: worse than unfair or dishonest. A Magister could conceal himself in perfect safety while he killed ungifted men, ordinary men, by the dozens. People without the talent for theurgy were helpless against sorcerers. Every act of sorcerous power was an atrocity.

Yet Belleger could not endure without sorcery. Magisters were essential to the realm despite the way they dishonored whatever they touched.

But if the riflemen's tactics proved effective, Prince Bifalt might live to see the day when every Amikan theurgist was dead. In another two or three years, Belleger could make more than enough guns, hundreds of them, thousands. Then Amika would be defeated. King Abbator's people would be able to savor their natural lives at last, as men and women and families should. They would have no need for Magisters themselves, and would be content without them.

If there were no sorcerers, a man like Prince Bifalt might finally have the right to an honorable life: a right he could not afford now because his homeland was assailed by theurgy. The rifle he carried was his own hope as much as Belleger's.

With his comrades, he went to his mount. When he had tested its girth and tack, and had murmured a few comfortable words to the warhorse, he secured his rifle in its plain leather scabbard, where it would rest unseen under his thigh until he needed it. Then he surged into the saddle, holding the reins in one hand, his bow in the other.

Arrows would be his first weapons. He might require every shaft in his quiver. Then he would have to rely on his saber—and on Gret and Jeck—until one or two or all three of them broke through the Amikan lines: until he or they neared the high wall of boulders, the ramparts, that closed the far side of the valley.

After that, he would be free to draw his rifle; and the true worth of King Abbator's eldest son would be measured.

※

It all came down to rifles, every hope, every future. But not to simple muskets, single-shot guns that wasted an eternity of fighting while they were reloaded. *Repeating* rifles. Prince Bifalt knew more about their discovery and development than any soldier of Belleger. The secret was stringently guarded. But as a member of his father's inner circle, he knew the name of the alchemist, three generations back, who had discovered the composition of gunpowder, aided by a sheaf of brittle papers found in an old trunk: papers written with fanciful diagrams, peculiar recipes, and obscure terms. He knew the names of the skilled iron-wright and the famous jewel-smith with whom the alchemist had shared his discovery. The Prince even knew the name of the apprentice who had been wounded when the three men had succeeded in using gunpowder to expel a lead ball from an iron tube. The King who had learned of this accomplishment, foreseen its possibilities, and imposed a severe secrecy on its improvement, had been Prince Bifalt's great-grandfather.

The work that followed had taken a long time. The subsequent kings and their advisers had scorned the use of any gun that could not match an archer for quickness. In addition, the obstacles to be overcome were unprecedented. Guided by the original alchemist's papers, Belleger's blacksmiths, iron-wrights, and jewelers were able to devise, first, the cartridges that held both gunpowder and bullet, then the breech that secured the cartridge so the triggering mechanism could spark the gunpowder, and finally the bolt action that ejected the spent casing and accepted a new cartridge. These innovations they were able to effect within a few decades.

Unfortunately, shaping iron for the barrel posed a more daunting problem. Year after year, the barrels ruptured themselves, or exploded the whole gun, when they had been used once or twice, or perhaps three times. No forge in the realm burned hot enough to harden the iron. Muskets, by comparison, were simple: their barrels had time to cool between shots. But muskets could not save Belleger's people.

Eventually, keeping the process secret became easy. Its failures made it seem trivial, too pointless to prolong curiosity among people who were either numbed or ruined by the enduring costs of the war. Only the succeeding kings of Belleger kept faith with Prince Bifalt's great-grandfather's vision—and they did so only because they were desperate.

This impasse persisted until one blacksmith in despair was inspired to consult a Magister. Their long experiments proved that the Decimate of fire could enable any forge to shape barrels durable enough to withstand the stress of rapid shots.

The fact that his hopes, and Belleger's, depended on sorcery made Prince Bifalt bitter. He accepted the contradictions of his position only because the stakes were so high. The plight of his people made nagging questions of honor meaningless.

❖

Mounted now, and eager because they could not afford fear, Captain Swalish's threes formed a wedge in the center of the Bellegerin lines. Around them, horses jostled, men cursed, officers shouted for order. As daylight filled the bottom of the valley at last, the two armies faced each other, Bellegerins on the south, Amikans to the north. The Amikan forces had crossed the Line River and come here because there was no better place for their battle than this. The bouldered heights that walled the lowland gave the commanders on both sides the advantage of being able to watch and direct the whole conflict from above. It also allowed their theurgists the opportunity to strike at will without hazarding themselves. But the armies also relied on the horsemen in their lines below the ramparts. Both forces needed open ground for cavalry. Foot soldiers had no hope of reaching the high positions like redoubts from which the Magisters fought.

In this confrontation, as in the entire war, Belleger's whole attention was fixed on its enemy. It had no other concerns. Any student of the heavens could have told his king that the world was wide: far wider than the lands claimed by Belleger and Amika. But Belleger knew nothing of this. Bordered on the west by seas and an unnavigable coastline too sheer and reefed to be sailed, to the south by mountains with jagged cliffs and peaks that clawed the sky, and in the east by a trackless desert, the Bellegerin realm had nowhere to look except toward Amika in the north.

If Amika knew more, no one in Belleger cared. The fight for survival stripped away other considerations.

Here Prince Bifalt was clad like any other soldier. None of the riflemen wanted to call attention to their unique purpose, their unprecedented tactics. In addition, King Abbator did not wish his eldest son singled out for death. The Prince was indistinguishable from his comrades in his boiled-leather jerkin and leggings; in his

helm and breastplate, both marked with the emblem of his homeland, the sign of the beleaguered eagle. In every obvious respect,
his weapons—his bow and arrows, his saber and dagger—were
identical to those carried by all the Bellegerins.

In full daylight, horns sounded from the Amikan lines. At once,
the enemy horsemen began to move. As they came down the slope
below their heights, they swept from a canter into a full gallop.

Almost immediately, King Abbator's lead commanders responded. When they gave their own signal, Prince Bifalt and the
entire Bellegerin army surged toward the plain.

Mounted on their armored chargers, they rode with the wild
hearts and severe discipline of well-trained cavalry. The sight of
the Amikan forces pounding to meet him made the Prince ache
to draw his rifle. But he had his orders: he did not touch his gun.

As he and his comrades drew within bowshot, the opposing
Magisters attacked. Without warning, a line of fire spread across
the Bellegerin front. It seemed to come from nowhere, feed on
nothing, yet it burned with the ferocity of a furnace. In an instant,
the screams of men and horses appalled the air. Heat made torches
of hides and heads. Flesh bubbled and ran like wax. Bones flamed
like tinder. In that instant, scores of Bellegerins died.

At once, Belleger's sorcerers countered. Wielding their gifts,
they answered fire with fire—and with other powers. Elsewhere a
deep cracking sound shook an Amikan company, knocking the
horses to the ground. Under them, the earth opened: it swallowed
men and mounts whole, broke the legs of beasts trying to avoid it,
pitched riders headlong to their deaths. When the surface of rocks
and dirt closed again, it claimed more victims.

From both sides, sudden winds with the force of hurricanes struck the riders. Blasts like battering rams punched horses and horsemen to the ground. And after the winds came waves of pestilence that sickened both beasts and men, covered them with oozing boils. The pain of those infections was so intense that some men clawed off their faces and even tore their eyes to escape the agony.

It should have been a cause for wonder that Belleger and Amika had not eradicated each other from the world generations ago. But sorcery had limitations. Its range was limited, as was the stamina of the sorcerers. The Magisters could not attack each other directly: the distance between their positions was too great. And they could not sustain their attacks. Their exertions drained them. Each wave of theurgy was horrific, but it was also brief.

In addition, the sorcerers were handicapped by their own cavalry. As soon as the charging armies met, the Magisters could not unleash their powers without killing their own men as well as their foes. The result was that sorcery could not rout either army. Despite the carnage on all sides, Prince Bifalt and his surviving comrades still had to fight for their lives.

As in past battles, the Amikan strategy was simple: kill Bellegerins, as many as possible. But now Belleger's defenders had a more definite objective. Supported by vicious spates of fire, by quakes that tore sections of the earth apart, by winds and pestilence, and warded by companies of their comrades, Prince Bifalt and the other riflemen strove to pierce the Amikan lines so they could approach the enemy ramparts.

The Prince loosed arrows until the battle engulfed him and his bow became a hindrance. Then he discarded it, snatched out his saber, and began hacking at his enemies.

Dodging through the chaos of screams, war cries, curses, his charger trampled charred corpses, skirted crippling pits and cracks in the plain, skidded in blood-drenched mud. The riders assigned to his squad's protection absorbed most of the Amikan force near him. Still, he had to cut and thrust savagely to keep himself alive. When his blade was batted aside, he turned his blocked slash into a swing against a different foe, trusting Gret and Jeck to guard him.

Abruptly, an Amikan dropped Gret and rushed close, mouth wide in a bloody howl. Prince Bifalt stopped him by driving his saber between the man's jaws. The Amikan died in a red spew; but the bones of his skull trapped the blade. As he fell, he wrenched the saber from Prince Bifalt's hand.

Snatching out his dagger, the Prince went on fighting as well as he could. Some soldier behind him would try to retrieve Gret's gun.

Stride by stride, Prince Bifalt's mount began to ascend the slope at the foot of the Amikan redoubt.

Then, suddenly, he won free of the battle. Several other riflemen had been forced back. Others were too heavily engaged to accompany him. But no one stood between him and the last rise, the stretch of ground where the high pile of the enemy's rampart reared upward. There or nowhere, he would be able to find his targets and take his shots. And Jeck still guarded his back.

Off to his left, he saw three members of his squad emerge from the fighting. At a glance, he knew they would fail. Amikans had rallied behind them—and the Amikans had not discarded their bows. Already arrows hissed in the air. One rifleman died with a

---

shaft in his back. His comrades were thrown when their mounts stumbled under them.

But they rolled to their feet, recovered quickly; turned their rifles on their immediate foes. That was necessity, not tactics. They disobeyed one order to obey another: keep their guns out of enemy hands. For the first time in the long war, shots cracked through the clamor. For the first time, Amikans were flung from their horses by bullets and rapid fire. In shock, nearby riders halted like men hitting a wall.

The Bellegerins would be visible from above. Surely, at least one or two sorcerers would come to the edge or rise from their coverts to see what was happening. If their comrades could not save them, those two riflemen were as good as dead.

But they might open a clear shot for the Prince.

His gun was more accurate than any bow loosed in combat. It had greater range.

He needed mere moments to reach the crest of the rise he sought. While Jeck dismounted to cover him, the Prince leapt from his charger. Taking only his rifle and his satchel of ammunition, he slapped his mount away, then ran to a boulder that he hoped would shield him from sorcery.

Quickly, he scanned the horizon of the redoubt. He looked for niches between boulders where a Magister could stand to survey the battlefield. In the distance, above the tumult of his heart, he heard the sharp stutter of rifle-fire as his comrades fought to keep the Amikans back; to protect each other, and their guns, and him. But he did not glance away from his sights. Holding his breath, he searched the heights.

———

There: the flicker of a Magister's slate-grey robe in a gap below the rim of the ramparts. Without hesitation, Prince Bifalt tightened his finger on the trigger. The gun bucked in his hands. While the muzzle flash flared across his vision, he controlled his rifle, aimed again.

A brief puff of stone shards and dust from the side of his target told him he must have missed. By good fortune, however, the ricochet was as effective as a hit. The robe toppled, fluttering, out of its covert. Limbs floundered until the body struck the ground and lay still.

Yes!

Working the bolt to chamber another bullet, the Prince scanned the rocks for another sorcerer.

Almost immediately, he was rewarded. A robed figure stepped into view; stood against the backdrop of the sky as if he had been etched there for killing.

Prince Bifalt's second shot did not miss. Spouting blood from his chest, the theurgist fell backward out of sight.

Yes!

Again he worked the rifle bolt. Again he searched.

If he had bothered to count his heartbeats, he would have reached ten or twelve when every hair on his forearms stood on end, and his scalp crawled inside his helm. In that instant, he knew what was coming. Only one form of sorcery had this effect. He had no more than a moment to pray this theurgy was not meant for him; to hope it would strike and melt the ground rather than take him or any Bellegerin. Then a wild blare of lightning from the bright heavens punched through him, and he understood that he was dead.

While that terrible discharge of theurgy claimed him, he saw himself as if from the outside. He saw his bones glow like iron in the forge; saw his eyes drip from their sockets. He watched his flesh melt from him, leaving only the coruscation of his skeleton. From a great distance, he felt an instant of absolute agony.

Then a voice spoke. Although it was not loud, it had the depth of a subterranean convulsion: it seemed to emerge from the foundations of the world. It took no time at all, yet every word was distinct, as if it had been written on his mind.

It said: **Are you ready?**

The King's eldest son rolled onto his back, staring sightlessly at the Amikan ramparts. His last thought was that he did not want to die. He had not accomplished enough.

PART ONE

Nearly two years after the day he had felt himself killed by lightning, and then—impossibly—had lived, the day when Bellegerin rifles had changed the world, Prince Bifalt and his company departed Belleger's Fist without announcement or display. Why risk raising hopes, he had asked his father, when success is hardly imaginable? And King Abbator had agreed. For that reason, there were no trumpets or banners. The company did not pass outward along an aisle of courtiers. The high balconies of the Fist were empty, apart from the King himself, his most trusted counselors, and his lead commanders. None of them waved or shouted encouragement. Some of them were probably swearing to themselves.

But someone had started a rumor. Stolle, an incurable gossip, may have said something to his new wife, who shared his taste for whispered secrets. He had surely felt compelled to give her *some* explanation to account for an absence that might not end. Or Captain Swalish's family might have overheard a low remark intended for someone else. In any case, the Open Hand was tinder for rumors. They spread like wildfires.

When Prince Bifalt left the Fist mounted on his favorite destrier, with his ten guardsmen, two supply-wains, and one former Magister, his road through the Hand was lined with crowds. Belleger's people—most of them failing merchants and tradesmen, destitute serving-folk and farmers, starving beggars and maimed veterans—knew nothing about the Prince's quest. They only knew he would not leave his place at his father's side, or in the army, for any trivial purpose. So they gathered to watch him go. If they guessed he went in search of some nameless power that might save them from Amika, they did not show it. They only watched in silence while he rode between them.

For his part, Prince Bifalt presented a countenance of resolute confidence. He could not offer hope, but he had no intention of encouraging despair. Shining in his bronze helm and breastplate, both marked with the beleaguered eagle of his homeland, he was the perfect emblem of a soldier who would redeem his people or die. His only concession to a long journey was the silk rather than boiled leather he wore under his armor to avoid chafing. And he had at his back as much support as King Abbator could spare. His ten guardsmen were all veterans, all armed with rifles as well as their more traditional weapons. The wains with their paired oxen carried stores and necessities enough for a season in unfamiliar lands. The oxen were managed by four teamsters chosen for strength and stamina as well as for devotion to their beasts. And the Magister with the company was an older man who had once been mighty, but who still knew a trick or three that might defend the quest from Amikan theurgy.

In addition, the Prince himself was far from helpless. His training, experience, and weapons were augmented by a chiseled visage, a piercing gaze, an unyielding nature, and the knowledge that his quest was desperate. Also, he loved his people as he loved his father. His homeland was dear to him. There was no man in Belleger better suited to his task than he.

Nevertheless, his air of confidence was a sham. Behind his façade, uncertainties gnawed at him. He had no map to his destination. Indeed, he had no assurance his destination existed. If he found it, it might not have what he needed. And if what he needed were there, he might not be allowed to use it.

Furthermore, he knew his limitations. Although he was as resolute as he appeared, he was not clever. He was not a man who outwitted his foes. His skills were hard-learned, the result of long repetition: they were not the product of quick thinking or inspiration.

But he had deeper problems as well. The catastrophe that had befallen Belleger had shaken him to the marrow of his bones. It had shattered every conceivable future for his people. And now he was responsible for answering it. That burden filled him with dread. More than ever before in his life, he feared to fail.

The signs of that catastrophe were everywhere around him as he rode. He saw them in the lines of privation that marred every face; in the disrepair of the homes, the merchantries, the streets, the very walls; in the thinness of even the most prosperous shopkeepers.

Elsewhere, he knew, grapes rotted on the vines because the vine-yards could not be adequately tended, while fields of wheat and barley were useless because there were too few able women and uncrippled men to plant and harvest them. Cattle were becoming as scarce as fresh horses. The panic of the first days, the confusion, clamor, and outrage, were gone, burned out by exhaustion and deprivation during the seasons that followed. What remained was hopelessness. Prince Bifalt saw it in scores of faces. His people were afraid to dream of survival.

If he failed them, they would all die.

The catastrophe had swept over Belleger almost a year after Captain Swalish and his squad had first used rifles in battle, and the Prince had killed two Amikan Magisters. Between one day's sunset and the next's dawn, all sorcery had vanished from the realm. *All* sorcery. While they slept, or caroused, or worked, or whatever they did at night, every Magister was rendered impotent. Fire and wind no longer answered the summons of their former masters. Quakes, lightning, and pestilence no longer came when they were called. In one night, all power was extinguished in the land.

The effects were devastating. Bellegerins did not know how to live without sorcery. It was essential to their understanding of their world; their understanding of existence. Even Prince Bifalt, who despised theurgy, was appalled. For him, however, as for King Abbator, and for everyone who had experienced Amika's enmity, the loss of sorcery was only the start of the catastrophe. There was worse to come.

It was this: Amika's eventual victory was now assured. That foe could direct its own savagery and power against Belleger whenever it chose, whenever it felt ready, now that its victim was helpless. Every Bellegerin knew that the headsman's axe could fall at any moment. While men and women still lived, they felt that waiting for death was more cruel than death itself.

Of *course*, King Abbator's counselors and lead commanders reasoned, *Amika* still had sorcery. Its Magisters could still wield ruin. There was no other explanation. Belleger's old enemy was its only enemy; the only other people in their world. How could the realm have been bereft of its only defense, except by theurgy? And who apart from Amika could have caused—or desired—the catastrophe?

The wonder, then, was not that Amika had committed such an atrocity. Its people were capable of anything. The wonder was that Belleger's enemy had not yet acted on its advantage. Prince Bifalt's homeland was ripe for the taking. Why had it not been simply overrun?

This was the subject of endless debate—and intolerable delay—in the King's council chamber: why?

Some advisers believed that Amika was biding its time until it had readied strength enough to overwhelm Belleger in a single assault. Most of the army's lead commanders—and the Prince himself—disagreed. They argued that the Amikans held back because they feared Belleger's ability to make guns. After all, only some men were capable of sorcery. Fewer still had the knowledge and training to develop their gifts. Also, their powers were singular. A Magister who could fling fire could not also raise winds or crack the earth. In contrast, any man able to stand up and point could kill his foes at improbable distances. A host of men with rifles could wreak appalling havoc. An unprecedented massing of

STEPHEN R. DONALDSON

sorcerers would be required to overcome them. Naturally, Amika feared a premature attack.

In truth, of course, Belleger had no host. When the catastrophe struck, the whole realm possessed no more than a few hundred rifles. And the alchemists, iron-wrights, and jewel-smiths could not produce more without sorcery; without the Decimate of fire. Their forges were not hot enough.

Considering this cruel contradiction often made Prince Bifalt so angry he wanted to froth at the mouth. At times, he bit the inside of his cheek until it bled. He did not know another way to grieve, except with rage. But in his present straits, he could not afford to dwell on his frustration. Eventually, some Amikan spy would discover Belleger's hidden weakness. Then the last battle would begin. Against any onslaught, a few hundred rifles might suffice to defend the King's city, but not his lands. To preserve the entire realm, Belleger required theurgy.

Hence the Prince's quest.

Yet even his own doubts and the threat to his people were not the sum of his burdens. He had a more personal fear, a private reason to distrust success as much as he feared failure. In the instant of his death—the instant when he should have died—a voice had spoken to him. **Are you ready?** It could only have been a sorcerer's voice. And it gave him cause to think that he had been singled out by an inconceivable power for an incomprehensible purpose: a purpose which might be fatal to Belleger. He had felt his own death. He had seen it take him. He did not know why he was still alive.

On that topic, however, he kept silent. Whom could he tell?

34

Anyone who had not heard that voice would dismiss it as the con-fusion of a mind unhinged by the Decimate of lightning.

After the catastrophe, the debates in the King's chambers had seemed endless despite their urgency. They had chewed on Prince Bifalt until he felt eaten alive. He needed to *fight*—and yet the council had entirely failed to determine a course of action. What could Belleger *do*? It could not overcome its foe. It could not shield itself. And it had no allies. It knew of no lands or peoples with whom it could have allied itself. If there were ships on the sea to the west, they did not come to Belleger's impossible coast. If there were passes through the southern mountains, the Realm's Edge, passes leading to inhabited regions, they had not been explored. The war with Amika had left neither time nor resources for exploration. A ruinous desert filled the east, and Amika held the north. There was nowhere Belleger could turn for help.

Early in the debates, a minor counselor had suggested timidly that perhaps Amika had also been bereft of sorcery. But this notion had been dismissed with derision. Who *else* could have caused Belleger's catastrophe? Who *else* hated Belleger so much? There *was* no one else.

Of course, spies had been sent into Amika. In fact, they had been sent for generations, one after another in a bewildering vari-ety of guises. But very few of them had ever returned, except those who had nothing useful to report. And none returned at all now. That harsh fact supported the conviction that Amika's Magisters still had power. How else had Amika detected and stopped or killed *all* of Belleger's spies?

King Abbator and his advisers believed that their realm was too weak to prevent certain doom. They had good reason.

But then an old man came forward. He had once been a powerful Magister, and a strong voice among the King's advisers. Since the loss of sorcery, however, he had fallen into senility, and had preferred the isolation of his scattered wits to the company of his fellow Magisters and advisers. Yet now he presented himself.

Forced by decrepitude to support himself on a gnarled staff, and clad in a tattered grey robe much soiled by various mishaps, he was the personification of lost efficacy. Most of the council turned away as he advanced, embarrassed as much by his uselessness as by his apparel and frailty. Nevertheless, he had served King Abbator faithfully for some decades. Respect for the old man's past stature commanded the King's attention, although it did not command the Prince's.

"Magister Altimar, welcome," said the King in a tone of patience already somewhat stretched. "You wish to speak? You have some counsel that may free us from our impasse?"

"Free you, Majesty?" replied the impotent sorcerer. "No." The strained wheeze with which he spoke made Prince Bifalt feel that his own breathing was constricted. "You decide nothing. You can decide nothing. You do not know your peril. While you debate and debate, you are lost."

King Abbator stroked his beard to soothe his frustration. "So much we understand, Magister. What we do not know—"

"Consider, Majesty," interrupted Altimar, wheezing. "Such power. The power to deprive an entire realm of sorcery. Who wields such theurgy? Who knows such things are possible?" For a moment, he appeared to drift. Then he coughed to clear his lungs. "None here can answer," he said with an old man's quavering sullenness. "None can name that power. None knows where the answer may be found. You doubt an answer exists."

Exasperated on his father's behalf, Prince Bifalt saw no reason for politeness. "What is your point, old man?" he demanded. He did not like any sorcerer. "We are *familiar* with our ignorance. We acknowledged it long ago. Now we have left it behind. We must choose our course in spite of it."

"Old man?" The theurgist's head jerked. Angers long burned to ash found embers in his eyes. His lips glistened with phlegm. "You call me *old man*? I hear your scorn. Yes, I am old. I was old while you were a mewling babe. But I was wise long before your birth. I have wielded powers beyond your foolish imagining. I am *Magister* Altimar, boy. I have no use now, but I *remember*. At last, I have *remembered*. I speak because no other will. No other can."

The King gestured his son to silence. "Then speak, Magister. We have heard counsel from jesters and mountebanks, having none worthy of repetition ourselves. We will surely heed you. Speak of what you can. Relieve our ignorance."

"*Old man?*" repeated the sorcerer. Petulance had knocked his wits awry. "I did not drag myself up from the depths of memory to be met with disdain. You, *boy*, deserve your ignorance. You will never escape it."

Again King Abbator commanded Prince Bifalt's silence. Wiser than his son, Belleger's ruler controlled his own vexation. Carefully mild, he replied, "You have not been met with disdain from *me*, Magister. You will not. Only speak. Tell me what you have remembered."

The frail figure shook himself. After more coughing, he cleared his throat. "Of course, Majesty. Why else have I come?"

Clinging to his staff, he began in a hectoring tone better suited to a hall of apprentices.

"Of Decimates, six are known. Fire, certainly. Wind. The plague of boils. The cracking of the earth. Also a drought that can suck the water from a man, or a company of men, leaving only corpses. And a lightning terrible to contemplate. It shatters stone as easily as wood, and the stone burns. Ask any who were once Magisters. They will tell you that the Decimates of sorcery are six."

The King nodded in silence. The Prince gnawed his cheek to restrain himself. Every man in the chamber knew of the six Decimates. Every lead commander, like every counselor who had ever served in Belleger's army, knew the horrors of theurgy intimately.

"But," continued Altimar, "they will not speak of the *seventh* Decimate. They do not know it. Only *I* remember."

That assertion drew a rustle of interest from the sorcerer's audience. "There is a seventh?" exclaimed King Abbator. "I shudder to think that there is a Decimate more virulent than those we have witnessed, to our great cost in blood and pain."

"And to the great cost of Amika," replied the Magister with an attempt at imperiousness, "until recently. We no longer do what is done to us because there *is* a seventh, and it is mighty. It is a power unlike any you have conceived. It does not harm flesh or wood or stone. It does not roil the heavens or shake the earth. Rather, it halts all lesser sorceries. It renders sorcerers futile.

"We are helpless because the seventh Decimate has been invoked against us."

This pronouncement produced no reaction. It hardly seemed worth hearing. Everyone in the chamber already believed Belleger had been deprived of sorcery by sorcerers. Prince Bifalt was sure of it. No one but a theurgist was capable of so much evil. The only surprise was that the evil had a name.

Fortunately, the King's wits were more acute. Leaning forward with his hands tangled in his beard so that they would not tremble, he asked urgently, "Where does this knowledge exist? Why is it unknown to us? How did Amika acquire it? How can we? If it is accessible to our foes, it must be accessible to us as well.

"How has such a secret been forgotten?"

While King Abbator spoke, the old man turned away as if he had accomplished his purpose and now had nothing further to contribute. However, when the King snapped, "*Magister!*" Altimar faced his sovereign again.

"Too many questions, Majesty," he wheezed. "Too many. I am old and useless. I have no answers." Before King Abbator could protest, the former theurgist added, "None but one.

"Where does the knowledge exist? Why, in a book. Where else? It must have been learned from a book. A book named—" He paused, apparently groping. His eyes rolled. He bit his lip. "I remembered only this morning. It will come to me. The author's name is"—abruptly he stamped his staff on the floor—"*Marrow*. There! I remember again. Hexin Marrow. A Magister at a time when the knowledge of sorcery was young. Or perhaps a descendant of the first Magisters. The book is Hexin Marrow's *Seventh Decimate*."

The King released his beard. He braced his hands on his knees. "Thank you, Magister. Once again, you have proven your worth. I will forego other questions. One remains necessary.

"*Where* is this book?"

The old man became petulant again. "You have to ask? Where are such tomes kept? In a library, of course." But then he appeared to relent. After coughing for a moment, he explained, "A repository of books. The great Repository of the sorcerers. My teacher's teacher's teacher studied there in his youth."

King Abbator summoned reserves of patience that seemed more than human to the Prince. "And where is this repository, Magister?"

Altimar fluttered a hand. "Who knows? None of us have been there. None of your Magisters. Not for generations. Only I remember it exists." He mused briefly. "If it still exists."

Prince Bifalt bit his cheek to stifle a snarl.

"But if I am asked to hazard a guess," continued the former sorcerer, "I would say—" His head sagged to his chest. For a few heartbeats, he gave the impression he had fallen asleep where he stood. Then he roused himself. "In the east." With lugubrious care, he turned away again. "Somewhere." Slowly, he tottered toward the doors of the chamber. "In the east."

The King let him go, which seemed to Prince Bifalt the greatest display of patience of the entire exchange.

❋

So it came to pass, two days later, that the Prince, his team of guardsmen, and their laden wains passed through the gates of the Open Hand's fortifications, heading east. Beyond the walls, they traveled the streets of the haphazard town that had grown outside the King's main defenses, and had continued growing until its inhabitants outnumbered the city-dwellers. Driven by loss, Belleger's people had gradually migrated away from the frontiers of the interminable war with Amika.

Outlying towns, villages, and hamlets had been leached of their men, their potential soldiers. Strong fathers and sturdy sons and even able-bodied grandfathers were taken by the army. Eventually, being too few to work the land and the flocks or herds themselves, the families had followed their men in search of employment or charity, leaving most of the north peopled only by stubborn farmers and horse-breeders; by women, grandparents, and children. Of course, women could do as much as men. But without men, the women could not do enough to supply both the army and the realm. Soon they could not do enough to supply their own families. The result around the King's walls was a stinking mess of a city, unplanned and undrained, and made more noisome by fires blaring from the smithies, by rank fumes rising from the workshops of the alchemists. Whenever there was rain, poverty streamed from the eaves of the ramshackle houses, and the gutters poured sewage into the lanes and alleys.

Prince Bifalt was considered a hard man. Certainly, he had done everything he could to harden himself. At the age when young boys became attentive to their fathers, he had watched pain erode the lines of his father's face, the strength of his father's arms, the firmness of his father's strides. Within a few years, he understood that King Abbator's pain was caused by Belleger's suffering. If the realm had been at peace, the King might have been a man in his prime. In a time of war, he was old, flensed of muscle and vigor by the poverty of his people and the threat to his lands. He carried the weight of every wound, every death, on his shoulders.

Seeing King Abbator diminish, the Prince had vowed with a youth's enthusiasm that he would not fail his father. But now Prince Bifalt was a man: he knew his vow had wider implications than he had first imagined. He knew what failure meant, not just to Belleger's king, but to Belleger itself. And he had learned a man needed a heart of stone to face Amikan cavalry—and Amikan theurgy.

The sight of Bellegerins living in such slums sickened him. From his mount's back, he saw eyes haunted by bereavement, faces lined with privation and woe, limbs made scrawny and draped in rags by destitution. If they were the cause of King Abbator's decline, they were also the reason for Prince Bifalt's vow. If or when he failed, they would pay the price.

For this, as for the war itself, he held Amika responsible. The conditions surrounding the Open Hand could not be improved until—unless—Belleger's enemy was defeated.

Amika's animosity defied his comprehension. He faced it without flinching, but he did not understand it. The tale he had told his comrades before the last battle did not suffice to account for Amika's savagery. It was only a tale—and in any case, its events had happened a long time ago. Yet the fury of Belleger's foe endured. It seemed as unnatural as sorcery. If the Prince had not seen Amikans rage and cower and charge and flee and bleed and die like ordinary men on the battlefields, he would have doubted their very humanity.

Nevertheless, he projected certainty while his father's subjects

---

watched his departure. Through mire and sewage, he held his head high and his mien stern as he led his escort among the throngs. Only when he had left behind the streets, and then the outbuildings, and then the fields, did he permit himself to acknowledge his doubts.

Of his vague destination, he had learned only two details since the King had commanded him to this quest. One of the older captains had shown him a map more explicit than any he had previously studied. In its outlines he had confirmed, first, that Belleger's borders to the east were imposed by a trackless and unmeasured desert, a boundary that extended north into Amika and perhaps beyond. In a general way, he had known of the desert's existence. But he had never had a chance to see it: it was too far to the east, and his training to serve against Amika had allowed him no leisure to explore his homeland. Second, the map had shown him that a direct line to the east would take him closer and closer to Amikan lands. From the sea to the desert, the Line River formed the border between the realms. Eventually, his only protection from his foes would be the terrain on either side of the Line.

In contrast, one less practical matter had become clearer to him. The seventh Decimate had been invoked against Belleger. Therefore, Hexin Marrow's book must still exist. Therefore, the library of the sorcerers must still exist also. Therefore, the Prince told himself, his only real challenges were to *find* that library—and to survive the intervening search.

He did not think about what he would do when he arrived there. If he arrived. Books and libraries where sorcerers studied were beyond his imagination.

———

Still, the most private of his fears clung to him. In his last audience with his father before he left Belleger's Fist, King Abbator had asked, "Are you ready?"

Hearing those words, the Prince had not been able to restrain a flinch. Glowering at echoes that resembled omens, he replied, "No, Majesty. I do not know what will be required of me. How can I be ready?"

The King put a hand on Prince Bifalt's shoulder. "I understand, my son. What I ask of you—what Belleger asks—is likely impossible. A book that may not exist, in a library that may not exist, with a destination we do not know at a distance we cannot estimate. Your quest is surely implausible.

"Nevertheless, I entrust it to you. What else can we do?"

Through his teeth, the Prince promised, "For you, Father, I will do what I can. For Belleger, I will do all I can."

King Abbator sighed. Like a dying breath, he said, "Perhaps it will be enough. It is our only chance."

Groping now for some insight that might improve his ability to ponder the imponderable, Prince Bifalt called the former sorcerer in his company to ride at his side.

His need to do so vexed him. Memories of his father's face, and of his own experiences in hell, nagged at him whenever he was in the presence of a man who could cause so much slaughter with such ease—and at such a distance. Even theurgists who had lost their power reminded him of who they were. For the sake of his quest, however, he was prepared to control himself.

By the standard of Magister Altimar, the former sorcerer was not old. Certainly, he did not lack vigor. Though his eyes were commonly downcast, and his beard drooped from his visage like gloom, he rode with easy balance and a light hand, mounted and dismounted without obvious exertion, and conveyed a general air of readiness. Instead of a sorcerer's customary grey robe, he wore a tan shirt and trousers woven of heavy wool.

Prince Bifalt knew nothing about the man except that he had volunteered. Indeed, he had declared himself the company's steward. He claimed the task of preparing meals, tending to supplies, and rationing the burdens of the wains for a trek of unknown length.

Swallowing distaste, Prince Bifalt spoke as the man joined him. "Magister Slack—"

Before he could continue, the older man interrupted. "Forgive me, Highness," he said without raising his gaze. "I am no longer a Magister. That title signifies all I have lost, and I cannot hear it without pain. You will do me a kindness if you discard it."

The Prince frowned. He had not considered the man—or indeed any former sorcerer—as suffering a bereavement. In truth, he had given no thought at all to the plight of those who had once been mighty. But they were still sorcerers, in their hearts if not in their gifts. He did not care what became of them. Nevertheless, he would need this man. He intended to be cautious.

"Slack, then," he conceded. "I meant your title to show respect, not cause distress. Captain Swalish will instruct my men to do as you wish.

"But I am curious. Perhaps you will answer a few questions, if you can do it without discomfort."

Slack looked everywhere except at the Prince. "You are generous, Highness. I am not reluctant to speak. I wish others would forget I was once a man of power. I cannot myself. What do you wish to know?"

Prince Bifalt needed a moment to consider his tactics. "Then I wish to know—" He wanted to understand why any Magister would set aside his former status in order to serve guardsmen and teamsters, but he tried to avoid being blunt. "The experience itself, Slack. The sudden loss of theurgy. How did it take you?"

Slack sighed. "In some respects, Highness, it resembled an instant blindness. Unforeseen. Incurable. For myself, however, I think of it as a door slammed shut. A door barred against me. If you imagine a man, any man, as a house of several chambers, some with few, some with many, then I have been locked out of the brightest and most desirable of mine, those with the best light and warmth, the richest furnishings, the clearest windows, the widest vistas. I have lost a great wealth. Now I am poor and inconsolable."

This assertion scattered the Prince's thoughts. He had always considered sorcerers to be men of small souls and large malice. How otherwise could they endure the horrors they performed in battle, the carnage they committed? Yet this man claimed an extreme loss—

Prince Bifalt abandoned circumspection. "Do you tell me you *prized*—?" A moment of ignorance halted him. "What was your gift, Slack? Did you toss men with hurricane winds? Did you crack the ground under their feet?"

For the merest flicker of an instant, Slack met the Prince's glare. Then his gaze returned to the dirt of their track.

"My gift was fire, Highness."

"Then do you wish me to understand," continued the King's son while memories beat in his veins, "that you *prized* your power to burn the flesh from men's bones?"

The former sorcerer sighed again. His posture drooped like his beard. "Allegiance demands much of those whose lands are at war. The needs of king and realm and home cannot be set aside." Then he drew himself more erect. "But have you not observed, Highness, that fire has many uses, and many of them do not wreak harm? The same can be said of every Decimate, but we are speaking of mine. Sadly, I cannot adequately describe the solace of being able to set a cold hearth easily alight at the end of a bitter day. I cannot name the value of being able to give my neighbors a similar comfort—or of being able to save their homes when some mischance threatens an inferno, for I could quench flames as readily as cause them. Until the door within me was sealed, I burned the stubble from fields to prepare them for planting—and did so without endangering other fields, or the woods at their borders. Our smithies now lack the heat to forge iron for rifles because gifts like mine are gone.

"Surely, Highness, I prize what I have lost. The killing I wrought in battle was a necessary evil for which I endeavored daily to make amends." His voice held a tinge of vehemence as he concluded, "A man is not a man at all if he cannot enter and enjoy every chamber of himself."

Prince Bifalt had not contemplated the subject from Slack's perspective. He was reluctant to do so now. But he remembered that he meant to be careful, polite; that he would have to rely on this man. He tried to find common ground between them.

"Here is another crime to be laid at Amika's charge. If our foes would allow us peace, men with your gifts would not be burdened with the need to make amends."

Speaking as if to himself, Slack inquired, "Do we not have peace *now*, Highness?"

"It is the peace before the pounce, Slack," snapped the Prince. "The peace before the pounce. When Amika is ready to spring, we will have no peace until we are in our graves."

The older man sighed yet again. "As you say, Highness." Then he continued more firmly, "But you did not call me to your side to discuss my life. You have other queries, Highness?"

The Prince gathered his original thoughts. "Indeed," he answered in a more neutral tone. "I was told you know some trick or tricks to ward us on this quest. What are they? They will do little good if we are not ready to take advantage of them."

"They are not *tricks*, Highness." Slack's words suggested umbrage, although he spoke them mildly. "One is a gift all former sorcerers share. If we can no longer perform theurgy, we remain sensitive to its imminence. I can forewarn you of a sorcerous attack."

Hearing this, Prince Bifalt allowed himself a moment of relief. Without question, he needed Slack. And now he knew how the first king of Belleger, Brigin, had survived his brother's betrayal. Fastule's attack on Queen Malorie had announced itself to King Brigin's Magisters.

But Slack was not done. "As for the rest"—he shrugged inside his loose shirt—"they are merely skills. I am an adept of the skillet and stewpot. You and your men will eat as well as our rations allow.

Also, I am wise with the balms and unguents that mend burns. We will have burns, whether or not we suffer by fire. In the desert, without sufficient water or any shade, our lips will crack, our skin will blister, and our strength will falter. While my balms and unguents last, they will ease us."

With every response, the older man showed himself in a new light. Prince Bifalt had not expected so much from him. Swallowing his dislike, he forced himself to say, "Then, Slack, you may be the most necessary member of our company." His quest required that admission. "Now hear my command. See to your own safety. If we are threatened, my men and I will face the danger. If there are obstacles in our path, we will deal with them. Keep to the rear. Seek shelter when you can. I do not mean to lose you."

The former sorcerer might be able to interpret Marrow's book if the Prince himself could not.

Like a man compelled, Slack stared at Prince Bifalt. In the former Magister's eyes, the Prince saw an instant of astonishment. Then the look was gone, and Slack turned his head away. With a hint of his earlier brief vehemence, he answered, "As you command, Highness."

Bowing his head, he left the Prince's side.

A man is not a man at all— If Slack were regarded as a dwelling, Prince Bifalt now wondered, how many chambers did he contain? If those that pertained to theurgy had been sealed, how many remained for his use? Could such a man be humble? Or show kindness? Was it possible?

The Prince doubted it. But he was prepared to be persuaded, if

Slack helped his quest succeed. If its success relieved King Abbator's distress, and Belleger's.

If the sorcerer who had spoken in Prince Bifalt's mind did not have some fatal use for the quest's outcome.

❖

At the company's first halt for food and fodder, the Prince spoke to Captain Swalish about Slack. He had chosen his former commander and teacher to lead his company of riflemen. This reversal of their positions eased the Captain's native deference. He understood discipline. He knew the value of following orders. But it was not in his nature to consider the circumstances that gave those orders meaning. He was grateful he did not have to make decisions which might determine the outcome of this trek.

After Captain Swalish had instructed his men to respect Slack's wishes, he and the Prince discussed their immediate road, comparing its perils and advantages on Prince Bifalt's map. The fact that the company's most direct track tended closer to the Line River and Amika posed an obvious danger. Captain Swalish observed, however, that the river in that region was tumultuous, racing through deep gorges between rugged hills. No battles were fought there because no army could effectively descend into the gorges, cross the wild water, and scale the cliffs beyond. In the Captain's opinion, the terrain would ensure the company's safe passage.

"Consider the scale, Highness," he added. "The map makes Amika appear closer than it is. If we hold to our heading"—Captain Swalish traced a line on the map with one stubby finger—"we will not come within ten leagues of the Line. I see no danger."

But Prince Bifalt could not share the Captain's confidence. "If those lumbering wains did not slow us," he growled, "we would be safer. I want speed, Captain."

Swalish shrugged his heavy shoulders. "Our speed will improve, Highness," he remarked sourly, "as our supplies dwindle. Even what we have may not be enough. Amika's nearness will not trouble us when our bellies ache."

The Prince nodded. He knew his company could not overcome even small obstacles without adequate water, food, and fodder. Nevertheless, his worries were a storm cloud on his brow, and his companions avoided him as they resumed their journey.

The road they traveled had been well used in earlier times. It remained clear for several days. Also, its heading was generally eastward, although it wavered to accommodate hills, gullies, and the crossings of smaller rivers that fed the Line. The quest traveled as fast as the oxen could plod.

The earth there was fertile: the region had once been populous. But now the towns showed neglect and decay on all sides, the villages reeked of poverty, and more than one hamlet was entirely deserted. All this demonstrated the growing ravages of the war, and Prince Bifalt cursed inwardly at the sights. He felt he was riding through the stages of a wasting disease, the increments of Belleger's inevitable demise.

And for that disease there was only one cure: knowledge contained in a book that might be impossible to find. If the seventh Decimate accomplished nothing else, it could be used to render Amika's Magisters as impotent as Belleger's. That might be enough. Amika had more men, but Belleger had a number of rifles. King Abbator's realm might endure.

However, Prince Bifalt hoped for more. He had no idea how many secrets the unknown library might hold. It might reveal powers or methods that could help Belleger overcome the inadequacy of its supply of guns.

If the Prince and his company lived long enough. If they could find the library. If the library still had the book. If it could be used.

If Prince Bifalt had not been singled out to betray his people.

If. Always if.

Although he rode a trusted steed, and his track was plain, he had the sensations of a man crossing quagmires and sinkholes. He chewed the inside of his cheek to prevent himself from barking at every man who spoke to him.

On the sixth day, trudging at the pace of the wains through an overgrown wood, Captain Swalish spotted a herd of deer. After a brief chase, Vinsid brought down a large buck. This stroke of good fortune raised the spirits of the Prince's men, spirits that rose still higher when Slack prepared a comparative feast at the end of the day's travel. If the wains had carried ale or wine, some of the men would have ended the evening drunk.

Around the campfire that night, Camwish, the horse-master, indulged his enjoyment of ribald tales, stories of such flagrant improbability that they made shy Klamath blush. To all appearances, Camwish's obsession with women was moderated only by his devotion to horses, and exceeded only by his relish in describing extravagant sexual misadventures.

In this, old Bartin was the horse-master's natural antagonist. His distrust of women bordered on terror. At other times, he and

Camwish worked well enough together. They served to keep each other sharp. But when Camwish felt like entertaining his comrades, Bartin's disgust overcame him. Snorting his scorn, he left the campfire. With the Captain's tacit consent, he went out into the night to stand guard.

In contrast, Vinsid and Ardval yelled laughter. They were unmarried, a condition Ardval ached to remedy. Unfortunately for him—or perhaps for the women he met—he was a playful man who enjoyed the chase too much to settle down. His closest friend in the company was Vinsid, whose sullen nature doomed any chase. Vinsid seldom smiled, and no one had heard him laugh, except when Camwish was telling stories. His friendship with Ardval seemed to rely on their ability to balance each other.

The remaining unmarried riflemen were young Flisk, who had only experienced one hell, Nowel, the company's stitcher and bonesetter, and Elgart. Flisk listened with wide-eyed incredulity. When he was provoked to laughter, he sounded faintly hysterical. Apparently, he was still uncomfortable with humor as raw as the horsemaster's; or perhaps he was simply unconvinced. But Nowel scowled humorlessly. He knew too much about the possible consequences—the diseases, duels, and ruined marriages—of adventures like the ones Camwish described. And Elgart, as he often did, seemed to be of two minds about what he heard. One eye glittered with glee while the other looked skeptical. When he was not chuckling, he added his own sarcastic commentary to Camwish's tales.

Captain Swalish was one of the only married men, and he doted on his wife and children. Perhaps because he was loyal to them, or perhaps because he was too unimaginative to enjoy extravagance, he gave Camwish nothing more than amiable disinterest. As for newly wed Stolle, his real interest lay in hearing secrets he could whisper to his wife. He laughed when others did. At other times, his lips moved as if he were memorizing what he wanted to reveal later.

They were a diverse company, but Prince Bifalt trusted them all. He and Captain Swalish had chosen them. He had trained with each of them; had fought beside some of them. They had their weaknesses, certainly. But they had proven their courage, and their discipline never failed. While Camwish talked, the Prince was content to stand outside the circle of his men and pay no attention.

Instead, he turned his thoughts to the teamsters.

He did not know them at all, apart from their names. They had been picked for him: a father and son named Spliner and—apparently—"Boy," and two brothers called Hught and Winnow. When the Prince spoke to them, trying indirectly to probe their loyalty, they looked to Captain Swalish for permission before they replied. Prince Bifalt noticed, however, that they had no visible interest in Camwish's tales. They were practical men, dedicated to their oxen, and quick to complain about their own exertions and discomforts, but unassuming otherwise. They may have been too stolid to appreciate the horse-master's flights of fancy.

Eventually, Camwish talked himself out, and Swalish sent the guardsmen to their bedrolls. But the Prince stayed awake for a while, pacing around the camp. He told himself he was keeping watch; but in truth he could not stop gnawing the dry bones of his worries. Slack had not joined Camwish's audience; and the former sorcerer's absence raised new questions about the "chambers" of the man—or of any man.

In himself, the Prince knew, there was a place that always feared hearing the words, **Are you ready?**

Then, on the seventh day, the pendulum of fortune swung the other way. By this time, the quest's road had become a dirt track unimproved by use. Shrubs clustered inconveniently down the center of the trail. The wheel-ruts which had once served distant towns and hamlets were now cluttered with rocks and potholes. In addition, the wood had become a forest, and the trees clustering close on both sides blocked any other path. The oxen were forced to strain along at a slower pace; yet even that laborious walk met hazards. The crack as one of the wain's wheels shattered dropping from a rock into a pothole sounded to Prince Bifalt like a nail driven into a coffin lid with one blow.

That wain was lost. The company carried tools for minor repairs, but no spare wheel. With their iron rims and heavy spokes, they broke too rarely. Interrupted by swearing, obscenities, and brief respites, the riflemen and the teamsters spent the rest of the day sorting the remaining foodstuffs, casks of water, bundles of fodder, and bedrolls, piling only the most necessary onto the intact wain, and rigging the two teams of oxen to pull together. The Prince and his companions were compelled to make a cold camp in the forest, where they were vulnerable.

The Captain set three guardsmen to stand watch among the trees. Other than the Prince, the rest slept the sleep of exhaustion. And with the dawn, the company prepared to resume its arduous plod.

Still, the pendulum of fortune swung against them. Before all the riders were mounted, a snake struck the leg of one of the horses. No doubt the tramping of the steeds as their riders began to mount had disturbed the serpent—and beyond question it was venomous. Screaming, the horse went mad.

Prince Bifalt's men caught and restrained the beast promptly; but even Camwish could not calm the animal. And his horse balms had no virtue against poisons. When he and the Prince smelled venom in the froth spurting from the animal's nostrils, they knew the horse had to be put down.

They had all killed horses on the battlefield, putting crippled animals out of their agony. The beast was dispatched quickly. Only Elgart cursed the necessity.

The company was now short a mount.

And the oxen could not bear more weight. Although they heaved at their burdens, they were scarcely able to draw the over-laden wain as it was. Spliner and Boy took the reins while Hught and Winnow pulled on the yokes, giving their beasts what aid they could; but still the wain's pace was little better than a crawl. The Captain's men had to take turns riding double.

When the questers emerged from the forest at last, they found their path had dwindled further. It was now no more than the sketch of a trail. Nevertheless, it offered several branchings, all no doubt leading to widely scattered villages, hamlets, and farmsteads, most of them deserted. The company might have been able to obtain more food and fodder from habitations in the south; but Prince Bifalt could not afford the time to go scores of leagues out of his way. Biting his cheek, he chose the track that ran most directly east.

It frustrated him by wandering widely. First, it veered to the northeast until it approached a horse-breeder's abandoned ranch. Next, it turned almost directly south to reach an equally forsaken farmstead. Only then did it drift more to the east.

These shifts added leagues to the trek. They consumed additional supplies and extended the exertions of the oxen. Prince Bifalt would have preferred to forsake the track entirely and pick his own way east. Unfortunately, the terrain forbade him. The trail was difficult for the oxen, but the surrounding rough hillocks, bracken, and wild grasses would be impossible. And where the ground was masked by vegetation, unpleasant surprises might lurk. Gullies might force the company to return to the track. More leagues would be added, more time lost.

Vexed and bitter, the Prince kept to the trail. On a direct heading, the desert—the true beginning of his quest—was still distant. The whims of his path made him fear he might not reach the border of Belleger for ten days or more.

It was all time lost: time during which the Amikans might finally find themselves ready to launch a killing strike against King Abbator in his city. And the Prince could do nothing to improve his progress.

The next day, however, the company came to a hamlet still inhabited despite its disrepair, its air of hopelessness. A few families with their children clung to life there. They emerged from hovels and failing houses to stare wide-eyed at Prince Bifalt and his companions. Halting, he found himself regarding four women and three men with a cluster of six or seven children.

The children must have been of various ages, but the penury of their lives had reduced them to similarity. All had the same gaping mouths, the same gap-toothed jaws, the same clumps of hair lost from their scalps, the same rags on their stick-thin limbs. All had the same helpless despair in their eyes, a look that seemed to preclude any possible wonder at the company's coming. Their parents fared no better, but the adults were stronger, or perhaps more hardened. They were able to show surprise.

After a moment's hesitation, Slack came to Prince Bifalt's side. "By your leave, Highness," murmured the former sorcerer.

The Prince nodded consent, although he had no conception of Slack's purpose.

At once, Slack dismounted. Approaching the wary adults, he spoke to them softly. At first, they appeared reluctant to respond. But then one woman nodded toward a half-fallen house on the opposite side of the track, and the man beside her pointed. Quick with thanks, Slack crossed the track and entered the house.

Captain Swalish nudged his mount closer to the Prince. "What does the sorcerer seek, Highness?" he asked in a low voice.

Prince Bifalt ignored the question. Instead, he commanded, "Look at them, Captain."

The burly man sighed. "Must I, Highness? The sight pains me."

"It should," retorted the Prince. "They are Bellegerin. The King's subjects. *Our* people." He had hardened his heart, but it was not hard enough. And he was not slow to make decisions. "They must be fed."

"Highness!" Captain Swalish tried to protest, but Prince Bifalt silenced him.

"Unpack the wain, Captain. I say these people must be fed. We will give them supplies enough for one good meal now, and for a lesser on the morrow." He spoke with muted ferocity, although his ire was not directed at the Captain. "If we are hungry later, I will not regret what I have given away." Gripping the Captain's arm, he hissed his frustration, wrath, and doubt into the man's ear. *"They must be fed."*

For him, sorrow and pity were anger.

His tone convinced Captain Swalish. The man turned away at once to obey.

The King's advisers, Prince Bifalt knew, would call what he did madness. They might accuse him of choosing to fail. But they were not *here*. They heard reports of conditions in the realm's outlying regions: they did not witness what the Prince saw. He gave more weight to the reactions of his veterans; and he was pleased to see them respond without hesitation. Even Elgart did not hold back. They had hearts as well as eyes, and they had all seen a surfeit of slaughter. If they did not wish to preserve the folk of Belleger, their presence—their quest itself—served no purpose.

As for the teamsters, they enjoyed any relief from goading their teams. While the guards obeyed the Prince, the teamsters cared for their oxen.

Shortly, Slack returned. Although his manner drooped more than usual, he lifted his gaze as high as Prince Bifalt's chest.

"Highness," he reported in a tone that resembled woe, "I have spoken with the oldest man here. I fear he will not live long, but his mind remains clear. I asked if he knew any tales concerning a library, a repository of books. Perhaps his father had told him of such a place, or had mentioned hearing of it from *his* father. But the old man shook his head. 'Books?' he asked me. 'What use are books when the land starves?'

"I assured him King Abbator has not forgotten the straits of his subjects. Then I left him to his decline."

Without awaiting a response, the former Magister hastened away to prepare a meal. Bartin and Nowel had already started a fire. Retrieving his skillets and pots, Slack went to work.

When the food was ready, Prince Bifalt watched the ravenous survivors eat. He could not look away. He approved as the parents cautioned their children to fill their mouths slowly, knowing he could not have shown so much restraint in their place. The need of the waifs transfixed him. It seemed to rule him.

If he could have destroyed the entire realm of Amika with a word at that moment, he would have done so.

❋

After the meal was eaten, and a bundle of provisions for the next day had been delivered to the adults, the Prince refused their gratitude. "We have done nothing," he answered gruffly. "In two days, your plight will be as it was. We cannot save you."

"Yet you have come, and are generous," replied one of the women. "When you are gone, you will still be generous. No doubt some great purpose has brought you this way. Perhaps in the end you *will* save us."

To the Prince's ear, her speech sounded strangely stilted. His immediate impression was that she was not speaking her native dialect. But that was mere fancy. Living so far from other folk, and in such deprivation, she had probably lost the habit of speech. Her awkwardness was an effect of disuse, nothing more.

Rather than reply to her, he signaled for his companions and the wain to resume their journey.

Groaning, the oxen and their handlers heaved the wain into motion. The guards and Slack mounted to resume their accustomed places behind Captain Swalish and the Prince. With a slowness that galled Prince Bifalt's nerves, the company left the hamlet behind.

An hour or two later, Flisk called for the Captain's attention. When Swalish, the Prince, and their companions looked behind them, they saw a smudge of black smoke in the distance where the hamlet lay.

"Captain?" demanded Prince Bifalt. Instinctively, he feared some calamity.

But Captain Swalish was not concerned. "A bonfire, Highness," he replied. "Most of those hovels are empty. They can spare the wood. Maybe the warmth comforts them. Or maybe they cook their food to make it last longer."

Risking a quick glance at the Prince, Slack said, "We left no live embers that might cause a blaze."

Slack's assurance, and the Captain's explanation, did not satisfy Prince Bifalt. He wanted to send one of his men to check on the villagers. But his frustration was mounting every day; it had been made worse by the sight of Bellegerin children starving; and he still had no idea how far he had to go to reach the desert—after which he would have to find his way without even a sketch of a map. He could not afford the time to wait for a rider to go and come back. He needed to keep moving.

Muttering curses to himself, he led his company onward.

�֍

Now the track straggled to the northeast, leading the company by small increments closer to the river boundary of Amika. On the following day, the Prince passed another hamlet. In every respect, it resembled the habitation he had encountered the previous day; but this one was entirely forsaken. Still the trail drifted northeastward. Studying his map, he marked how far he had to go before his true difficulties began, and how near lay the lands of his foes. He felt a tribe of rats chewing on his vitals, but he could do nothing to expel them.

Late the next day, however, a place that had once been a village became visible ahead. When he reached it, he found at least twenty people living there, defying the decayed condition of their homes. As a group, they seemed less destitute than the folk of the hamlet two days past, but the difference was slight. The men and women were somewhat better clad, and the children showed fewer lost teeth, fewer bald patches on their scalps, less sunken cheeks. Still, the children might have been made of kindling, their limbs were so thin, their bellies so hollow. Where their eyes were not filled with despair, they held a mute animal greed for food.

Fortunately, the adults included one old woman, one older man, and one man positively ancient. When Slack asked his leave, Prince Bifalt did not hesitate. Pausing only to instruct Captain Swalish sternly, "*Feed* them," he dismounted with Slack and accompanied the former sorcerer.

Addressing the village's old ones courteously, kindly, Slack drew the woman and the two men aside. "Good folk," he began as the Prince listened, "we see your privation is desperate. His Highness Prince Bifalt will spare what he can to feed you. While his men prepare a meal, will you speak with us? We have a question, or perhaps several. Your answers may aid us."

The woman chewed her toothless gums for a moment. Then she replied in a voice made querulous by want, "You are lords of this realm. We will answer. We would answer if you did not feed us."

To the Prince's ear, her speech resembled that of the woman who had offered him gratitude in the hamlet. But she was obviously starving: he would not fault her for her accent.

Slack thanked her, then ventured, "Our question concerns books—or rather, a storehouse of books, a library or repository. Have you heard talk of such a place, perhaps from your fathers, perhaps from your grandfathers? Any word or tale? Any legend?"

"Books?" the older man snorted. "What use have we for books? Our lives are survival, nothing more. At one time, we fed ourselves. Now we fail at our only task."

"But you are not the oldest," chided the woman. Prince Bifalt heard more reproach in her tone than he expected. "Ambrost is. Perhaps he can answer." She prodded the ancient's ribs with one finger. "If his wits have not strayed."

Ambrost shook himself. Briefly, he gaped at Slack and the Prince with confusion in his milky eyes. Then he seemed to rally.

"Books?" he croaked. "Did you say books?"

"I did, good sir," replied Slack with more calm than Prince Bifalt could have managed.

"Great piles of books?" persisted the ancient. "Whole mountains of books?"

Slack nodded. "Indeed." His demeanor gave no hint of impatience or excitement.

After a long moment, Ambrost sighed. "Yes."

He lapsed into silence.

"Remember for us, if you will," urged Slack, still gently. "What tales have you heard concerning whole mountains of books?"

Ambrost appeared to consult the dimness of his sight. "Books, you say?" he muttered. "Books and sorcery? Oh, yes." His tone was sour. "My grandfather told wild tales when I was a lad at his knee. A great storehouse of books against the mountains. A storehouse like one castle piled on top of another to reach the heavens. Sorcerers with unimaginable powers. He told such tales, my grandfather. I was a lad. I listened. Others did not."

Now Prince Bifalt felt a suggestion of eagerness; but he remained silent. He could not make his tone as soothing as Slack's.

"Wondrous tales," remarked the former Magister. "I am not surprised they remain in your memory. I would gladly hear them myself." Then he asked, "Did they suggest where this storehouse might be found?"

The ancient pursed his lips. His eyes wandered like those of a man trying to trace some recollection to its source. With an air of triumph, he pronounced, "The Repository. The great castle of the sorcerers. Yes." Abruptly, he flung out his arm, waving indiscriminately northward. "It lies in Amika. Against the mountains. As I said."

———

The Prince's dismay made his jaws ache with the strain of containing it. In Amika? *Amika?* Fighting for calm, he said, "Do not be alarmed if I appear distressed. You have told us enough"—the words threatened to choke him—"and I am grateful. Slack will now oversee the cooking. You will have the best meal we can provide. I must consult with my men."

He could not say more without vehemence. Wheeling away, he strode toward Captain Swalish and the horses. At his back, he heard Slack express better thanks. Then the former sorcerer hastened to join the preparation of food.

Prince Bifalt's black glower warned the Captain to meet him halfway. As they came together, the Prince gripped Swalish's arm and drew him farther until they were beyond hearing. There he released the Captain, crossed his arms to conceal the trembling of his hands. Without preamble, he growled, "They say the Repository—the great castle of the sorcerers—is in Amika."

Captain Swalish stared. "Do you believe them, Highness?"

The Prince swallowed curses. "The oldest of them heard tales from his grandfather, who may have been ancient himself when he told them. The grandfather may have invented those tales to give himself stature. How can I believe him? Yet they are Bellegerins starved near to death by Amika's wars. How can I doubt him? He has no cause to lie."

Swalish considered the dilemma. He appeared to stretch his mind in unfamiliar ways. "The cause," he replied slowly, "may be nothing more than a desire to please you. If he did not have an answer, he might have imagined it. Maybe he feared you would take back your offer of food."

"I think not," snorted Prince Bifalt. "Slack assured them they would be fed before he spoke of our search.

"And if the old man sought only to please or placate me," he continued with growing exasperation, "why *that* lie? Did he suppose I would be *gratified* to hear my quest is hopeless?"

The Captain looked baffled. "Then, Highness, we must guess whether to trust what he heard. Or what he remembers."

Hells! Glaring at everything under the sun, Prince Bifalt commanded, "Summon Slack. We will hear his thoughts."

Relieved to be spared responsibility for decisions based on speculation, Captain Swalish turned and shouted to Bartin.

Bartin addressed Slack. The old soldier gestured commands. The former sorcerer mimed vexation. But he did not refuse. Consigning his preparations to Stolle and Flisk, he came at an older man's trot to join the Prince.

Briefly, Prince Bifalt explained his dilemma: could he trust what he had heard about the library and its location? Then he asked, "How does this riddle strike you, Slack? I need counsel."

Slack made a show of hesitation. He frowned in one direction, then squinted in another, always avoiding the Prince's gaze. He held his hands with his fingers tangled together as if they echoed a mind twisted by contradictory impulses.

Speaking like a man who tested each word before he uttered it, he answered, "There is this, Highness. If the library indeed lies in Amika, that might explain how our foes gained access to Hexin Marrow's book and mastered its secrets before we knew of its existence."

Now Prince Bifalt cursed aloud, violently, and with a veteran's precision. When he had vented his dread and indignation, however, he chose his immediate course. Dismissing Slack, he waited until the man had resumed his cooking. Then he addressed Captain Swalish again.

"To my eye, Captain," he said, rigid with restraint, "our trail appears to continue northeast."

Swalish nodded. "Evening is near, Highness, and my sight is not what it was. Also that hill"—he indicated the northeastern horizon—"hides what lies beyond it. I can send Flisk to scout the track for a league or two. His eyes are the keenest we have."

Prince Bifalt nodded. "Do so."

Together, the two men returned to the clamor of the guards and Slack as they gave the villagers a better meal than those poor folk had tasted in many seasons.

Urged by Captain Swalish, Flisk mounted his steed and rode away. As the youngest of the veterans, he still felt a desire to prove himself among them. Spurring his horse, he soon dropped beyond the rise of the hill.

Rowels of a different kind goaded Prince Bifalt. While the villagers, hungry as wolves, devoured their meal, he commanded his men to reload the wain. When the pots and skillets had been emptied, the plates and utensils licked clean, and a quantity of water the company could ill afford drunk, the Prince was ready to depart. He only awaited Flisk's return.

In his acid mood, he sent Slack to deal with the gratitude of the villagers. He wanted none of it. His mind was full of intimations, none of which seemed clear or credible. Would he find himself forced to dare the lands of his enemies? If so, how? How could he cross the barrier of the river and its gorges? Even if he found a trail that allowed him to cross the Line—him and his men and their horses—how could he take the wain with him? And how could his purpose survive the dangers of Amika?

How could he determine whether Ambrost had lied?

However, he had made the first of his decisions. He would not spend the night where he was. No. The needs of the villagers asked too much of him. Soon he would have neither food nor water to sustain his men. When Flisk came back to report that a league beyond the hill the trail branched, one path continuing northeastward, the other tending more to the southeast, Prince Bifalt hailed his train into motion. To Captain Swalish, he announced his intention to make camp at the branching. He would choose his heading on the morrow.

Ponderous as men bearing the wounded and the dead from a battlefield, the Prince and his company left the village, ascended the gradual slope of the hill, and sank beyond it into the obscure embrace of evening.

※

At the branching, they halted. Watches were set. The horses and oxen were tended and tethered. Bedrolls were tossed down from the wain. Rejecting the small tent provided because he was the King's son, Prince Bifalt set out his bedding under the stars. Although he had no use for astrology, he hoped—contrary to his nature—that the slow wheel of the heavens might guide his thoughts. His blankets he wrapped tightly around him against the night's cold, but if he slept, he did not know it.

By his estimation, he was no more than five leagues from the gorges of the Line River, the only barrier between him and his enemies.

With the dawn, he rose and packed his bedroll. He watched the teamsters rouse themselves, grumbling while they went about their tasks. Captain Swalish reported that the guards on watch had seen nothing to make them uneasy. With more than his usual alacrity, Slack rolled from his bedding and went to feed the men. And still the Prince, who was not accustomed to indecision, doubted himself.

But he refused his uncertainty. When at last the company was ready to resume its trek, and Captain Swalish asked for orders, Prince Bifalt said only, "The track to the northeast, Captain."

Perhaps the terrain closer to the border of Amika, or the Line River itself, would render Ambrost's assertion moot. The only question then would be, How long should he search for a crossing before he gave up? Before he faced his failure?

Accompanied by a cacophony of curses from the teamsters, groans and snorting from the oxen, and fragmentary muttering among the guardsmen, the quest lurched into motion.

Within an hour, Camwish called out that his mount had gone lame. Although he examined his steed with care, he found no treatable injury. The beast was simply lame: it could not bear his weight. And it would not heal without days of rest. With Prince Bifalt's irate consent and the Captain's rueful approval, Camwish unburdened his horse of its saddle, tack, and halter, then turned it loose.

So another hour was lost.

The company of guards now had eight mounts for ten men, and the boots of the men were poorly made for long treks on foot. However, Prince Bifalt had foreseen this. From the first, he had assumed that a time would come—in the desert if not before—when the horses would no longer be worth the weight of water and fodder they required. At his command, the wain carried a set of sturdy knee-high moccasins for every rifleman. Wearing them, unmounted men could match the pace of the oxen without harming their feet.

Chewing the inside of his cheek mercilessly, the Prince led his companions forward. To the rhythm of his destrier's steps, he asked himself, Enter Amika or turn back? Enter or turn? But he had no answer.

Then, toward noon, Flisk raised a cry that halted the company again. Waving an arm, he pointed back in the direction of the village.

Despite the distance and the tugging breezes, smoke showed above the horizon.

Prince Bifalt stared. His thoughts eddied in circles he could not escape. What reason could the villagers have for setting any of their homes ablaze? And the earlier hamlet had done the same. The coincidence was too great. True, the night had been chill—but not cold enough to justify such a large fire. After all, the wood could not be replenished. What possible reason—?

Hardly daring to acknowledge his alarm, the Prince sent Flisk to scout the way ahead. "Ride hard," he commanded. "If you sight another village or hamlet, study it until you know if it is inhabited. Do not approach it. Return at speed."

At once, Flisk sketched a salute, dug his heels into his mount, and obeyed at a gallop.

"Highness?" asked Captain Swalish quietly. "What troubles you? Any chance can set a village like that burning. It has been neglected for years. It is tinder."

Prince Bifalt said nothing for a moment. Like a man holding his breath, he watched the track where Flisk had ridden out of view. Then he observed, "The speech of those villagers. It had a strange sound. I have not heard it before."

While Swalish looked away, unsure how to answer, old Bartin volunteered, "Folk speak that way in the north. When I was a boy—before you were born, Highness—my family lived near the Line. A league or two farther east. We left when I was called to the war. But while we were here, we spoke like those villagers. I did not know we had an accent until we reached the Open Hand."

The Prince shook his head. He had spent his whole life in the vicinity of the Hand. He could not argue with Bartin's explanation. But still, that smoke troubled him—

Slack came to him with a different question. "As we are already halted, Highness, and must await Flisk's return, shall I prepare a meal? The beasts need rest, and guardsmen are always hungry."

For that query, the King's son had a curt reply. "No. Unpack nothing. Remain ready."

A burning village could set the grasses and bracken around it on fire: an obvious danger. Was that what disturbed him? No. How could a blaze reach him at this distance? True, this region had not seen rain for at least a fortnight. But the high grasses seemed lush, the bracken flourished, and the wildflowers were bright with color.

He did not believe the overgrown hills and lowlands would take flame.

Nevertheless, the pressure in his chest expanded as if he were indeed holding his breath.

In the distance, Flisk reappeared, galloping furiously. Prince Bifalt did not need to hear the man's shout to understand his haste. At Flick's back, he saw fresh smoke begin its rise into the cloudless sky.

The Prince's world reeled. It veered into a new shape. Wheeling his destrier, he roared at his men.

"Ambush! We will be attacked!"

"Highness?" asked Captain Swalish, gaping.

"The smoke!" retorted the Prince. "Those are signal fires! They mark our progress! Now we are bracketed! The Amikans know where we are!"

His yell confused the teamsters. Fortunately, their only duty in a fray was to hide under the wain. The riflemen and their Captain understood the Prince better.

Barking orders, Captain Swalish called his men into formation against the north. They unslung their rifles and steadied their mounts in a protective arc to ward the wain, the oxen, and Slack. Some sighted their guns on the horizon of the nearest hill. Others held their rifles ready while they loosened their sabers, preparing for close combat.

They were cavalry veterans, trained to fight from horseback. Obliquely, Prince Bifalt wondered whether it might be wiser for his men to dismount and engage on foot, trusting their guns to drive off their attackers while their horses were shielded behind the wain.

But he could not be sure that his foes would come from the north. His company might need to change its formation in an instant.

The sky looked unnaturally clear. Even the low winds seemed to pause, waiting to see what would happen.

How did Amika know? he asked the empty air. Who betrayed us? How were we found?

In the distance, two men rose from hiding places in the tall grass. They threw what might have been rocks at the Prince's company—if rocks had trailed burning fuses. At once, the men ducked back into the grass.

Their grenades struck some thirty paces short of the company. The concussions as they exploded shocked the Prince's hearing. They seemed to startle the ground under his destrier's hooves. Flames erupted from the impacts. Clods of earth, clumps of grass, shreds of bracken: all burst into the air like frightened birds. But the blasts did not touch the Bellegerins.

Nevertheless, Prince Bifalt was shaken. Clearly, Amika had discovered gunpowder. And Amikan alchemists or soldiers had devised an unexpected use for it. There were references to such weapons in the old papers that had inspired Belleger's efforts to make rifles. But the idea of grenades had been dismissed early. No *thrown* explosion had enough range to threaten enemy sorcerers. Everything Belleger had done to create rifles and keep them secret had been aimed at countering Amika's Magisters.

One purpose. No distractions. Bellegerin single-mindedness.

The Prince considered it his greatest strength. He was not afraid. No sane foe would waste gunpowder when it could use theurgy. Therefore, the ambush did not include a sorcerer.

All around where the grenades had exploded, the grasses and bracken caught fire. And where they burned, they emitted clouds of dense smoke. In moments, smoke the colors of ash and soot veiled the north. Prince Bifalt glimpsed nothing more than obscure shapes behind or within the fume.

Instinctively, he believed those shapes were horsemen.

"Open fire!" he roared, although his men could only guess at their targets.

At once, rifles shouted flame and lead into the smoke. The guards snatched back their bolts to eject spent casings, then slammed the bolts home to fire again. Each rifle held a clip of six cartridges. Each veteran carried a satchel of loaded clips. If the Prince's men sustained their rate of fire, they might disrupt the Amikan charge without ever seeing their foes.

Through the rattling din of the rifles, he heard a horse's scream. Another cry may have come from an attacker.

Then a volley of arrows flew out of the smoke, men and horses among the company went down, and the defense became chaos.

Arrows by the score. Arrows sent by skilled archers who nocked and loosed their shafts almost as quickly as the rifles fired. It was conceivable that the Amikans had left their mounts behind. On foot, they would be slower than horses; but they could hold their bows steady and take better aim. The smoke would give them more cover if they were closer to the ground.

Camwish was already dead, a shaft jutting from his throat. Flisk had taken an arrow in one shoulder. Now he struggled to fire his rifle and work the bolt with one hand. Stolle lay writhing under his stricken mount.

Prince Bifalt fired a shot at random. Lowering his aim, he fired again, and had the satisfaction of seeing a shape as vague as a shadow fall.

A cruel breeze carried the smoke toward the Bellegerins. But it was thinning, dissipated by the wind; or perhaps the grasses resisted burning. On impulse, the Prince slung his rifle over his shoulder, drew his saber, shouted to his mount, and sent the destrier into the thickest of the fumes.

This was fighting he understood, man against man. It was honest. There was no safety in it. Amikans would die, or he would. He slashed fiercely, down on one side, down on the other, hacking at foes he saw or did not see from one blow to the next. When his blade bit flesh, he did not pause. When he cut only air, he continued swinging. He struck down two of his foes, then a third, before he burst through the smoke to clear air.

There he found a score of Amikans advancing, mounted, behind their obscured comrades. Random bullets had left three dead among them—three men and two horses. The rest were unscathed.

Enemy commands responded to Prince Bifalt's arrival. Five archers wheeled to pierce him with flights of arrows.

His training saved him. He dropped from the far side of his horse, tossed his saber aside, snatched up his rifle. Shooting at speed from the cover of his destrier, he felled one Amikan and winged another before his clip was empty.

While he scrambled to set another clip, arrows thudded into his horse. Squealing its agony, the beast collapsed toward him. It could have trapped him under it; but as it fell, he kicked out his legs and sprawled beyond it. Although the impact knocked the air from his lungs, he did not let it slow him. He was already in position to resume fire, concealed behind his dying animal.

His foes were closer now. Fighting for breath, he ended two of them with three shots. The winged Amikan and his comrade veered away, racing now to outrun his bullets.

The Prince ignored them. In the distance, at the far edge of the failing flames, he saw archers loose fire arrows across the smoke. They were aiming at the wain, trying to set it alight.

If the company lost the wain—or its supplies—Prince Bifalt's quest would end here, whether or not any of his men survived.

The range was too great for accurate rifle-fire. Still, the Prince did what he could. He emptied his clip—three more bullets—at the fire-arrow archers. One fortunate shot hit a horse, forcing the Amikan to leap free. Then the Prince sprang to his feet and sprinted forward, discarding his clip and slapping another into place as he ran.

Now he was able to see his company through the fading smoke. Stolid as a stone, Captain Swalish sat his horse and directed a fragmented fusillade toward the fire-arrow archers. At the same time, Elgart stood atop the wain with a water cask, splashing every fiery shaft as it struck.

In a moment, Captain Swalish and his remaining men drove off the threat to the wain. At once, Elgart took up his rifle and began to shoot at the nearest Amikans.

Abruptly, the ambush ended. The last of the fire arrows must have served as a prearranged signal. As one, the unmounted attackers turned and ran, racing to reach their horses before Bellegerin bullets hit them. In unison, the mounted Amikans near the

Prince wheeled to flee. Captain Swalish and a few guardsmen continued shooting. They took down two more men before the rest passed beyond reasonable range for the rifles.

The Captain ordered a cease-fire. Other attacks might come, and the company's supply of cartridges was limited.

Prince Bifalt was closer to the Amikan flight. He took aim. Before he could fire, however, his attention was caught by Slack.

Ducking out from under the wain, the former Magister dashed to his horse, flung himself into the saddle, and followed the attackers at a desperate gallop.

Again the Prince's world reeled. Slack was not pursuing the Amikan forces. What harm could he do them? He had no theurgy.

He meant to join them.

Bartin fired at Slack's back; missed. He slammed home another bullet and fired again. This cartridge exploded in the breech, shattering the rifle. Hot shards of iron ripped through Bartin's hands, his chest, his face. He fell screaming.

Without a glance at the Prince, Slack sped to distance himself from the betrayed quest.

He was not fast enough—and Prince Bifalt was not slow in decision. For him, rage was speed. It was steadiness. In one quick motion, he aimed and fired.

His shot punched Slack forward. For an instant, the former sorcerer clung to his mount's neck. Then he toppled aside and flopped to the ground, left there by his frightened horse.

None of the Amikans returned to retrieve their fallen ally. They could not outface rifle-fire.

Running, Prince Bifalt approached Slack. He heard horses behind him—Captain Swalish and another guardsman, Vinsid—but he did not wait for them to cover him. As soon as he reached Slack, he flipped the man onto his back.

He was still alive.

At once, the Prince crouched at the man's side, gripped his shirt, jerked his head up. "Traitor! Spy! You *dared*?"

Slack did not meet Prince Bifalt's bitter gaze. The dullness of dying filled his eyes. He would meet no living gaze again.

Close to his last breath, he gasped, "I know what you do not. I will not enlighten you." The blood bubbling from his mouth promised that he spoke the truth. "But I will tell you this. My teacher was an Amikan Magister."

Again Prince Bifalt's world took a new shape. Vague alarms and intimations gained substance. He heaved Slack from side to side as if he sought to snap the man's neck.

"The villagers we fed? Amikan? *All* Amikan?"

"Belleger's victims," breathed Slack wetly. "They volunteered. To stop you."

"Victims?" shouted the Prince. "Amika makes victims of *us*!" Almost weeping with fury, he cried, "We *fed* them!"

"Your generosity—" Slack spoke weakly. The Prince had to stop shaking him and lean close to hear. "It astonished me. But I could not turn from my purpose.

"You must not find the book."

He drew one last gurgling breath. Then his life slumped out of him, leaving him limp in Prince Bifalt's grasp.

Captain Swalish and Vinsid approached. Their mounts stamped to a halt. "Highness!" croaked the Captain.

The Prince released Slack's body. He needed to understand, but he could not compel answers from a corpse. The memory of his talk with his supposed comrade made him writhe. *You may be the most necessary member of our company.* He had said that after Slack had said, *A man is not a man at all*— He should not have trusted the former Magister. He should not have chosen the northeast track.

He should not have been commanded to lead this futile quest. He had no instinct for treachery. He had imagined that a powerless sorcerer could be honest.

Captain Swalish dropped to the grass. *"Highness,"* he insisted. "He is dead. We must *go*. They will regroup. They have more than enough men. Our losses—"

Prince Bifalt did not raise his head. Looking at Swalish and Vinsid required too much effort. Slack's betrayal held him. As if to himself, he muttered, "They fear our rifles." But he knew the Captain was right. More strongly, he repeated, "They fear our rifles."

Captain Swalish started to protest. The Prince demanded silence with a gesture. "Vinsid," he ordered, "go after them. If you can drop a straggler or two, do so. Make them think we give chase. But do not risk yourself. See how far they go before they gather themselves. See if they have reinforcements. Come back and tell us how much time we have."

Vinsid nodded. His sullen glower cracked uncharacteristically, baring his teeth in a feral grin. He had lost his best friend. Without a word, he rode away, following the track left by the Amikans.

His departure eased Captain Swalish. The Captain came to Prince Bifalt's side. Clearing his throat, he said hoarsely, "A just

end, Highness. A bullet in the back is a kinder death than he deserved."

Prince Bifalt rose unsteadily to his feet. The weakness in his
limbs undermined him, but he ignored it. "*How*, Captain?" he
demanded, disguising his frailty with ire. "How was this done to
us? We were told the river and its gorges are impassable."

Swalish rasped a curse. In his fashion, he was as angry as the
Prince. "We were mistaken, Highness," he snarled. "That is all.
We were mistaken. We have never scouted this boundary. Why
should we? No army attacks us here. Cunning and treachery we
could expect—but not *here*.

"A fault of judgment, Highness," he declared with more assurance, "but not a fault of *ours*. Our commanders think what their
commanders thought. None of them studied this terrain. They did
not know enough to warn us. With an Amikan spy among us, we
were exposed to some attack from the start."

Yes, the Prince thought. From the start. Because we have always
relied upon sorcery. We did not imagine we could be made helpless
so easily.

But he did not speak that thought aloud. Instead, he replied
harshly, "We are still exposed, Captain. How many men do we
have?"

Swalish looked away. His flesh seemed to sag on his bones.
Hoarse again, he answered, "Come, Highness, and count our
losses. See what has become of us."

Prince Bifalt knew then that his losses were severe.

PART
TWO

However, the Prince did not return at once to the wain and his men. First he went to his destrier—his fallen favorite—and searched the tall grasses until he recovered his saber. Only then did he mount behind the Captain and ride to see what price his company had paid.

He had left Belleger's Fist with ten guardsmen. He now had five, although only Swalish, Vinsid, and Elgart were uninjured. The arrow in Flisk's shoulder prevented him from performing even such tasks as saddling his horse. Fortunately, the fifth, Klamath, had suffered nothing worse than grazed ribs. The cut bled heavily, and the pain made him wince, but he assured the Prince that he would be able to fight once his wound was bandaged.

Camwish was among the dead, as was Nowel. The explosion of Bartin's rifle had killed him instantly. Ardval had taken an arrow in his face and lay close to death. He still drew shuddering breaths, but the interval between them stretched as Prince Bifalt watched.

The last loss was Stolle, who had been crushed by his horse. Even Nowel at his best could not have treated the man's internal bleeding. He would not whisper secrets to his wife again. But while his life and pain lasted, he wept. "She will not understand," he moaned between gasps of blood. "She will not. Dead? she will cry. For what? *For what?* I cannot get her to understand."

Captain Swalish ignored them all. Like a man who could not bear the sight of his dead and dying, he watched the north, studying the hills for some sign of Vinsid.

Despite his hurt ribs, Klamath tried to make Stolle more comfortable. But there was nothing that could save him.

Weighted with grief—a burden he carried as smoldering fury—the Prince went to join Captain Swalish.

For their part, none of the teamsters had been harmed. The wain had covered them. But the beasts had not fared so well. Two more horses were dead, one urgently needed to be released from its agony, and one ox would have to be put down. Slack's mount was gone; the Prince's, slain. The company was left with four horses for six men, three oxen for the wain. By Elgart's efforts, the wain itself and its burden of supplies had taken no significant damage.

Prince Bifalt neither knew nor cared how many Amikans had been killed, or would die soon. Only those that remained concerned him.

They were enough to strike again.

"*I* do not understand," protested Klamath in a cracking voice. "How was this done to us? How can Amika know what we do?"

"Spies," snapped Elgart. "Amika did not need many. One would be enough. Slack volunteered to join us. He knew when we would depart. He knew where we hoped to go. He could guess our heading. A spy took his report to Amika.

"The villagers we fed. Those starved and dying children. Those decrepit elders. They were all Amikan. They crossed the gorges and the Line into our lands, groups of them. All sent to affect our choices. They found abandoned homes, where they pretended to live. When they saw us—when they knew where we were—they waited until we were gone. Then they fired the houses. The signals warned other groups. They warned the force that ambushed us.

"It was simple enough. If they knew trails and river crossings. They could wade shallows. People on foot could use goat tracks in the gorges." He shrugged. "Horses could not. But those soldiers had days. They could have brought the horses across one at a time."

Trembling, Klamath asked, "Will they send more?"

Elgart snorted. "They do not need *more*. We left enough of them alive to finish us."

Prince Bifalt found himself nodding. He knew that Elgart was right.

There was still no sign of Vinsid.

When Ardval was gone, and Stolle had too much blood in his mouth and throat to speak, Captain Swalish tried to cast the company's straits in a less ruinous light. Loud enough to be heard by the others, he said gruffly, "We were fortunate, Highness. They did not bring a sorcerer."

The Prince thought that Amika had better uses for its theurgy. Every Magister would be needed to overwhelm Belleger. The only encouraging conclusion he could draw was that Hexin Marrow's book was *not* in Amika. The Repository was not. If it were, the ambush—and the starving villagers—served no purpose. His foes and Slack had not needed to risk those losses. They could have ignored him until he tried to cross into Amikan lands.

However, the Captain had other concerns. Faintly pleading, he continued, "But we will not survive another attack. Highness, we must go on. We have our orders. We cannot remain where we are. Perhaps the Amikans will miss our trail."

"King Abbator," said Elgart heavily, "does not know our straits. If we go back, he will not fault us. He cannot want his eldest son killed for nothing. And the Amikans may let us pass when they see we have given up. They will be reluctant to lose more men."

"Elgart!" Captain Swalish was shocked. "You would give up? You would betray your king's trust? You would let Amika slaughter your homeland? I do not *believe* you. I *will* not. The Elgart who has ridden into hell with us and paid the price"—he gestured at Elgart's scar—"would not go back. The Elgart who saved the wain would not."

"But I am not *that* Elgart," retorted the rifleman. "I am *this* one." He thumped his chest. "The one who still lives.

"*This* Elgart wants to hear what Prince Bifalt will say."

But the Prince said nothing. Biting his cheek, he watched the north. He needed—

Behind his back, Stolle's struggle came to an end. In spite of what he had just said, Elgart went to work with Captain Swalish and Klamath. Together, they did what they could for the dying beasts, the slain men. They treated Klamath's side, using cloths and balms from Nowel's supplies. Then Swalish broke the arrow in Flisk's shoulder, wrenched it out by its ends, bound the wound as best he could. The pain turned the young veteran pale, but he bore it without complaint.

In this season, the afternoon sun slanted across Prince Bifalt's sight. His eyes blurred when he needed them to be clear. For a moment, he thought he saw a moving dot on the line where the sky met the hills. Then he was sure he had imagined it. Then a dull flash like sunlight on bronze crossed the bracken and tall grasses.

"Captain," he said: a low growl from the back of his mouth.

Leaving Flisk to Elgart and Klamath, Captain Swalish joined his prince.

"Hells," breathed the Captain. "Is that—?"

The dot waved an arm.

"Vinsid," pronounced Prince Bifalt. "It is Vinsid."

At once, Elgart and Klamath came closer, supporting Flisk between them. The five men watched the rider approach. They saw him punch the air with one fist, brandish his rifle with the other. A less sullen man would have shouted.

As Vinsid rode nearer, the Prince was finally able to see that the guardsman had not been wounded.

A moment later, the man dismounted. He seemed to be having trouble with his habitual glower. At intervals, it broke into flickers like grins. Even scowling, he gave an impression of exuberance.

"Highness," he said formally, "I did what you asked."

Prince Bifalt prompted him. "And?"

Vinsid lost control of his visage for an instant. "One of them rode a lamed horse. I shot him. There were other stragglers, but the sound of my shot made them ride harder. I followed until they dropped into a wide hollow among the hills. I left my horse and crawled to the crest to look without being seen.

"They were gathering themselves, as you said. Shouting at each other. Counting arrows. I saw sixteen men on good horses."

The Prince interrupted him. "Supplies?"

"Not that I saw, Highness. They had no mules or packhorses. There were no other Amikans. They did not take bundles out of hiding, or dig them from the ground."

When Prince Bifalt nodded his approval, Vinsid continued.

"The hollow is two leagues away. But I was not content with that distance. They could return against us too quickly. I fired a full clip. I was too far for good aim, but one lucky shot dropped a rider. The rest scattered for the far hills. I could not follow without being seen in the hollow."

Once again, the Prince said, "They fear our rifles."

"And, Highness," added Vinsid, "they will not return galloping. They do not know where we might hide." Just for a moment, he let himself smile. "When they come, they will come cautiously. If we go now, I do not think they will find us before sunset."

Prince Bifalt clapped Vinsid's shoulder. "Then we will go." Vinsid had restored his decisiveness. He knew what to do now. Behind the slow seethe of his anger at what the ambush had done to his company—behind his dismay at what he had lost, and his grief—he felt almost eager. "We will go as soon as we can."

Now at last he turned to consider the problem of Flisk's wound. The color had returned to the young veteran's face. He held his rifle like a man who meant to use it. His jaw jutted with determination, despite his obvious pain. But the Prince was not persuaded.

Coldly, he ordered Flisk to ride away. In addition, he asked the teamsters to send Boy on another horse to watch over the guardsman.

Boy objected until Spliner silenced him with a cuff to the side of his head. "It will make your ma glad," muttered the teamster. "Do not take that lightly."

Flisk braced himself to refuse an order. Gripping his gun, he began, "No, Highness—"

The Prince had no patience for an argument. He needed to *go*. He interrupted the young veteran by demanding, "Clean your rifle."

Sweating in pain, Flisk tried. But the condition of his shoulder crippled his whole arm. Unable to disguise his failure, his face twisted with chagrin. "Pardon, Highness," he sighed. "I am useless. I will go."

Prince Bifalt could not afford sympathy. "Do only what you can," he said. "Do not follow the track. Ride southwest, away from the Line. Look for aid. If you reach the King, report what you know."

Sternly, he sent Flisk and Boy on their way.

Once they were gone, Captain Swalish and Elgart shifted as many of the wain's burdens to the last horses as they could carry. Spliner, Hught, and Winnow again rerigged the oxen so that the three could pull the wain together.

Glowering like a clenched fist, Vinsid spent a moment with Ardval's body. To no one except himself, he muttered, "I have lost friends before. But I *liked* him." Then he turned away.

Because it was his place to do so, the Prince gave the Bellegerin army's traditional farewell to the men he had lost. "Your blood for your comrades. Your blood for your people. Your blood for your king. No man can be asked to give more."

He did not know what else to say.

When the men had eaten a quick meal, donned their moccasins, and fed and watered their animals, Prince Bifalt announced his intentions.

"Those Amikans will not harm us again. We will not permit it."

"How will we stop them?" It was Elgart who spoke. He had always been a lean man, but now he looked positively emaciated by indignation, as if he had taken the ambush as a personal affront. Although his quick thinking had saved the wain, he did not congratulate himself. Instead, his manner challenged the Prince. "We have done what we can. They still outnumber us. And they are mounted."

Prince Bifalt studied the old scar that divided Elgart's face from the center of his forehead to the point of his chin. It made him look like a man with two natures that had been imperfectly joined. Two *chambers*—

The Prince ignored Elgart's insolence. "We will leave this track," he replied, "and head south until we gain the other road." He meant the more southeasterly branching the company had passed. "There we will make better speed."

"And that will save us?" snorted Elgart. "I think not. In this grass, we will leave a trail a blind man could read. And the Amikans will still be mounted."

Now Captain Swalish snapped, "Elgart! You forget yourself.

You address Prince Bifalt. He is the eldest son of King Abbator. I will have your hide if you cannot show respect."

Elgart chewed curses for a moment. Then he ducked his head. "Highness."

But now Vinsid and Klamath supported their comrade. "Still," said Vinsid carefully, "Elgart speaks truth, Highness. We cannot outrun our foes. We cannot outfight them. They will strike at us when they have decided how to counter or avoid our guns."

Holding his side, Klamath nodded.

Captain Swalish opened his mouth to shout down objections. The Prince silenced him with a gesture. "They will not," he answered. "We will turn their tactics against them."

"How, Highness?" protested Klamath. "We are only five."

Grinding his teeth, Prince Bifalt emulated the patience of his father.

"They will not come on us in daylight. You judged them rightly, Vinsid. They will require caution. If they come now, we will see them. Or we may have hidden ourselves to waylay them. They will not attack until nightfall. Until we have made our camp. And they will approach with care, sending scouts to be sure of our position. *Those* men will not outnumber us.

"They hid in this grass to surprise us. We will do the same to them."

Briefly, he described what he had in mind. Then he concluded, "They have already come too far from their lands. They cannot hope for more supplies or men. We will kill their scouts, or drive them off. Then the Amikans who remain will attempt a concerted attack. They will have no choice. They cannot stop us by any other means.

"If we can catch them in our cross fire, they will learn what rifles can do against numbers and horses and arrows."

The Prince's men were veterans. They saw that the tactics he described might succeed. Elgart seemed to scowl with one side of his face, grin with the other. Vinsid's glower promised killing. With one hand, Klamath wiped the pain from his face.

"They will try to surprise us again," warned Captain Swalish.

Prince Bifalt nodded. "They will. When they do, try for a single shot. If you fire more than once, one of us will come to help you. But no more than one. The wain must be protected from other scouts.

"And remember. The flash of your muzzle will show where you stand. Shoot and move. Shoot and move."

The guardsmen agreed. Apart from the teamsters, no one in the company would sleep this night. But perhaps one night would be enough.

Like his men, the Prince shouldered his burdens: his weapons and bedroll, his satchel of clips, a leather canteen. When the diminished quest was ready, Swalish commanded the wain into motion. Sullen and fretting, Spliner and Winnow flicked their whips to start the oxen while Hught pulled on the yokes. Trailed by two laden horses, the heavy wain left the trail and began to plow arduously through the earth's thick mantle of grasses, bracken, and wildflowers.

Watching the rear, Prince Bifalt chewed his cheek and prayed he would not encounter some insurmountable obstacle—a deep gully, perhaps, or a swollen stream—before the sun set. He did not much care whether he reached the other trail or not. More than a faster pace, he wanted terrain that would suit his plans to repay the Amikan ambush.

※

When evening came, they were still forcing their way through dense grass blades that sawed at the legs of the oxen. The teamsters had contrived padding to protect their beasts, but the animals were exhausted nonetheless. Prince Bifalt judged the company had gone no more than a league—an easy distance for mounted foes—and now night was near.

Captain Swalish wanted to push on until the wain reached the shelter of a low escarpment dimly visible ahead. There the wall of higher ground would provide a measure of protection on one side. But the Prince decided otherwise. "The wain is our bait. It must be an easy target." Also, he wanted time to eat a cold meal and rest before he and his men crept into hiding. "We will halt where we are."

While some light remained, he pointed Swalish and Elgart, Vinsid and Klamath, to their positions in the defensive cordon he desired. In effect, they would conceal themselves at the four points of a compass centered on the wain. His own task would be to support any of his men who needed help. Perhaps unnecessarily, he warned the teamsters against lighting any flames. If the wain could be located too easily, the Amikans would suspect a trap. Then, when all the men had fed, and the teamsters had gone to their bedding under the wain, he set himself to rest until the stars unrolled their uninterpretable map across the heavens.

———

Fervently, he hoped for moonlight. It would aid him and his men more than their enemies.

The sky remained cloudless, allowing the stars to shed their vague illumination; but the moon had not yet risen when Prince Bifalt's tension forced him into motion. In whispers, he told his men to check their weapons and ammunition. Then he sent them to dare the night.

Although they were not foot soldiers, they understood stealth. They made rustling sounds as they departed, but soon the Prince could not hear their movements.

With his rifle in his hands, he left the wain as well, walking quietly along the company's back trail. Eagerness and uncertainty rode the beating of his heart. He was sure of himself, and of his men, but of nothing else. He expected the scouts to be widely scattered when they came, but one of them might follow in the marks of the wain's passage. He meant to be ready.

If they came.

When he had gone far enough to be sure he could spot archers before they came within arrow range of his bait, he turned aside. Slowly through the clogging blades and branches of the vegetation, he took ten steps, paused to gauge the visibility, then took ten more. There he crouched into a tall clump of wildflowers. Aiming his rifle toward the trail, he confirmed what he could see and what he could not. After that, he tried to relax.

He hoped the scouts would come soon. They might. Their approach had not been threatened yet. They might believe that they could catch the Bellegerins unprepared.

Time passed. By slow increments, a crescent moon climbed the east, bringing a subtle shift in the starlight. Prince Bifalt closed his eyes to ease the strain of peering endlessly at shapes he could almost see, shapes that seemed to shift and waver while he studied them. He counted his breaths until the tightness in his chest became too great to contain.

When he looked again, he thought he saw a darker shape in the vicinity of the trail. He thought it moved. He imagined it was a horse and rider; but he was not sure.

The stars were everywhere. The moon added a tint of silver so delicate it was almost invisible. The Prince's finger curled on the trigger. Surely, the shape was a horse and rider.

Surely, it was a bush. It had not so much as twitched a leaf since the evening breeze died away.

If he fired prematurely—worse, if he fired at nothing—he might betray his position. His tactics. His men.

Grim as stone, he held himself still.

The crack of a rifle in the distance resolved his doubts. Warned by the sound, the shape he watched reacted. As it turned, it became unmistakable: a man on horseback.

At once, Prince Bifalt's rifle spoke. The flash blinded him. But it cleared quickly. In a moment, he knew he had hit the horse, not the rider. Both of them toppled into the grass and vanished. Only the horse cried out.

Other scouts must have reacted, must have given themselves away. He heard a shot far to his left, another closer on his right. He ignored them. Swalish and Vinsid had more experience than he did. Elgart and Klamath were more accurate. None of them were fools. As fast as he could through the whipping grass, the stiff

STEPHEN R. DONALDSON

bracken, the Prince sprinted toward the place where his target had fallen.

In his own ears, he sounded like surge, like the crash of heavy seas or the pound of a waterfall. Every stride announced his coming. At any instant, an arrow would sprout from his chest, and his quest would be done.

Instinctively, he flung himself to the side, rolled heavily, and came up on his knees with his rifle aimed. Urgency and sudden movement sharpened his vision. Star-etched in the night, the darker shape of a man fled along the wain's back trail.

For the second time on this journey—the second time in his life—Prince Bifalt shot a man in the back.

Heartbeats later, another rifle fired. After that, silence. The Prince heard nothing except his own breathing.

He counted backward. Including his own, there had been six shots. Five scouts? Were they all dead? Had the Amikans truly sent five? If he had been their commander, he would not have risked so many. No more than three? One should have been enough. The wain was easy to find.

Why had the Amikans sent *five* scouts? Were they that desperate? Or did they have some new surprise waiting for him, a danger he had not foreseen?

Hells! Had his foes outwitted him again?

Still holding his rifle to his shoulder, Prince Bifalt trotted back toward the wain.

Captain Swalish joined him along the way. The Captain was grinning fiercely. For an instant, moonlight glistened faintly on his teeth. He had done more than kill a scout. He had captured the

96

Amikan's horse. Led by its reins, the beast followed Swalish at the Prince's side.

Prince Bifalt set his teeth on the inside of his cheek so that he would not ask aloud, Why did they send so *many*?

Klamath appeared, an incarnation of moon- and starlight. "One, Highness," he reported, whispering. Glancing at the Captain's new mount, he added, "The horse ran."

The Prince said nothing.

As they neared the wain, Vinsid caught up with them. Breathing hard, he panted, "I felled one, Highness, but I am not sure of him. I could not find a body. He may have crawled away."

"His horse?" asked Captain Swalish.

"Gone," replied Vinsid. "It panicked when he fell."

"Then he will not crawl far enough to harm us," declared the Captain.

Together, they reached the wain. Like the Prince himself, his men smelled of gunpowder in the motionless air. But there was also a pang of blood.

Elgart's return distracted him momentarily. The lean guardsman reported success. "A long shot, Highness. I would not have chanced it, but he was moving away."

Prince Bifalt shook his head. He did not understand. Why had the Amikans sent five men to scout an obvious trail?

Suddenly, Captain Swalish whispered, "Highness! The oxen. They are gone."

"*What?*" The Prince whirled to look.

By starlight, he saw the traces lying limp in the grass, the yokes empty.

The sight smote his heart. The beasts had disappeared. Set free—or taken.

While visions of Amikans leading oxen into the night spun in Prince Bifalt's head, Captain Swalish demanded, "The teamsters?"

Yes, the teamsters. Why had they not called out? Had they been killed in their sleep? *All* of them?

Had they aided the Amikans? Were they as false as Slack?

He would have staked his oath on them.

Klamath was already crouching to peer under the wain. "Highness!" he croaked. "Come!"

Three strides took Prince Bifalt to Klamath's side. When he dropped to his hands and knees, the cloying metal scent of blood filled his nose.

Under the wain, two men lay where there should have been three. The nearer was Hught. A cut gaped across his throat. Blood drenched the grass under his head; but it no longer pulsed from his wound. He was dead.

The other man carried the bow and wore the garments of an Amikan: the orange headband, the orange scabbard.

Elgart had run to the far side of the wain. As he dragged the body out, Prince Bifalt hastened to examine the Amikan.

Like Hught, he was dead. But he had not been cut. Even in the faint illumination, the marks of blows were visible. In addition, his neck had been broken. The teamsters were powerful men. They had killed their foe with their hands.

But there was no sign of Spliner and Winnow. Like their beasts, they were gone.

While Captain Swalish swore, the Prince's world reeled yet

---

again. Pieces of his confusion fell into new patterns. The teamsters had fled, or they had not. In either case, they did not serve Amika. That was obvious. The death of Hught's killer proved it.

"The scouts," he rasped. "Hells! Decoys, all of them. The Amikans guessed what we would do. The scouts demanded our attention. They were a distraction to cover this one. He crept to the wain." Another piece became clear. "But not to kill teamsters. That would not stop us. And setting fire to the wain would not. We would see the flames.

"Also, he did not plan to drive off the oxen. We have horses. We could overtake them. And killing them would take too long." Cutting the throat of an ox was not easy. Stabbing it deeply enough to reach its heart was not. "He meant to hamstring them. We could not go on without abandoning our supplies."

"Aye, Highness," assented the Captain. "That would have been the end."

"But the oxen are gone," put in Vinsid.

Prince Bifalt ignored this detail. He was not ready to consider it. "He did not reckon on the teamsters," he continued. "He must have believed they would keep guard atop the wain, or rest at a safe distance. As he crept close, Hught caught at him. In the struggle, he killed Hught. Then Spliner and Winnow killed *him*."

"Where *are* they?" insisted Vinsid.

Quickly, Elgart climbed onto the wain, took a quick inventory. "Their bedrolls are gone," he announced. "Some supplies. A canteen." Then he added, "And fodder."

Unsurprised, Prince Bifalt nodded.

The Captain grunted. "I am baffled, Highness. They risked their lives to protect the oxen, then abandoned us? Why? And why *now*? They have had other chances."

The Prince had no answer. He had not chosen the teamsters. He did not know them. But his instinct was to trust them. "If they have not fled," he muttered, "they will return at dawn. Otherwise, we will hunt them down. We must."

His thoughts were already elsewhere. He had not expected even Amikans to be so cunning—or so cruel. As cruel as Fastule's attack on King Brigin's new bride. Oxen could be hamstrung quickly. One leg each would be enough. The beasts would be crippled—and in terrible agony.

Perhaps Prince Bifalt should have anticipated the danger. Men who killed their own wounded after a battle—men who used their starving children as bait—were capable of anything.

Abruptly, he turned from the bodies. Speaking as much to the night as to his companions, he declared, "The fault is mine. I did not imagine this tactic. I did not plan to defend the oxen.

"We will do better."

He spoke with his usual decisiveness. He was not a man who hesitated. Yet what he was thinking dismayed him. He did not understand men who would aim to cripple oxen.

"The night is long," he said, "and they do not need scouts to find us. They will not hesitate to send more men—and more surprises. They are sure to attack when their riders do not return.

"We waste time here." Hells! "We must re-form our cordon."

His men stared at him, grappling with the same fears that wracked him. Were the Amikans truly willing to spend so many lives? Were they that desperate? If so, *why*? They had no obvious cause. If they feared the quest so much, they could have brought a Magister to their initial ambush.

No. All of their sorcerers were needed elsewhere. They were massing for Belleger's ruin.

But that alone did not account for Amika's tactics. Theurgy could ravage the whole of Belleger before the Prince's company found the library and the book. The Amikans were desperate for some other reason.

The book, he thought. Marrow's *Seventh Decimate*. It must contain knowledge more powerful than he had imagined. The knowledge to block Belleger's sorcery, yes—but also, perhaps, the secret of its restoration.

The book might enable Belleger to trade places with its enemy at one stroke. Amika would not simply be made helpless. At the same time, Belleger would regain its strength.

That prospect would inspire any amount of desperation.

Angry at himself—at Amika—at the whole world—Prince Bifalt snapped his commands. "*Go*. Hide again. But stay close. They will not attack the same way twice.

"I will guard the wain."

Captain Swalish was as troubled as the King's son; but he knew his duty. Without hesitation, he assigned Elgart, Klamath, and Vinsid to new positions. When they were gone, he, too, faded into the grass and the darkness.

Quickly, Prince Bifalt climbed onto the wain. There he replaced his rifle's clip with one fully loaded. He worked the bolt to chamber a cartridge. With his thumbs and a small pouch of loose bullets, he refilled the used clip. Then he made himself small among the wain's burdens and strained his senses for any hint of movement in the night.

❋

The night was indeed long. He may have dozed while the uncaring stars wheeled overhead. But he was instantly alert at the first sound of horses.

The sound of horses charging.

In the grass, they made a low noise like a wave that rose and rose and did not break. Vegetation tore at their legs. It muted their hooves. Gripping his rifle, Prince Bifalt rose high enough to scan his surroundings. He saw shapes too vague to be sure, too indistinct to shoot. They came in two squads, one on each side of the wain. He could only be sure that they were Amikan because arrows began thudding into the bedrolls and supplies under him.

An instant later, a rifle uttered a lick of flame, a sharp boom. Another gun answered it, and another. Muffled cries stained the darkness.

Still the horsemen pounded closer, lashing their way through the cling and tangle of bracken, grass blades, wildflowers.

The Prince chanced a shot himself, risked betraying his position. His only reward was the louder soughing of the charge. But when he fired again, one of the approaching shapes plunged headlong to the earth.

The rifles spoke again, and again. If they took a toll on the riders, Prince Bifalt could not discern it.

Then a small flame showed among the horsemen. That faint

light revealed a rider rearing back with an object like a ball in one hand—a ball that trailed sparkling fire from its fuse.

Hells!

Near it, Vinsid rose from the grass. He, too, had seen the flame and the fuse. He fired while the rider began his throw; while the ball was still in his hand.

The man lurched in his saddle. He tried to complete his cast, but he had lost control of his arm. Floundering through the air, the ball and its fuse fluttered like a wounded bird toward Vinsid.

When the grenade exploded, it took Vinsid with it.

The Prince stared. Chagrin pounded through him. He had forgotten the grenades. Slack's treachery had obscured that memory. And his dismay at the threat to the oxen had driven other dangers out of his head.

If just one hit the wain—

That possibility took over Prince Bifalt's mind. Thought and fear no longer troubled him. He became his training, his learned certainty. While his men increased their rate of fire, he searched the night for another lit fuse.

There.

As he spotted it, he fired. But he did not pause to see whether he had hit the rider, or to look for the grenade. From the ground, Swalish, Elgart, and Klamath could not watch the whole area around the wain; and Vinsid was lost. The guardsmen could only shoot at Amikans and pray. The Prince had to protect the supplies.

The second grenade exploded somewhere as Prince Bifalt located a third rider lighting a fuse. Instantly, the Prince fired. With his whole being, he willed his bullet to rupture the Amikan's heart.

———

His shot tugged at the rider's shoulder, at the arm that held the reins. The man nearly toppled from his mount. Then he righted himself.

Other rifles fired at other foes, but they had become irrelevant. Only the Amikan with the lit grenade mattered. Working his bolt with practiced speed, Prince Bifalt sighted again, fired again.

Too late, the horseman fell dead. He had already finished his throw. The spinning trail of the fuse marked the grenade's progress as it arced toward the wain. When it detonated, it would destroy—

Without a heartbeat's hesitation, the Prince sprang from his place, leaping to intercept the grenade like a man who believed that he could preserve the wain with his body; believed that his desire alone would suffice to save his quest.

The grenade exploded near him. Its concussion slapped him to the ground as if he had fallen from a height measured in leagues. Shards of hardened clay shredded him before he hit the grass. For the second time in his life, he knew he was dead. No man could survive the force of his fall, or the damage of his wounds.

For the second time in his life, a voice spoke. It sounded like the grenade's blast, like his impact with the earth, like the last beat of his heart. Loud as thunder and silent as a grave, it asked: **Are you ready now?**

Prince Bifalt had no answer.

✤

When he opened his eyes in the dawn of a new day, he found Captain Swalish sitting beside him, propped against one wheel of the wain.

104

The Captain did not turn as Prince Bifalt, groaning, tried to lift his head from the ground.

The movement ignited pain in his forehead. Briefly, it overcame him. Apparently, he had suffered a deep gash. But at least the hurt assured him that he was still alive.

Lying still, he consulted his limbs for other wounds, his chest and abdomen. To his surprise—a dull sensation, but distinct—he found none. His only injury was the throbbing line across his brow. The dawn's chill emphasized the feel of wetness.

Scalp wounds bled copiously, he knew. When he tried to estimate the severity of the cut, however, he was able to determine only that he could not hear. The world around him had become mute. No men moved or spoke or called out. Breezes ruffled the grass in silence. If there were horses nearby, he heard no sign of them. Swalish breathed without a sound; without lifting his shoulders or expanding his chest.

The Prince considered the notion that he was surrounded by enemies. Then he discarded it. No Amikan would leave any Bellegerin alive—and certainly not a son of the King.

Wary of more pain, he raised his hands to the sides of his head. There he felt blood still oozing from his forehead. It spread downward to fill his ears. Its clotting made him deaf.

With his fingers, he spent a moment scraping at the crust. Then, carefully, he pressed one palm to his brow and tried again to lift his head.

This time, he mastered the pain. Still holding his forehead, he rolled until he was able to draw his knees under him. Gritting his teeth, he knelt upright.

His shift appeared to disturb Captain Swalish. Slow as a drunkard's, the Captain's head lolled to regard the Prince. But there was no sight in the Captain's gaze, and the trail of blood from the corner of his mouth had ceased dripping. The arrow driven through his breastplate proclaimed that he was dead.

Prince Bifalt smelled blood. It was stronger than the reek of gunpowder. Anguish thudded in his head. His vision blurred. His cheeks felt wet.

He refused to acknowledge what he felt.

Despite the stabbing above his eyes, he tried to look around. The wain appeared intact. But he saw no sign of Klamath or Elgart. Vinsid was already gone. And now Captain Swalish—

A groan escaped him. It made his head hurt worse. Had he lost all of his men? *All* of them?

He needed them. Belleger needed them.

Are you ready now?

Beyond question, he had been singled out. Twice now, he had been snatched back from the threshold of death. Only sorcery could have saved him. A sorcerer had chosen him. Or sorcerers. Magisters with powers that exceeded every theurgy he knew.

Alone and wounded, the Prince felt ready to burst into flames.

Ever since he began to understand his father's pain—the anguish of a king whose realm was dying, and who was helpless to save it—Prince Bifalt had been a conflagration in the making. He had wood enough for any fire. Belleger's growing privation and misery. His own frustration. Slack's betrayal. Death after death: Nowel and Camwish, Bartin and Stolle, Ardval and Hught; and now Captain Swalish, who had been the Prince's teacher. Elgart's absence, and Klamath's, both likely killed. And to this was added the certainty that he had been chosen by theurgists he did not know for a purpose he did not understand.

What he felt deserved other names: names like grief and despair. But he had turned his back on his own emotional wounds long ago. He did not acknowledge them. They were little more than ash. The breeze blew them away. Heedless of his injury, of the way his brow bled afresh when he removed his hand, of the unsteadiness of his limbs, he surged to his feet like a man poised to burn.

In the silence of his mind, he demanded of the empty sky, Do you want me? Come and take me. Tell me what you think I will do for you. Let me give you my answer.

There was no reply.

For a few moments, a mist of weakness obscured his vision. When it cleared, he found himself staring at oxen. They were still some distance away, coming from the direction of the escarpment. Spliner and Winnow led them.

Bellegerins, he thought. The teamsters had not forsaken him. They had saved the oxen.

And they would not have left the covert where they had spent the night unless all of the Amikans were gone: dead or fled.

Then he saw another welcome sight. As the teamsters and oxen approached, Elgart rose from his hiding place in a tangle of brush. The dawn sun made a red streak like a cut along his scar, but he had no obvious injury.

When he saw Prince Bifalt standing, he came at a run.

"Highness," he panted as he arrived. "I thought you were dead."

The lingering effects of exploding gunpowder and blood distanced his voice, but the words were clear. "The grenade—" Peering at the Prince's brow, he asked in wonder, "Is *that* all? It needs care. A few stitches. But it will heal. How did you—?"

"Elgart," the Prince interrupted with as much authority as his weakness allowed. "Where is Klamath?"

The guardsman grimaced. "I sent him to watch the north. The Captain was dead. We believed you were. You know how he is after a fight. He needed someone to tell him what to do. I hid to protect the wain." Hesitating, he added, "He can tend you better than I can."

The Prince nodded. Every motion sent a flare of pain through him. "The Amikans?"

He wanted to call them butchers. Despicable. No Bellegerin would consider hamstringing oxen an acceptable tactic. It was more than cruel: it was dishonorable. As dishonorable as Slack's betrayal. As using starving children for bait. As theurgy itself.

Sorcery was dishonorable because it allowed a sorcerer to wreak harm without risk to himself. Crippling the oxen would have had the same effect for most of the Amikan force. Only the scouts were in danger, and the result for Prince Bifalt's quest—for all of Belleger—would have been ruin.

The outcome would have been the same if the scouts had used grenades. One would have been enough. The Prince knew that now. But his foes had *not* known it when they sent their scouts. No doubt they had feared the lit fuse would expose the scouts to rifle-fire prematurely.

"Gone, Highness," replied Elgart. "I counted ten dead or dying.

The rest rode away. They will not come at us again. If they meant another attack, they would have struck while darkness still covered them."

Prince Bifalt allowed himself to support his unsteadiness on the side of the wain. "We need their mounts." His voice sounded faint in his ears. The ground seemed to shift on its foundations. He had lost too much blood. "Recall Klamath. Do what you can for me. I must rest."

Slowly, he slumped to the grass. His thoughts faded into the comfortable earth. But he continued to hope for conflagration.

✳

Later, he learned that Winnow had more experience stitching cuts than Klamath did. When the Prince returned to consciousness, his brow felt like it was being gashed repeatedly, but it was bandaged and no longer bleeding. Klamath was preparing a meal. Elgart had gone to look for horses.

Only three of us, the Prince sighed privately. Three trained to fight. And he himself was useless, at least for the present. He had to trust Elgart's assertion that there would be no more attacks. Fortunately, the guardsmen could ride now. The company had escaped the ambush with two horses; and Captain Swalish had caught a third. Elgart might find more. But Prince Bifalt could not sit a saddle. He was too weak to walk or ride. He would have to lie on the wain.

If the teamsters had not saved the oxen—

Resting among the bedrolls and bundles of fodder, he ate what he could stomach. While Spliner and Winnow readied their beasts,

Klamath retrieved the Captain's rifle and ammunition. Vinsid's gun was twisted beyond use, and his clips had been fired or otherwise ruined by the blast that killed him. Then Elgart returned, disgusted at his failure to capture any mounts. When he, too, had eaten, the teamsters took the reins of their animals, and the wain moved at last.

Passing around the escarpment, the small company turned east across the rough terrain. The Prince had no more use for the south-easterly track. It would not help him now. His destination was somewhere in the east. Any trail he encountered in this region would take him out of his way. He remained watchful until he saw Elgart riding ahead of the wain, Klamath guarding the rear. Then he let himself doze.

He needed to heal. He no longer suspected that he would die on this quest. In fact, he now believed that the quest itself would not fail. Men or powers who had saved him from death twice would not discard him without reason. But he wanted both his wits and his strength for the moment when the sorcerers claimed their prize.

When that moment arrived, he meant to be ready. He believed that he was capable of more than fire. He could be an inferno.

❊

As Elgart had foreseen, the Amikans were gone. They had lost too many men. The wain's progress was hampered only by the weight of its burdens, and by the rumpled grasslands it crossed.

After two days of rest and increasing impatience, Prince Bifalt joined Elgart and Klamath riding. On the third day, he began to smell the parched breezes gusting from the eastern desert. During the fourth, the grasses and bracken started to fail, slowly giving way to patches of hardpan and small mounds of sand. And on the fifth, after less than an hour's travel, the company crested a rise to gaze for the first time at the baked expanse of the wasteland.

On the border of known lands, the Prince halted to consider his course.

Across a distance that was difficult to estimate, confused by the shimmer of heat, he saw low dunes piling higher as they leaned eastward. Nearer at hand, however, the ground was true hardpan, a flat plain scoured to its foundations by desert winds. It might support the weight of the wain's wheels. Then the oxen would be able to haul their burden more easily for a league or more, until they came to the dunes.

But Prince Bifalt owed a debt to the teamsters. He felt reluctant to prolong their exertions, or to extend the straining of their beasts. Eventually, they would have to go back the way they came. Studying the future through a haze as misleading as a mirage, he decided against asking them to go farther. He and his riflemen would make do with horses.

When he told Spliner and Winnow to take their beasts and Captain Swalish's rifle and return home, they shrugged without any signs of gratification or relief. They hardly seemed to care what they did or where they did it. But they kept their usual complaints to themselves as they helped Elgart and Klamath unload as much food, water, bedding, and fodder as the horses could carry. And after finishing that task, they did not depart. Instead they lingered to care for the oxen. In a sidelong fashion, they watched Prince Bifalt and his comrades.

When the guardsmen were ready, Spliner offered the Prince an unexpected farewell. He was a big man, not so much tall as broad, and solid as a boulder. His face twisted as if he were uncomfortable speaking to people of higher birth—or perhaps to anyone at all. Studying his boots, the teamster said only, "I will tell Boy. The tale will please him."

Prince Bifalt surprised himself by bowing. Apparently, he was capable of gratitude, despite his unbending nature.

❊

Soon he and his veterans walked down off the verge of the desert onto the packed plain, leading their laden mounts.

The region was as brutal as he had feared, and more desolate. Erratic winds gusted and cut at the hardpan, but raised no whiff of dust. Instead, they had a desiccating effect like the Decimate of drought. Before long, the Prince felt his eyes parching in their sockets. His skin became old parchment. Although he set a moderate pace for his companions, an immediate thirst sapped their strength. And around them, nothing grew. No living thing forced its way out of the earth. The plain seemed to be a place where sorcerers of wind and drought had been at play, reducing a once-verdant world to blank death.

Within half a league, the Bellegerins had discarded their helms. The metal served only to cook their brains more quickly. Later, they rid themselves of their breastplates, the last of their armor. They could not bear the weight.

For an hour or more, they led the horses while the sun's heat accumulated and the air's shimmering made the horizons vague, strangely unattainable. Then Prince Bifalt called a halt. Already, he felt like he could drink a lake.

As he and Elgart gave rations of water to the beasts, Klamath wiped his brow, squinting through the haze in all directions. After a moment, he mustered his courage to address the Prince.

"Highness, may I ask? Do your maps show the extent of this waste?"

Elgart snorted unkindly. "We have hardly begun. Are you defeated so soon?"

But Prince Bifalt was not inclined to rebuff Klamath. He had come too far, lost too many men. He was tired of gnawing dumbly on his fears and frustrations. "Ask what you wish," he replied. "We are alone. Our lives depend on each other. I have no use for secrets.

"I have seen two maps. I have the better one with me. It shows we have left Belleger. But the men who made it did not know how far this desert extends, or what lies beyond it. Our only choice is to go on until we find the library—or until we can go no farther.

"One of the Amikans we fed—" He cursed to himself at the memory. "An old man named Ambrost. He described the library as 'A great storehouse of books against the mountains. A storehouse like one castle piled on top of another to reach the heavens.' If any word of that was true, there are mountains beyond the desert. But he also said our goal is in Amika. It is not. If it were, those butchers would not have needed to ambush us. How can we believe him?

"From the start, every step of our quest has been uncertain."

Klamath winced. "Then, Highness," he asked, "how will we survive? This desert looks vast. We have water for three days, food for four, fodder for two at most. But the horses will founder on those dunes. We will be forced to turn them loose." Distress mounted in his voice. "And without them, we will not be able to carry so much water and food. The mountains may be a hundred leagues away.

"We are going to die."

He might as well have said, Belleger is going to die.

Again Elgart snorted. "*You* are going to die, Klamath, if you waste your strength counting obstacles. I am not such a fool. I prefer to let them surprise me." Then his manner softened. With half his mouth, he smiled ruefully. "Still, you have it right. I may outlast you for a day or two. Not more. The heat alone will finish me."

Glancing at Prince Bifalt, Elgart concluded more harshly, "But the Prince is not like us. He will not die."

Klamath stared at his comrade. "How not?"

With his arms folded on his chest, the Prince waited for Elgart's answer.

The thin man considered what he would say. When he replied, he addressed himself to the King's son. "Highness"—he stressed the title sardonically—"I have waited to speak until there is no one left who might carry the tale. It is not mine to tell. But Klamath will not reveal it. I will not. And you surely will not. I wish to speak before I am too weak to think."

Prince Bifalt nodded his consent.

Elgart studied him. "That grenade should have killed you. I *saw* it. You were too near the blast to endure it. Yet you suffered only a cut forehead."

"It was night, Elgart!" protested Klamath. "And we were beset. Amikans were everywhere. How did you *see*—?"

Elgart silenced his comrade brusquely. "There is more." Still facing the Prince, he said, "You did not know it, Highness—you were unconscious—but I was among those who retrieved you during the last battle, when we used our rifles for the first time. You shot two Amikan Magisters. I was near. I saw a bolt of lightning burn the flesh from your bones. I saw you *fall*. But when we reached you, you were only *unconscious*. The bolt melted stone until it looked like glass. It was near enough to scald your skin. Yet you were unharmed."

Now Klamath gaped. Still waiting, Prince Bifalt held Elgart's gaze.

The guardsman's tone was a sizzle of fury. "How did you survive *then*, Highness? How can you withstand grenades *now*?"

Softly, dangerously, the Prince countered, "How do *you* account for it?"

"The answer is plain, Prince of Belleger," snarled the cynical veteran. "You have been spared by sorcery—by sorcerers so strong that distance does not affect them. You are in league with Magisters.

"I thought the one who protected you from lightning was Amikan. Their Magisters were near enough to see your peril. They must have intervened somehow. But now I am forced to reconsider. There was no theurgy in the ambush. No Magister witnessed your attempt to save the wain. Yet you were saved from a blast that would have ended our quest. I have to believe your allies do *not* serve Amika. They live where you wish to go. They act to protect you because you are in league with them."

Prince Bifalt's response was direct. Without warning, he punched Elgart in the face.

The guardsman hit the ground like a man flung against a wall.

Before he could rise, the Prince stood over him. Ignoring Klamath, who had drawn back a step and covered his mouth, the King's son held up his fist, ready to strike again.

"Now hear me, Elgart," he rasped at the rage on the fallen man's visage. "Hear me well, Klamath.

"I am *Bellegerin*. I would die for my king, or for my homeland, or for either of you. I am not a traitor. *I will not fail my father*.

"And sorcery is an *abomination*." He had flames in him. They demanded an outlet. "It is as dishonorable as *treason*. Magisters in safety butcher men in peril. It makes them arrogant. It makes them *despicable*. Look at Slack and see the truth." He thought of his father flayed by pain and helplessness; dependent on theurgists who were his only defense, although they could not save his realm. "If I had the power to end all sorcery with a word, I would do it.

"Your accusation is *offensive*. I repudiate it. I am not *allied* with sorcerers. I do not *serve* them."

Then he made an effort to master himself. Opening his hands, he showed his palms to Elgart, a gesture of placation.

"Also there is this. What possible purpose would an alliance with sorcerers serve? If it does not help us against Amika, what is the *use* of it? Have they and I gone to such lengths to cause the deaths of a few guardsmen? Or perhaps to feed a few Amikans? Do you suppose I led you here to watch you die? For *what*? If I am in league with sorcerers, both they and I are insane, and everything we have done is stark madness."

When the Prince saw Elgart's anger fade, he stepped back. Speaking now as much to the broiling heat as to his men, he said grimly, "I have indeed been chosen by some sorcerer. Or sorcerers. I have been protected just as you claim. And I have heard a voice in my mind, asking if I am *ready*. I do not know how it was done, or why. We all know the limitations of Magisters. I have never heard of one who could cast his awareness or his power farther than he could see. But this I swear.

"I am *not* ready. I was selected without my knowledge"—he brandished his fists as he shouted—"and without my consent!"

He let his cry fade into the desert air. When it was gone, he continued more quietly, "I have promised myself I will give them the reward they deserve. But I fear I will not be able to keep my word. I am only one man. How can I want your deaths? I need you. If I had sorcerers for allies, sorcerers with incomparable strengths, our comrades would still be with us, Camwish and Vinsid and Captain Swalish and Nowel, all of them. I would know Slack's secrets. And I would *defy* any Magister who tried to make me his servant."

There he fell silent, waiting to hear how his men would respond.

"Well, Highness," murmured Elgart before Klamath spoke. Watching the Prince closely, he clambered to his feet. With one hand, he rubbed his bruised cheek. "I am answered.

"I am a divided man." He rubbed at his scar. "Anyone can see it. Despair and urgency. Curiosity and anger. Also I am quick. Too quick at times. I often speak faster than I think. My accusation was stupid. I regret it."

Prince Bifalt nodded. "I have no use for secrets," he repeated.

"Not in this extremity." With a gesture, he indicated the wasteland. "Now you know mine. I do not fault you for your doubts."

"Yet yours is a heavy fist," replied Elgart, grinning.

The Prince faced him without flinching. "My *burden* is heavy. It wearies me. It infuriates me. I know who I am. I know I have been chosen. But I do not know *why*."

"You are the King's eldest son," ventured Elgart. "King Abbator's heir. If you cannot do what these sorcerers want, no one can."

"Yes," snorted Prince Bifalt. "Of course. But why was I singled out *privately*? Why does the voice speak only in the silence of my mind? Why did these sorcerers not make their wishes known to my father?"

Elgart seemed to stare with one side of his face, scowl with the other. "I have no answer, Highness. What do you fear?"

Through his teeth, the Prince said, "I can only think of one explanation. I am my father's son and heir, yes. No one else can do as much harm to Belleger. No one else can do more to assure Amika's victory. If this is not the reason I was chosen, there was no need to summon me in secret."

"Highness?" asked Klamath weakly. "Harm to Belleger? How?"

Prince Bifalt did not respond. He kept his attention focused on Elgart.

Now Elgart's whole face scowled. "And you are sure these sorcerers are from the library?"

"It is their Repository," retorted the Prince. Magister Altimar had said so. "Where else can they be from? There *is* nowhere else."

After a long moment, Elgart nodded. "As you say, Highness."

At last, Prince Bifalt turned to Klamath.

"Highness—" began Klamath. Then he stopped, clearly bewildered. Taking his time, he admitted, "I did not know what Elgart knew. I do not understand it. How can you harm Belleger? In this desert?" Then he took a deep breath, released it in a sigh. "But you are my prince. My king is your father. *That* I understand. While I live, I will follow you. What else can I do?"

With a quick glance at Elgart, the rifleman risked adding, "Only, Highness—if I may ask—? Do not strike Elgart again. He is my comrade. I serve you, and he is my friend. I cannot choose between you."

The Prince disguised a smile. "I will not. I was wrong. We are Bellegerin. We must not fight each other. And if I do—if I forget myself—Elgart may return my blow. If he does, he will have cause, or he will not. In either event, you may find choosing is not so difficult."

For Prince Bifalt, Klamath's frown of consternation was oddly comforting—as was Elgart's sour laughter. Bellegerin veterans, both of them. His people. He might have picked other men to accompany him in this desert, but he could not have picked better.

With his darkest secret spoken, he was able to walk for another league across the plain before heat and thirst drove every other thought from his mind.

❈

Toward midafternoon, he and his companions reached the dunes. Two steps on the shifting sands confirmed that the horses were useless here. They were too heavy: their hooves would sink deep. Before they gained the nearest crest, they would founder in exhaustion, if they did not break their legs first. And forcing them upward against their will would cost strength the Bellegerins could not afford.

The Prince did not flinch from the prospect of releasing the beasts. He had no wish to watch their struggles and suffering. Still, he regretted the necessity. Now he, Elgart, and Klamath would have to carry as much as they could lift on their backs: a scant half of their remaining supplies. Their feet, like the horses' hooves, would sink in the sand, sucking the vitality from their muscles. And the sun would continue its pitiless assault. Their thirst would grow while their rations of water shrank: it would work to drive them mad. In addition, Slack had spoken of burns. Without the traitor's balms and unguents, the Bellegerins would be fried until their skin blistered and peeled away.

Discarding the fodder so that the horses could eat their fill, the men prepared their own burdens: their bedrolls, as much water as they could carry, their rations of stale bread, cured meat, and dried fruit. From their small bundles of garments, they took shirts to cover their heads. But they kept their weapons: their daggers, sabers, and rifles, their satchels of loaded clips and extra cartridges.

When Elgart and Klamath were ready, Prince Bifalt turned his back on the horses, the plain, and Belleger, and began to slog upward. What else could they do? The Prince had been singled out. The sorcerers who had summoned him would not relent now. He needed to know *why*. And he needed to save his people. The conflagration waiting in him required an outlet. It could not be satisfied, except by succeeding in his quest—and by humbling the arrogance of his summons.

✳

Trudging ever more slowly up the slopes, then floundering to control their descents on the steeper eastward sides, the men conquered two dunes before their strength failed. In the valley at the foot of another rise, they sank to the sand. The crest behind them blocked the sun: they stretched out in the comparative bliss of shade. In another hour, night would fall. Its chill would bring a deeper relief. Already, the sand around them was giving up its heat. Still, they felt like small furnaces themselves, retaining the sun's fire while it faded from the world.

After a time, the Prince announced hoarsely, "We cannot endure this. We must change our efforts.

"When night comes, we will attempt another dune, or perhaps two. I will hope for three. Then we will dig into the sand for shelter." Their bedrolls would provide a measure of protection from the sand as well as the cold. "There we will rest through the morning. After that, we will do as little as possible by daylight. In darkness, we will do as much as we can."

"Sorcerers willing," muttered Elgart, a low scrape of sound. He did not say more.

Unsteady as old men, the three veterans each drank a little water. They gnawed on hard bread, fruit like leather, slices of dried meat. They drank again. Then they sprawled where they were to rest until darkness and stars came to cover the wasteland.

Stunned by weariness, Prince Bifalt was slow to realize that Klamath was talking.

The guardsman seemed unaware of his own voice. He spoke in

a low, blurred rasp, like a man in a reverie or dream. He did not ask to be heard. Perhaps he did not hear himself. But what he said made it clear that he was thinking about Prince Bifalt's assertions. *Sorcery is an* abomination.

"Where I was born," murmured Klamath. "Three days on horse-back from the Hand. Farmers, most of them. Horse farms. Wheat and barley. Less prosperous than it was. There was a healer.

"I never heard his name. He called himself a healer, nothing else, but he did not mend broken bones or mangled limbs. He did not touch cuts unless they festered. Men who fell from wild stallions with their heads cracked, he ignored. He insisted he could not treat most pains. Still he was a healer. Fevers faded when he laid hands on them. Chills. Rashes. Infections. Instances of plague. Any affliction with no obvious cause—any except madness and idiocy. They all left when he made them go.

"I knew a man. A friend of my father's. He had a swelling in his belly on one side. Hard and hot to the touch. The pain twisted him until he leaned like a drunkard when he walked. The healer spent an hour with him, stroking his belly. An hour every four days, or five. Only that. In a fortnight, he was able to walk upright. In two, the pain and swelling were gone. Just—gone.

"Or a woman. I only knew her by sight. The whole town knew her by sight. She had an ugly tumor on her throat. It grew until she could only swallow water. Not food. Not even gruel. The healer offered his touch, but she refused. She thought—" Klamath was silent for a time. Then he admitted, "I do not know what she thought. But she lost weight until her skin hung loose, and her strength was gone. She changed her mind.

—

"She sat on the porch of her house. Any passerby could see the healer did not molest her. He only rested his palm on her tumor, and bowed his head, and hummed to himself. He did this for an hour daily until she could take soup. After that, he visited her every other day. Every third. Every fourth. Finally, the tumor was gone, like my father's friend's swelling.

"He was a healer. We thought he was our healer, nothing more. Only when the King summoned him to war—" Klamath sighed. "Then we learned he was a Magister. His gift was the Decimate of pestilence."

Without lifting his head from the sand, Elgart looked at Prince Bifalt.

"A healer, was he?" rasped the Prince. "That changes nothing. Sorcery is sorcery."

He was whispering. His throat was too dry for vehemence. He had forgotten he spoke to Klamath. He was remembering what Slack had told him. With every sentence, he heard an echo of Slack's explanation. Slack's confession.

"It is abhorrent. Unnatural. And cruel." *If you imagine a man, any man, as a house of several chambers, then I have been locked out of the brightest and most desirable of mine.* "When your healer went to war, he slaughtered men and beasts by the dozens. They died in terrible pain." *The needs of king and realm and home cannot be set aside.* "And he did it without peril to himself." *A man is not a man at all if he cannot enter and enjoy every chamber of himself.* "If he fought for Belleger, that was his only virtue."

Despite his certainty, however, Prince Bifalt found himself thinking that Slack may not have been the only Magister who had felt a need to make amends.

————

But Slack's "amends" had led him to treachery. When he spoke of *The needs of king and realm and home*, he was speaking of Amika.

That the Prince still did not understand. What did Amika have to fear? Its Magisters had not lost their power. And Belleger did not have Hexin Marrow's book.

Klamath said nothing. He did not seem to hear.

While the shade deepened, and the first faint sprinkling of stars showed overhead, Elgart propped himself up on one elbow. Peering through the gloom, he ventured, "A question, Highness. Curiosity."

The Prince nodded, saving his strength.

"You said," began Elgart, "you would end all sorcery if you could. But Belleger has depended on it since the first Magisters showed themselves"—he waved a hand vaguely—"oh, centuries and centuries ago. We would be hard-pressed to live without it, even if we did not have to fight Amika. We *are* hard-pressed. You have seen it. We have all seen it.

"What would you do if you had a gifted son? Would you end his power as well?"

Like Klamath, Prince Bifalt sighed. He had not considered his abhorrence in those terms. But he had an answer.

"I will not have sons. Or daughters. I will not wed. If my enemy sorcerers will not let me die, they also will not let me live. They will attempt to use me. They will succeed or fail. If they succeed, I will be lost to myself. And if they fail, they will not permit me to escape them."

Elgart held his gaze. "No doubt, Highness. I believe you. But

124

I am still curious. Let me put my question another way. Is there any limit to your revulsion? Can you imagine a sorcerer you would not make impotent?"

Vexed now, the Prince retorted, "I have given my answer, but you did not heed it. I will state *it* another way. My abhorrence is limited because it is *mine*. Must I say again that I am only a man? Only *one* man? My desires are empty. I do not rule the world. I do not rule Belleger. And if by some strange quirk I became King after my father's passing—if my enemies let me keep my life—we would still be at war with Amika. My desires would still be empty. I would still need Magisters—if I could get them.

"Have you forgotten our purpose? I wish Amika deprived of theurgy. Absolutely, I do. But that would not end the war. It would only make the war more equal. We have rifles. Amika has more men. The war would go on. We will not be done with it unless we can arrange matters so that Belleger has sorcery and Amika does not."

To Prince Bifalt's surprise, Elgart chuckled sourly. "Then I have misjudged you, Highness. You call sorcery dishonorable, but you do not shrink from it. You want to lift the dishonor of sorcery from Amika's shoulders and place it on Belleger's."

The Prince felt a sting in his vitals. He had not said he wished dishonor on his homeland. How had his companion twisted his meaning this way? What manner of man did Elgart think he was?

He had been reared from birth to fight for Belleger. As he would on any field of battle, he met challenge with challenge.

"You insult me again," he snapped. "Do you want me to doubt

myself? Do you think I will falter? I will not. I will not abandon my quest, or refuse my father's commands, merely because you choose to think ill of me."

Elgart gave another of his humorless laughs. "Forgive me, Highness. I do not mean to insult you. I am only curious.

"But at times curiosity is like despair. Or anger. It burns hot. A soldier's life is hard. You know that as well as any man. Training and more training, followed by battle and death. There are days when curiosity is all I have to keep me on my feet. It holds back my despair. I satisfy it when I can.

"I want to know what the stakes will be when you confront the Magisters who demand your 'readiness.'"

The Prince turned away, disgusted as much by his own ignorance as by Elgart's probing. "How can I answer?" he muttered to the coming night. "I cannot imagine what their purpose may be. They ask if I am ready, but they do not say what they want me ready *for*.

"We have spoken of this. Why was I chosen? Why was I chosen secretly? If I am preserved from death, why are the companions who keep me alive not protected as well? And you know my fear. I was chosen to do Belleger some fatal harm." He shivered as he said, "They want to make me a traitor.

"For all their power, they do not know me."

Despite Prince Bifalt's impulse to ignore the man, Elgart's reply reached him. "As long as they want you, Highness, you will learn the truth eventually. If they insist on preserving your life and asking if you are ready, and then do not tell you what they want you to do, they are insane."

Clearly, they are insane, thought the Prince. Or I am. There are no other possibilities.

Even in darkness, the desert fostered hallucinations. The obscure shapes of the dunes appeared to squirm under the uncertain stars. Like Elgart's questions, they made Prince Bifalt gnaw at himself.

PART THREE

For two days, the companions did what they could to endure the brutality of the wasteland, plodding up and down the dunes primarily at night, resting in the scant shelter of their shirts while the sun was overhead. From the highest of the dunes late in the afternoon of the second day, they caught their first glimpse of mountains, a jagged line across the east. But the range of peaks was still distant. Squinting at it, Prince Bifalt knew with the certainty of acute thirst and growing hunger that his men would not live to reach it. Their bodies would lie among the sands until the winds covered them, or the sun cooked their bones.

Now, he thought to the sorcerer or sorcerers who wanted him. If you mean to continue saving me, do it now.

He did not have more than another day in him.

Then the terrain changed. While the sun crested the line of mountains on the third day, the men stumbled down a last dune and found themselves on a bare plain. Beyond it, more dunes rose, blocking the peaks from view; but some strange trick of wind and weather had swept clean a swath of native rock wide enough to serve as a road for armies. It stretched far to both north and south, but it was not straight: its ends were hidden by gradual curves and sharper turns, as if the plain had been shaped to accommodate variations among the desert's bones.

It promised easier walking. If the Bellegerins followed it, it might extend their strength for a while.

Down its center ran a track that must have been made by generations or centuries of wheeled wains and shod hooves. There were ruts, some deep; and everywhere around them, the rock held the scars of hundreds or thousands of iron horseshoes.

At the edge of the track, Prince Bifalt halted, wavering on his legs. For a time, he could not find words.

Elgart found them for him. "Now what?" asked the lean guardsman.

Now what, indeed. Blinking at the blur on his vision, the Prince peered along the track in both directions. He was too drained by thirst and thin rations to ask, Who made this? or, Why is it here? But "Now what?" he understood. The library of the sorcerers was said to be in the east, but this track did not go that way. True, it promised another day or two of life. If he refused it, he and his comrades would spend the last of themselves on more dunes. But if he accepted it, should he go north or south? Which heading would take him closer to the Repository?

Prince Bifalt solved the riddle by letting himself sag until he sat spread-legged on the stone.

Dropping their burdens, Elgart and Klamath joined him.

Klamath bowed his head, holding his burned face in his hands. Elgart took up his waterskin, drank two quick swallows, then passed what was left to his companions. Klamath had already emptied his waterskin: he took more than the Prince. Prince Bifalt saved his small supply for his company's last need.

After a time, he croaked, "Shelter." Following his example, the riflemen pulled their spare shirts, sweat-stained and stiff, over their heads. Then the three men stretched out on their backs and tried to gather the dregs of their stamina.

The Prince could not think. The heat was ferocious. No breezes reached him, although the faint whisper of shifting sands suggested there was movement in the air high on the dunes. His lips were cracked and bleeding, his throat felt scraped raw, his blistered skin oozed fluids he could not afford to lose. In his sun-blasted state, he imagined that his quest—his search for Belleger's future—had finally come to an end. From the first, he had feared failure more than death. Now his men were done. They were like the horses, like the teamsters and their oxen: he could not ask more of them. He had to trust or pray or dread that the sorcerers who wanted to make use of him would intervene. If they intended him to betray his homeland, he would find a way to disappoint them. But first he needed them to save him. Without help, Elgart and Klamath would die. Even he would die.

Lying dry-eyed in the sand, he wanted to weep for Vinsid, for Captain Swalish and Nowel and Camwish, for Bartin, Stolle, and Ardval. He wanted to weep for Hught, whose throat had been cut. They had all given their lives to help him accomplish nothing. But the wasteland did not permit tears.

When he imagined hearing hooves on stone, he wanted to weep for his favorite destrier. It had fallen with a thicket of arrows in its side. But while it lived— Ah, while it lived, he had found pleasure on its strong back, delight in its quick movements and willing heart. When the fighting became an embodiment of madness, it had shared his courage. The beat of its hooves still echoed in his mind—

—and in his ears.

He spent a time wondering whether mirages made sounds. Did they confuse all the senses, or only sight? Then, suddenly, he snatched the shirt from his face and sat up.

There to the south, between the ruts: a figure on horseback.

A hallucination. How could it not be? No one could travel this desert. Certainly not alone.

Nevertheless, the clack of shod hooves on stone was clear until the rider halted. The Prince imagined that the rider was staring at him. The clatter of galloping as the beast wheeled and raced away was too distinct to be imaginary.

In moments, both horse and rider disappeared around a bend in the track.

Klamath raised his head like a man struggling out of a deep sleep. Blinking his parched eyes, he murmured, "What? Highness?"

Elgart was already sitting; already squinting south. "A rider?" he panted hoarsely. "Was that a rider? *Here?*"

"Fled," replied the Prince. He felt a deranged desire to laugh. "From us." The sight of three dying men had filled the rider with terror. "From *us.*"

A preposterous notion. If he could have found the strength, he would have laughed aloud.

Elgart scowled. "I think not. Who would flee us *here*? He must be a scout. An outrider of some kind. He goes to warn his people. They will come in force."

"To help us?" groaned Klamath. "They must help us."

"Help us or kill us," replied Elgart in a low snarl. "One or the other."

Prince Bifalt had a different question. What were *any* riders doing in this wasteland? Were they a figment? Was their appearance caused by sorcery? Or had they simply been *sent* by sorcerers?

His hands shook as he took up his rifle. His whole body trembled as he opened the breech, made a weak attempt to blow grains of sand from the barrel, then set a loaded clip in place.

"Why, Highness?" asked Klamath plaintively. "What use are rifles now?"

"Help us or kill us," echoed the Prince. "I do not want strangers to think we are defenseless."

Why would any man or men travel here? What innocent purpose could they have?

Sighing, Klamath readied his rifle. Elgart did the same with less reluctance.

Together, Prince Bifalt and his companions watched the south. None of them made the effort to stand.

Soon the rattle of hoofbeats came again. They were too numerous to be made by a single animal. The sound was too crisp to be distant thunder.

Cantering, three horsemen rounded the bend and drew closer.

"Stay down," commanded Prince Bifalt as he forced himself to his feet. "Do nothing they will see as a threat." His rifle he held across his chest, its muzzle pointing nowhere.

The riders slowed as they approached. They had heavy cutlasses on their hips and bandoliers of throwing knives over their shoulders. On their heads were turbans hung with gauze they could use to cover their mouths and noses. They wore loose blouses, scarlet sashes, billowy pantaloons tucked at the ankle into dull black boots. And their bronze skin seemed to leach into their eyes, giving the orbs a yellow cast. The Prince had never seen men like them. Certainly, they were not Amikan. But he had no notion where they had come from, or where they were going.

One of them carried what appeared to be a cask. It might hold water. Prince Bifalt could hardly take his eyes off it.

The leading newcomer guided his mount a few steps closer. With a flourish of his arm, he began to speak. He spoke volubly, uttering a liquid stream of words that ran without apparent pause like a brook rushing over slick stones. Unfortunately, his speech was incomprehensible, a foreign tongue. The Prince did not understand any of it.

With an effort, he straightened his shoulders, raised his head. Through lips stiff with dried blood, he announced hoarsely, "I am Prince Bifalt, son of King Abbator of Belleger. We are lost. We need help."

The spokesman's eyes widened in surprise. "Ah!" he exclaimed. "*That* tongue. I know." With obvious awkwardness, he said, "You stranger. From far. Wayfarer. I Suti al-Suri, caravan chief scout. You much need. Generousness gods command. Also caravan master. Travel perilous. Generousness make stranger friend.

"Behold!"

A second flourish indicated his companion with the cask. At once, that rider came closer. Dismounting, the man bowed his head to his knees—an act that Prince Bifalt would have considered nakedly obsequious in King Abbator's court. Then the man offered the cask.

The Prince smelled water before he heard it sloshing.

Elgart and Klamath were at his sides, ignoring his command to remain seated. Elgart accepted the cask eagerly, unstopped it and drank until water spilled on his face. Then he passed it to Klamath.

The prospect of so much water made Prince Bifalt giddy. He tried to match the bow he had received. "You speak our tongue, Suti al-Suri," he managed. "Your generosity saves us. We—"

"Drink!" ordered the spokesman, suddenly imperious. "Talk after. You think we heartless? We much generousness. Wait a time. Wait, see."

In his fluid language, he poured out another speech, this time addressing his other companion. With a nod, the man turned his horse and trotted back the way he had come. After a moment, he urged his mount into a gallop and was gone.

The Prince did not need a second invitation. Taking the cask from Klamath, he tilted it and drank, swallowing water and life until he had to pause for breath. At once, sweat beaded on his forehead. Its sting in his healing cut and its coolness on his skin were blessings. He had forgotten such things existed.

Suti al-Suri grinned approval. The contrast with his bronze skin made his teeth gleam.

Trembling with relief as well as weakness, Prince Bifalt handed the cask back to Elgart. The lean guardsman drank again, as did Klamath. The Prince took another long draught before he returned the cask to the waiting scout.

———

With a second deep bow, the man remounted his horse.

Now Prince Bifalt showed the chief scout a Bellegerin bow. "Suti al-Suri," he said as distinctly as he could, "accept our thanks. Our need is great. If you have more generosity to give, we will gladly wait for it."

"More?" The first scout waggled his eyebrows in mock surprise. "With assurance. More comes. Bounty comes. All need aided. Also caravan master eager tidings. All caravan eager. All caravan make welcome. Only wait."

The King's son bowed again. Groping among forgotten regions of his mind for courtesy, he added, "I have not named my companions. They are Elgart and Klamath."

While his men bowed as he did, he scrutinized Suti al-Suri and tried to think. If the caravan and its master were as openhanded as the chief scout claimed, the Bellegerins could afford to accept any offered hospitality, at least for a day. He had too many questions, but none of them were as urgent as life.

To the riflemen's names, Suti al-Suri gave a nod. Frowning now, he watched the veterans. Some thought had apparently occurred to him, a thought that had not troubled him earlier.

The Prince made an effort to forestall uncomfortable inquiries. "You will understand," he croaked, "we expected to die. We are far from our lands. We do not know the desert. We did not imagine a trade route here. You are a miracle." He did not add, Or an effect of sorcery. "Where have you come from? Where do you go? Who are your people? Who is in your caravan?"

As the Prince spoke, Suti al-Suri's frown became an exaggerated scowl. Instead of answering, he countered with an air of pugnacity, "You hold strange stick, king son. Why? Weapon? Scepter? Magic?"

Prince Bifalt considered lying to conceal his one advantage, but falsehoods did not suit his nature—or his situation. Perhaps knowing that he and his men were still dangerous despite their condition might provide a measure of protection from the uncertain motives and impulses of strangers. He glanced a warning at Klamath and Elgart, then addressed the chief scout.

"It is a rifle, Suti al-Suri." He held it out, still pointing nowhere. To the scout's look of bafflement, he explained, "It is like a bow that looses leaden arrows."

The chief scout assumed an air of skepticism. His companion stared in bewilderment.

Sighing to himself, the Prince asked, "Will you watch a demonstration?"

"Yes!" snapped the scout. "Show bow. Show leaden arrows."

Over his shoulder, Prince Bifalt commanded, "You, Elgart. You are our best marksman."

Elgart nodded. While the Prince struggled to stay upright, the scarred guardsman moved a few paces away from his comrades and the scouts. There he picked up a loose rock the size of his fist and pitched it to the far side of the track: a small target at twenty paces, one the Prince would not have been confident of hitting. With his rifle in one hand, Elgart removed the clip and held it up. "The arrows," he announced. Then he reset the clip, worked the bolt.

Klamath put his hands over his ears, encouraging the horsemen to do the same; but they ignored him.

In one smooth motion, Elgart brought the stock to his shoulder, aimed, and fired.

The bang lifted an echo like a flicker of shadow from the hard stone of the track. Dramatically, both scouts flinched, startled by the sound of the gun, or surprised by the way the target shattered. The animals shied until their riders controlled them.

When the horsemen had steadied themselves, and the report of the shot was gone from Prince Bifalt's ears, he said, "Our rifles keep us alive. Perhaps they can perform some service for you. Do you have enemies?"

In response, Suti al-Suri unleashed a spate of language like invective. Then he and his companion wheeled and left, galloping hard.

The Prince swallowed an impulse to shout after them. His need for their help was absolute. But what purpose would shouting serve? If the scouts ran because they were afraid, no word of his would call them back. Had his demonstration been a mistake? Perhaps it was. But if so, he could not correct it now. Like all of his misjudgments, this one would haunt him until it was swept away by another. The next would probably be worse.

"They took the water," muttered Klamath unhappily. "That was cruel."

Elgart snorted. "They will come back. They have never seen a rifle before. They need to warn the caravan. Get new orders.

"They have to pass this way. There cannot be another road through the dunes. But they may try to capture or kill us before the caravan comes in range. That is our real danger."

"I agree," said Prince Bifalt, thinking aloud.

"Then we should move," groaned Klamath. "Try to hide. Guess how they will come at us."

"No," answered the Prince. If he was doomed to make poor decisions, he would continue to make them. He could not cease to be himself. "Our only hope is to remain here. Let them see how helpless we are, despite our rifles. Let them see we are willing to be at their mercy.

"Scouts who know this desert can outmaneuver us easily. We cannot pretend otherwise. It will be useless."

Responding to Klamath's chagrin, Elgart nudged his comrade's shoulder. "Take heart, Klamath," he said sourly. "Sorcerers have preserved the Prince so far. They will do so again. And they may preserve us as well. They may think he needs us."

That thought made Prince Bifalt shiver despite the heat and his still-avid thirst. He agreed with Elgart, but he dreaded the implications.

❋

An hour later, a horseman resembling Suti al-Suri appeared on the crest of a dune beyond the trade route. A slide of sand above and behind the Bellegerins suggested the presence of another rider.

The Prince and his men kept watch from under their shirts, holding their rifles across their knees. They did not rise.

He expected more signs of scouts gathering to surround his position, but he saw none. Instead, a team of four horses came around the bend to the south, drawing an immense and ornate carriage with iron rims on its wheels and heavy springs supporting its axles. To him, it looked as big as a mansion. Its sides were carved with vividly painted symbols edged in gilt. Silver lanterns hung over its doors. Its occupants were shielded from the sun by supple leather window shades. King Abbator himself did not travel in such luxury.

The old ruts enabled the horses to pull the carriage with comparative ease despite its size and bulk. The man driving the team lifted a hand in greeting when he spotted Prince Bifalt, Klamath, and Elgart, but he did not alter his pace.

From one window of the carriage, a woman's shapely hand fluttered a silken scarf for a moment, then withdrew.

Prince Bifalt resisted the impulse to stand. He allowed himself only a brief wave to acknowledge the driver, and another to answer the scarf.

After that, he was too busy staring to lift his arms.

Behind the carriage, the first wagon of the caravan hauled into view. It was several times the length of the quest's abandoned wain, and loaded twice as high: a huge-wheeled vehicle drawn by six strange beasts tusked like boars, animals as massive as bullocks and as shaggy as sheep. Tight sheets of canvas concealed its burdens. Perched on their bench, two teamsters kept their beasts close to the rear of the leading carriage.

Another carriage followed, less ornate than the first, but large enough to bunk a family of eight. What it lacked in gilt and carving, it made up for in ribbons and streamers. They fluttered from every available edge and corner, all brightly colored, all different. Riding the ruts, it kept pace with the wagon.

These three proved to be the vanguard of a caravan so long that it made Prince Bifalt gape in heat-dulled amazement. A dozen or more wagons and wains in a line came next, some piled high with goods and provisions, some wearing tents like homes for nomads, some straining under the weight of elaborate contraptions with no obvious use. Then came five carriages, one after the next, all so plain that their rough boards might have been hammered together on a whim, and so poorly sprung that they were jolted like hammer blows by the unevenness of the ruts. Next followed a long string of wagons apparently belonging to a carnival, although the Prince could not read the gaudy promises written on their sides, or inter-pret the curious shapes of the wagons themselves. And behind them were more wagons, wains, and carriages as motley as their leaders, too many to count. Some were pulled by horses or oxen, others by the strange tusked beasts.

Together, they conveyed the impression that they were a num-ber of separate caravans which had joined at some mustering point far to the south, traveling as one to protect or guide each other across the desert. This impression was reinforced by the scattered throng of their scouts, at least fifty men, all of whom resembled Suti al-Suri in raiment, weapons, bronze skin, and yellowed eyes.

As the carnival wagons neared Prince Bifalt's position, the chief scout himself approached on his mount. If he had been the man on the far dune, he had made his descent while the Prince's atten-tion was fixed on the caravan. His manner was wary, but he no longer scowled.

Clearing his throat, he announced, "Master say not fear rifles. All safe. Welcome ready." When the Prince, Elgart, and Klamath only stared at him, he beckoned vigorously. "Come."

Under his breath, Elgart muttered, "What choice do we have?"

"None," answered the King's son, "if we want to live." He could do nothing else until the sorcerers revealed themselves.

Groaning, he climbed to his feet. Unsteadily, he pulled his sweat-crusted shirt from his head and tucked it under his belt. As Elgart and Klamath struggled to join him, he slung his rifle over his shoulder with the last of his burdens: his satchel of ammunition and his bedroll. Hoping that Suti al-Suri would understand the gesture, he slapped the hilt of his saber to set the blade more tightly in its scabbard.

When the chief scout turned to lead the way, the Bellegerins followed, wavering like figments in a mirage.

Suti al-Suri guided them to intercept a wagon behind the carnival conveyances. Although it was tall enough to admit a horse, its unusual length made its ceiling appear low. As the chief scout approached, a wide door slid aside, but shadows prevented the Prince from seeing who opened it.

Beside the wagon, Suti al-Suri dismounted. "Enter," he instructed the Bellegerins. "Refreshment there. Water. Food. Also rest. Healing. Sleep." After a moment, he added firmly, "No harm. This Suti al-Suri promise. Caravan master promise."

Briefly, Prince Bifalt met Elgart's uncertain nod, Klamath's glazed stare. Then he obeyed the chief scout.

One by one, their guide helped the comrades clamber into darkness.

At once, the door slid shut against the heat. For a moment, Prince Bifalt was blind. But as his eyes recovered from too much sun, he found a few small oil lamps lighting the long space.

"Highness?" asked Klamath.

The Prince had no answers.

The air was blessedly cool, perhaps because a number of pans filled with water had been set along the walls. Six pallets lay on the floor, one occupied by a man obviously asleep, the others unused. There were several cisterns: if they, too, held water, the Bellegerins might be allowed to wash as well as drink. Bronze trays here and there on the floor were laden with a variety of fruits and roasted meats; with breads Prince Bifalt could not smell through the sand and dust clogging his nostrils. Near the trays were flagons of ale.

Clearly, the caravan master meant what he said about aiding needy travelers.

At one end of the wagon crouched four figures. Prince Bifalt guessed that they were women, although they were hooded and cloaked as if to disguise themselves. Their bent backs and lowered heads gave them the look of crones. They spoke softly in a language he did not recognize—a tongue unlike Suti al-Suri's—but their gestures made their meaning plain. They were urging the travelers to eat and drink.

Their speech told Prince Bifalt that the caravan had gathered its people from more than one strange land.

With an effort of will, he forced himself to wonder whether he had any cause to be suspicious of the ready feast. But his men did not hesitate. Klamath dropped to his knees beside a tray and began to fill his mouth with fruit. Elgart snatched up a flagon and drank like a man who could not be filled. When he paused for breath, he gasped approval.

Like a man falling, the Prince sat down and reached for a flagon. To his shame, he could not steady his hand enough to lift it. But he did better with a few sections of a fruit that may have been a tangerine. With its sweet juice in his abused mouth and throat, he found enough strength to take up the flagon.

After that, he ate and drank like his men, ravenously, forgetting caution; forgetting the figures at the end of the wagon; forgetting that he did not know where he was being taken, or why. His only thought was to ease his thirst and hunger.

Later, his body's reaction to prolonged exertion and deprivation asserted itself, and his attention wandered. He did not notice when three of the hooded women rose to their feet. They did not impinge on his attention until one of them knelt in front of him. In her hands, she held a sponge and a basin of water. Wetting the sponge, she began to stroke days of sweat, sand, and grime from his face.

Somewhere in the background of his mind, an imaginary Prince Bifalt stopped her; insisted on tending himself. The real King's son let her do whatever she wished. When she removed his burdens from his shoulders and began to open his garments, he did not demur. The sensations of moisture and gentle stroking urged him deep into himself until he fell asleep without realizing it.

❋

Yet when he awoke, he was instantly alert—and soon conscious of being both clean and rested. Draped in soft muslin, he lay on one of the pallets with his head pillowed and his limbs outstretched. In ways that he could not identify at first, he felt like he had been made new. Then he realized that the heat and pain of his worst sunburns had been replaced by a tingling freshness. The ministrations of the woman had done more than cleanse him, more than encourage him to sleep. They had treated his burns as well.

Under the muslin, he was naked, a fact that inspired a momentary alarm. When he raised his head to look around, however, he found his weapons, satchel, bedroll, and moccasins beside him. As for his clothing, it hung from a line stretched across one end of the wagon. Even in the soft light of the lamps, he could see that his garments had been washed.

Lowering his head, he relaxed for a little longer while he tried to gather his thoughts. All of his earlier uncertainties remained, and he did not know where the caravan might take him. In a strange way, the fact that he and his men had been rescued did not comfort him. It felt like another implausible effect of theurgy.

Resolved to question the women, he rolled over and rose to his knees, holding the muslin around him. But a cursory glance was enough to assure him they were gone, as was the man who had been sleeping nearby earlier. Prince Bifalt, Klamath, and Elgart were alone.

Then the Prince noticed the wagon was not moving.

Klamath still slept on his pallet, but Elgart was awake. When he saw Prince Bifalt rise, he sat up. "Are you surprised, Highness?" Sleep lingered in his voice. "I am. Men say sun-sickness causes improbable dreams. Maybe this is delirium."

Prince Bifalt had no use for the guardsman's question. Instead of answering, he asked, "Did you see the women leave?"

Elgart shook his head. "They were gone when I awoke. But the wagon had already halted. They must have left when we stopped."

After a moment, he added, "The air smells like evening. And I hear voices calling. The caravan is making camp."

"Then," decided the Prince, "we must speak with the caravan master. If he is not more familiar with our tongue than Suti al-Suri, he may have other interpreters. Where is this train going? Our good fortune may be taking us farther from our goal." He searched for his purse, found it. "Some aid I can purchase. It may not be enough."

"If," observed Elgart, "our goal exists."

"It must." Prince Bifalt rehearsed old reasoning to help himself think. "Amika used the seventh Decimate against us. They learned that knowledge somewhere. But if they had the book itself, our search would not threaten them. They would not have troubled to ambush us."

Elgart nodded. "Therefore, the book remains where Amika found it." The shadows of the lamps seemed to divide down the length of his scar. "Therefore, the library must exist. As you say.

"But that does not aid us." He chewed his thoughts for a moment, then said, "Is this caravan aware of the library? Our hosts may know nothing of it. If they have heard of it, they may be ignorant of its location. We cannot be sure of them."

The Prince shook his head. "They know *something*. They must.

"The world is larger than we knew. This caravan is proof." Suti al-Suri himself was proof. "Sorcery must be larger as well. How else have sorcerers kept me alive at such distances? How are they able to speak in my mind? Their powers surpass our understanding of them."

"Therefore—?" asked the guardsman.

"Therefore, these sorcerers have acted to save us. How else could help come to us just when we were on the edge of death?" Of failure? "The desert is vast. The caravan has come a long way. The coincidence is too great.

"Our rescuers were *sent*. If they were not instructed—or not aware that they were instructed—then they were spurred or slowed to reach us when our need was desperate."

After a silence, Elgart admitted, "I understand that much, Highness. The caravan may not be aware of the library, but the sorcerers of the library are surely aware of the caravan. They are aware of *us*.

"But our question remains. If our hosts do not know the library, how can they help our search? If they do, *will* they help it?"

Prince Bifalt spread his hands. "I have no answer. We must learn where we stand with the caravan master and his people. We must test their attitude toward us. And we must do it *cautiously*. They may be theurgists themselves. If they are not—if they are ignorant—they may resent hearing that they have been used by sorcerers. Or they may be suspicious of us for other reasons.

"Suti al-Suri promised welcome, but we cannot expect the caravan master to trust men with rifles."

The guardsman scowled around his scar, but he did not argue. "I understand, Highness," he repeated. "But I do not like it. We are too few. Any half dozen of Suti al-Suri's scouts can overwhelm us. How can *we* trust *them*?"

"They could have let us die," retorted the Prince.

Elgart sighed. "As you say, Highness."

While Prince Bifalt rose and gathered his clothing, Elgart went to rouse Klamath.

Taking his garments from the line, Prince Bifalt discovered that the desert air had dried them thoroughly. Grateful for the feel of clean cloth on healed skin, he dressed himself. Briefly, he regretted the loss of his discarded armor. Then he pushed the thought aside. Like all his regrets, it was wasted. Being who he was, he could not have made his choices differently.

Still the weight of his rifle in his hands and his satchel on his shoulder reassured him. His homeland remained unconquered because it had invented rifles. He, Elgart, and Klamath lived because they had rifles. Let the world be as large as the heavens, and as little known. With his strength returning and his rifle ready, he was not defeated.

While Klamath arose, and the two guardsmen readied themselves, Prince Bifalt warned them, "We are at the mercy of the caravan master and his men. We must threaten no one, offend no one. We have been treated as guests. We must behave as guests. But we must say nothing of our quest. We do not know how these people will respond.

"We must accept whatever we encounter until we learn who these people are, where they go, what they want—and whether their generosity requires anything in return. If their goal is ours, I will offer them any service we can give. If it is not, we will still need their help. Without food, water, and some form of guidance, we will remain lost."

Klamath received this caution with a look of consternation. "Surely they will not spurn us, Highness? Suti al-Suri said 'gods' command generousness. I do not know what 'gods' are, unless they are high sorcerers. But the caravan master commands it, too. How can they turn their backs on us?"

With unusual kindness, Elgart told his comrade, "It is too soon for worry. Nothing will be resolved tonight. For the present, we have no reason to doubt our welcome. Just smile and nod. Let yourself enjoy what you are given. Listen. If what you hear troubles you, report it privately. The Prince will decide how to act on it."

Frowning, Klamath studied the scarred guardsman. Then he admitted, "We have too many enemies. And I have killed too many of them. I have seen too many Bellegerins die." He risked a glance at Prince Bifalt, then faced Elgart again. "I will fight if I must. But these people have been good to us. I hope we can be good in turn. Maybe they will offer us friendship."

"I do not expect friendship," declared the Prince. He was impatient to leave the wagon; to meet the conglomeration of foreigners who comprised the train. "It is too much to ask. We do not know Suti al-Suri's tongue. We may not understand anything said to us. But we must remember we are guests." Awkwardly, he added, "We must remember to be grateful."

Unwilling to remain where he was, he moved to the door and slid it open.

The noise of throngs and the light of fires greeted him as if while he slept the wagon train had become a bustling town.

By the last glow of evening and the flames of cook fires, he saw wagons, wains, and carriages settled in semicircles among each other, their teams unharnessed and led away, their passengers busy. Surveying as much as his vantage allowed, Prince Bifalt observed that the semicircles were formed by conveyances and people who clearly belonged together. Nearby were the five flimsy, poorly made carriages, and the folk around them were all men. They were all clad in dun cassocks with white ropes knotted at their waists, all of them wore their hair shaped into tonsures, all were sedate and purposeful in their movements. Prince Bifalt did not see them speak to each other. But when he showed himself, they turned as one and bowed to him gravely.

Opposite those carriages, in a larger curve, the carnival wagons had disgorged a host of individuals who resembled each other only in their peculiarities. While some were obviously laborers, most appeared to be performers of many varieties: clowns, acrobats, contortionists, jugglers, weight-lifters, dancers. Their costumes were gaudy and singular, some voluminous enough to disguise their wearers, others so scanty nothing remained secret. They were boisterous and comradely, and their polyglot shouting back and forth suggested they had been collected from several different realms or races. At Prince Bifalt's appearance, their shouts became a babble of halloos, or perhaps catcalls.

The tented wagons he had seen before made another arc. There the men tending their gear and preparing food were like Suti al-Suri, bronze-skinned and yellow-eyed, bearing similar weapons, wearing similar garments: surely his fellow scouts. That they slept in tents suggested they belonged to a nomadic race. When they saw the Prince, they stared openly; but he had the distinct impression that they were more interested in his rifle than in him.

Between these half rounds and others, in a space of open stone perhaps fifty paces wide, a high pile of wood had been raised for a bonfire, but it had not been lit yet. Beyond it, on the far side of the open space, the Prince made out several carriages. One was the ornate vehicle which had led the caravan; another, the beribboned conveyance. Others had joined them, all elaborately decorated in one fashion or another. Around them, servants hastened back and forth, but none of the occupants emerged.

The leading carriage, Prince Bifalt guessed, belonged to the caravan master. But the others— Did they carry wealthy merchants? Princes like himself? Highborn maidens traveling to consummate advantageous marriages?

Until now, his world had contained only Belleger and Amika. Here he saw how small his conceptions had been. And only a fraction of the whole train was visible. Other carriages were out of sight, and other wagons, including the huge, covered vehicle following the lead carriage, and those conveying unrecognizable constructs. Presumably, those vehicles and their animals formed the periphery of the large encampment, along with the wagons, wains, and beasts transporting more familiar goods, supplies, and other burdens.

In his immediate surroundings, Prince Bifalt counted five distinct races and at least twice that many styles of dress. Too many. Faced with so much diversity, so much lying outside his experience, he felt an unexpected impulse to draw back. Instinctively, he wanted to retreat to his pallet and sleep until the world shrank to more comprehensible dimensions.

But Elgart and Klamath stood at his shoulders, staring. Elgart gauged everything with eager curiosity. In contrast, Klamath's anxiety a few moments ago had become a child-like delight, open to wonder. They, too, had never seen so many *different* people. They had never seen so many people in one place, except in the Open Hand—and when they were riding into hell.

Settling his rifle on his shoulder, Prince Bifalt stepped from the doorway and dropped to the ground.

As Elgart and Klamath joined him, Suti al-Suri appeared around one of the wagons and approached. The chief scout had set aside his weapons—apart from his cutlass—and also his turban, letting his long hair drape down his back. Perhaps characteristically, he hid none of his emotions. His face showed amusement, curiosity, and wariness in quick succession.

His bow lowered his head to his knees, but it was brief. Upright again, he waited for the response of the caravan's guests.

The Prince returned a less exaggerated bow. When his comrades had copied his example, he said formally, "You honor us, Suti al-Suri. Our lives are in your hands. We hope to repay your generosity, but we do not know your ways. We do not know what you will accept."

The chief scout grinned, then frowned. "Come." He gestured toward the clearing around the piled wood. "Talk later. Eat now." His manner suggested that he did not understand everything the Prince had said.

In the open space, large blankets to soften the stone were being spread to form a wide circle. A variety of men and women clad in half a dozen divergent styles prepared seating on the ground, while others emerged from and between the semicircles carrying ewers and trays. Apparently, these were the servants of the train, although—like the train itself—they had been gathered from different lands.

Then the caravan's travelers began to arrive: a few teamsters; personal servants accompanying richly dressed masters and mistresses; carnival performers and laborers; others less easily identified, like the tonsured men in their cinched cassocks.

Obeying Suti al-Suri, Prince Bifalt and his men started toward the growing throng. After a few steps, however, the Prince paused. Hoping to spot some personage who might be the caravan master, he scanned the crowd and tried to believe that he would not lose himself in it.

"Come," repeated the chief scout. "Come."

The Prince remained where he was. "May I ask a question, Suti al-Suri?" Without waiting for permission, he said, "Your caravan is large. Where do so many people come from? Where do they go?"

What kind of trade required the train to cross this terrible desert? What form of communication between merchants or rulers was possible across such a distance? Was the trek permitted or encouraged or needed by sorcerers?

Suti al-Suri's wariness became a fierce scowl. A threatened scowl? "South north," he answered brusquely. "North south. A year journey."

Before Prince Bifalt could request a fuller reply, the chief scout pointed at the Prince's gun. "Rifles," he demanded. "Your people. How many?"

The scout's scowl was unquestionably a threatened one. Already, the Prince had misjudged his escort. But he allowed himself no sign of regret. Facing Suti al-Suri squarely, he matched the man's tone. "Enough."

The chief scout stepped back; unleashed a torrent of words in his own tongue. Then he appeared to recall his assigned role. Bowing a second time, he said again, "Talk later. Eat now." After a moment of hesitation, he added, "Caravan master commands."

Without softening his tone, Prince Bifalt replied, "I mean no offense, Suti al-Suri. I will not question you again."

The scout nodded. His expression implied relief.

But it lasted for only a moment. Then Elgart said, "I have a question." His tone was as casual as he could make it. "Those men." He pointed with a jut of his chin. "Shaved heads. Ropes for belts." He meant the men in the cassocks. "What are they?"

Prince Bifalt wanted to cuff the guardsman. With an effort, he kept his displeasure to himself. Apparently, Elgart could not contain his curiosity. And the Prince had told his men to behave like guests. It was natural for guests to ask questions.

Suti al-Suri's frown expressed disapproval. "Monks," he said curtly.

Almost simultaneously, Elgart and Klamath asked, "What are 'monks'?"

The King's son suppressed a groan.

The scout's frown changed. Now he was clearly struggling for words in a language he hardly knew. When he replied, he managed just three words.

"Give lives gods."

Then he repeated more strongly, "Talk *later*. Eat *now*."

Turning his back, he strode toward the unlit bonfire.

At once, Prince Bifalt followed. Over his shoulder, he commanded in a fierce whisper, "Be silent. He has no patience for us. He takes offense. Do not anger him."

———

156

"But, Highness," hissed Klamath. "'Gods'?"

Under his breath, Elgart added, "Does he mean they make gods live? Or do they give their lives to gods?"

Fuming, the Prince snapped, "Not now."

With his men in his wake, he pursued Suti al-Suri toward the throng taking places around the ring of blankets.

The scout guided the Bellegerins to an unused blanket. Many others were occupied by men and women sitting cross-legged. The tonsured, silent men, the monks wrapped in their dignity, had one to themselves. Merchants or nobles and their consorts or wives, attired in wealth, sat in loose clusters, claiming enough space to sit comfortably. In contrast, the carnival people packed themselves close together, apparently trying to fit as many of their comrades on each blanket as they could. They jibed and jostled constantly, raucous with laughter, complaints, and hunger in a complex cacophony of conflicting languages. Other folk sat where they could, mixing ebony women among men with skin the hue of moonshine, maidens demurely cloaked with gallants decked in feathers, brazen-eyed matrons with teamsters in cotton shirts and canvas trousers.

Among them, Prince Bifalt noticed, were none of Suti al-Suri's bronze-skinned race. Although a few scouts roamed between the wagons and carriages, and their chief remained nearby, most of them must have been on duty guarding the encampment. Even in this lifeless desert, apparently, there were dangers serious enough to threaten the caravan.

The Prince could not imagine what those dangers might be, if they did not involve theurgy.

Deliberately, he seated himself on the blanket reserved for him and his guardsmen. Hiding his uncertainty behind a visage studiously blank, he unshouldered his rifle and satchel, unhooked his saber in its scabbard from his belt, and set them behind him: a gesture meant to express peaceful intentions. Then he beckoned Klamath and Elgart to join him.

When they were sitting at his sides, and had put their weapons at their backs, they tried to relax, while he did his best to look confident in his apparent role as guest of honor. No other blanket around the ring was as uncrowded as his. And all of the travelers, including the servants, watched him as if they expected him to vanish suddenly, burst into flames, or begin raving. Clearly, he was as strange to them as they were to the Bellegerins.

Exposed to so much attention, speculation, and suspicion, Klamath stared around with undisguised excitement. Restored by water, food, healing, and sleep, he absorbed every peculiar sight with pleasure, almost with happiness. Left to himself, he might have tried to talk with the nearest foreigners. His interest in "gods" seemed to be forgotten.

Elgart's manner was more reserved, but his fascination was no less keen. If he shared Prince Bifalt's impulse to draw back from the size of the gathering, or from this evidence of a larger world, he did not show it. His gaze flashed everywhere, studying every individual and group as if committing them to memory. At every snatch of an alien tongue, he cocked his head like a man who wanted to learn it.

For his part, the Prince concentrated on his search for some sign of the caravan master. But he found no one who appeared to take precedence over the travelers, or to instruct the train's servants.

Then a man with a torch entered the ring to set the bonfire alight. On that signal, an array of servants carrying ewers of water, clean cloths, and trays approached the blankets so that all the travelers or guests could wash their hands. Prince Bifalt followed the example of people seated nearby, discarding his used cloth on the tray. And when that ritual was complete, other servants delivered plates, utensils, and goblets of brass, and began to carry around large platters of food, offering the guests a chance to serve themselves.

The fare resembled what the Bellegerins had eaten earlier. As the platters came to them, however, the Prince realized he was hungry again. One meal was not enough to relieve days of scant rations. He helped himself to polite portions, then saw how Elgart and Klamath piled their plates, and allowed himself to take more. Suti al-Suri had assured him that he and his men were guests; that they were safe. For one night, at least, they could take the risk of indulging themselves.

After the meats, fruits, and breads, the ewers returned, now brimming with a ruby wine. While the flames of the bonfire climbed higher, the goblets were filled. Seeing his neighbors drink heartily, the Prince tasted the wine and found it odd, as unfamiliar as the gathering itself, rich with spices and other flavors he could not name. But it was not unpleasant, and he took a few modest swallows, hoping that it would not cloud his mind.

Elgart and Klamath were not so circumspect. They drank the way they ate, enthusiastically, and raised their goblets to request more wine. A short time ago, Prince Bifalt had felt like slapping them both. Now, however, he did not begrudge them their excesses. He had done as much as they, endured as much, lost as much;

earned as much. Still, the principal responsibility for their quest was his. The burden of caution was his as well.

And he could not forget that his life was no longer his own. It had been claimed by sorcerers he did not know, men or powers beyond his ability to imagine them. If Klamath and Elgart ate too much and drank themselves fuddled, he could leave them to sleep while he sought answers. They might blurt details he wished to conceal, or ask questions that would cause trouble later, but they would not be harmed. *All safe.* The watchful presence of Suti al-Suri and the other scouts promised that the caravan master's welcome would be honored.

The Prince ate well, drank sparingly, and waited for whatever would follow the communal meal.

Soon the heat of the bonfire reached him, and he began to sweat. Fortunately, he did not have to wait long.

From among the servants and scouts, a tall man—a *very* tall man—came across the clearing. His skin was burnished ebony, and its look of having been oiled and polished was emphasized by the nakedness of his chest. Like the crown of his head, his torso was entirely hairless. For clothing, he wore a long sheet of many-colored cotton wrapped several times around his waist, then around each of his legs, and finally secured by a leather thong. His feet were bare, and he bore no weapons.

A glance was enough to assure Prince Bifalt the man was pro-digiously strong. Perhaps he did not carry weapons because he did not need them.

Approaching the Bellegerins, he nodded to the Prince, then knelt at the edge of the blanket and sank back on his heels. His grin exposed strong teeth a startling white in contrast to his black skin.

In a voice with the depth and resonance of a distant landslide, he said, "Suti al-Suri informs me that you are Prince Bifalt, son of King Abbator of Belleger." He spoke the Prince's language without accent or flaw. "My employer, Set Ungabwey, master of this caravan, asks the pleasure of your company for an hour. Your men may rest where they are, or enjoy the evening as they see fit." His grin broadened. "There will be dancing. Many of our maidens dance delectably."

Taken aback, Prince Bifalt stared. The man's strangeness, strength, and amusement unsettled him. A reply was expected, he knew, but he could not think of one. He barely retained enough presence of mind to answer by bowing his head.

The caravan master's emissary laughed. "You appear surprised that we understand each other. The mystery is easily explained. I am Set Ungabwey's interpreter. I speak all known languages, and others as well. Our good chief scout means well, but his pidgin grasp of your tongue is inadequate for pleasant conversation and full comprehension.

"For convenience, you may call me Tchwee."

With an undignified effort, the Prince recovered his voice. "Thank you," he said when he could control himself. "You do surprise me." Everything about the caravan surprised him. "We are far from our homeland. I did not expect your caravan master's generosity, or your ability with our tongue." Trying to gather the shreds of his composure, he asked, "Does the word 'Tchwee' signify 'interpreter'?"

The man laughed again. "Truly, it is only a convenience. My name is too elaborate for courtesy, and my full title is an embarrassment of riches. I am content to be known as Tchwee."

Then he repeated his query. "Will you accept Set Ungabwey's invitation? His curiosity is as great as yours, and as harmless. Also he would consider himself rude if he did not welcome you in person. Alas, his condition prevents his attendance at these festivities."

Prince Bifalt wanted to ask, His condition? He wanted to ask, Festivities? More than that, he wanted to ask if Tchwee used the word *harmless* with a double meaning. His own purpose—like the purpose of his quest—was neither unharmed nor unharmful.

But he sensed impatience in the background of Tchwee's genial manner. Or perhaps he simply feared the interpreter's strength. Rigid behind his regained blankness, he replied, "Certainly, I will accept. I am eager to meet the man who saved our lives."

However, he did not rise at once. Instead, he leaned close to Elgart. In a low voice, but distinctly, he told the rifleman, "An hour. No more." Then, trusting Elgart's wits to reach the obvious conclusion, Prince Bifalt reclaimed his weapons and stood.

Tchwee cocked an eyebrow at the Prince's rifle and saber, but offered no objection. With a florid gesture, he directed Prince Bifalt around the bonfire and past the overflowing blankets on the far side.

There, the caravan master's rich carriage was no more than twenty paces away. Despite Tchwee's long strides, however, and the Prince's determination to keep up, they acquired a following. Suti al-Suri trailed a few steps behind, accompanied by one of the tonsured men. Soon they were joined by a foppish individual dressed like a leader among the carnival folk: their herald, perhaps, or their ringmaster. In addition, the Prince and Tchwee were trailed by two women. One was hardly taller than a child, clad in a demure cloak of white silk, with her hair unbound and her hands clasped hidden in her sleeves. The other was taller, yellow-skinned and bold-eyed, and had elected to attire herself in the bright colors and revealing garments of a trawling courtesan.

Apparently, they, too, had been invited to attend the caravan master. Set Ungabwey had separate reasons to speak with them— or he wanted an audience to hear his Bellegerin guest.

Near the carriage, Tchwee paused. His group stopped while the interpreter addressed them.

"A moment, Prince." Prince Bifalt felt Tchwee's voice in his bones. "Set Ungabwey is the master of this caravan. His will rules. Nevertheless, he welcomes the counsel of his chosen advisers. These dignitaries share the benefits of their insights. They command their own folk among the caravan.

"Introductions can be cumbersome among strangers, especially when each speaks a different tongue, or when they are not all fluent in yours. I will name them to you now, so that Set Ungabwey's welcome will not be hindered by awkwardness."

Prince Bifalt had the sensation he was holding his breath. He had been ill prepared for the hazards and frustrations of his quest: he was more so now. Although he was his father's son, he was still only a soldier. He felt entirely unready to play his role here; to act the part of a diplomat, probing others while concealing himself.

With an effort, he kept his hands away from his weapons as he acknowledged Tchwee's courtesy.

In a variety of tones and inflections, the interpreter explained the words *Prince Bifalt*, *King Abbator*, and *Belleger*. When the five advisers had signified their understanding, Tchwee said to the

Prince, "Suti al-Suri you already know. His folk are the el-Algreb, nomads of the southern steppes, great horsemen, trackers, and scouts. For many generations, they have watched over caravans in these and other lands. For many years, they have performed the same service for Master Ungabwey.

"The man with him is a monk of the Cult of the Many. His order does not use names, and seldom speaks, but when he does offer counsel, his observations are prized. The Cult of the Many travels widely, seeking peace wherever it may be found."

Monks, thought Prince Bifalt. *Give lives gods.* Like his men, he had no idea what the chief scout's description meant.

But Tchwee was still speaking. "Their companion is Alleman Dancer, who owns and leads a troupe of performers grandly styled the Wide World Carnival. He brings insights concerning matters that lie outside the experience of monks and nomads."

The interpreter gave Prince Bifalt time to bow to each of the men. Then he continued.

"These women are dignitaries of another kind. You might think of them as priestesses, although they eschew such terms. They are Amandis, most holy devotee of Spirit"—he indicated the tiny woman—"and she wishes it known that she is an assassin." Tchwee chuckled. "Pity the man who trifles with her. Her gifts would astonish you.

"Her companion or partner or antagonist is Flamora, devotee of Flesh, also most holy. She teaches peace to those who have the wit to learn. Though their disciplines are distinct, she and Amandis are never far apart. They believe, or so I imagine, that they ward each other from excess."

Grinning as if his white teeth were a threat—or a promise—the tall linguist asked, "Are you content with the presence of Set Ungabwey's advisers, Prince of Belleger?"

The Prince bowed twice more. "I am a soldier," he replied gruffly. "I do not know the world." Words like *monk* and *priestess* were like *gods*: he could not guess what they signified. "But in my father's court, they would be welcomed with more warmth than I can offer. Perhaps they will counsel me as well."

Tchwee translated smoothly. To Prince Bifalt, the interpreter seemed to speak several languages at once. Nevertheless, he was understood. The monk lowered his head farther, Alleman Dancer smiled with a sparkle of relish in his eyes, and Flamora wet her generous lips with the tip of her tongue. The assassin nodded without looking up, while a succession of emotions played across Suti al-Suri's features, some friendly, others not.

"Then I will announce you," Tchwee told the Prince. Turning, he reached the door of the carriage, opened it, and ascended the steps to enter through a dazzling spill of light.

"Master Ungabwey," he declaimed, "I bring Prince Bifalt, son of King Abbator of Belleger, to accept your welcome."

Obeying a gesture from the chief scout, Prince Bifalt took the steps and went into the caravan master's ostentatious conveyance.

In the doorway, he froze, overcome yet again. By the blaze of a dozen lanterns, he gazed around a compartment more sumptuous than any chamber in Belleger's Fist. Rugs as rich as feather beds covered the floor. Except where they were punctuated by shaded windows, the walls appeared to ooze brass or gold. Starscapes had been meticulously painted across the ceiling. At both ends of the

compartment were doors studded with gems and chased with silver, but the Prince was too stunned to guess what lay beyond them.

There were no chairs. Instead, an abundance of satin pillows,
some in emerald hues, others in sapphire, were strewn around the
floor and piled along the walls. Among them, trays of beaten brass
held ewers and goblets, all intricately engraved.

Prince Bifalt could not have imagined that one carriage in a
long caravan camped in the middle of an immeasurable desert
might hold such wealth. And if the caravan master's carriage alone
displayed riches to this extent, the caravan itself must be beyond
price, more valuable in hard coin than all of Belleger and Amikan
combined.

Caught by what he saw, he was slow to notice the occupants of
the conveyance. But then Suti al-Suri nudged his back, encouraging him to make way for Set Ungabwey's counselors, and his attention shifted. His eyes skidded past four young women, all
slender, all modest in ochre robes, with brown skin and flowing
hair. They were too unformed to demand his gaze. Rather he stared,
gaping indecorously, at the individual who commanded the
chamber.

Seated on a profusion of pillows against the far wall was the
fattest man Prince Bifalt had ever seen, a personage so corpulent
that he looked too heavy to stand on his legs. Even seated, his belly
bulged to his knees. His cheeks extended down his neck, and his
pendulous earlobes reached his shoulders. Squeezed by fat, his eyes
were visible only as pinpricks of reflected lanternlight. His head
was entirely hairless, lacking even eyebrows and lashes. The rest of
his form was wrapped in long swaths of ochre muslin.

Tchwee's posture kneeling at his side identified him as the caravan master. Clearly, he did not attend feasts, or leave his carriage to welcome guests, because he could not. That was his *condition*. Only the brown hue of his skin, and what could be discerned of his features, suggested that he might be the father of the young women.

Grinning at Prince Bifalt's reaction, the interpreter addressed his master in yet another foreign tongue, crisp sounds among which the Prince recognized only his own name, his father's, and *Belleger*. Then the black man continued, "Prince Bifalt, I present Set Ungabwey, master of this caravan and all who accompany it. He expresses his pleasure in your presence. He is ever eager for knowledge of new lands. And he is glad of this opportunity to share his many blessings with those less fortunate than himself."

As far as Prince Bifalt could tell, Set Ungabwey had not moved his lips or uttered a sound.

While the Prince strove to summon a response, the caravan master's advisers entered the carriage. Three of them seated themselves on pillows around the walls, the monk close to Tchwee, Amandis and Flamora among the young women. Impervious to dignity, Alleman Dancer sprawled on his side and spent a few moments arranging pillows to make himself comfortable. Suti al-Suri remained standing near the door.

"Master Ungabwey," said Prince Bifalt finally, "since your chief scout found us, my men and I have experienced amazing things. We were as good as dead—and yet we are here. We have been fed and refreshed. And we are surrounded by people and conveyances like none we have ever seen. Your bounty is beyond our understanding.

"How is it possible for *any* caravan to cross this terrible wasteland? What imperative calls you to this trek? There must be more accessible lands with which you could trade. The size of your train suggests *many* more. Master Ungabwey, we are in awe.

"Belleger is a humble land. It holds nothing to compare with such luxury and ease." Struggling with the awkwardness of his role, Prince Bifalt concluded, "In our realm, wonders are only accomplished by theurgy."

Set Ungabwey appeared to nod. Certainly, his flesh wobbled. He made a distinct spitting noise.

At once, one of his women—his daughters?—hurried to his side, wiped his lips with a delicate cloth, then resumed her seat.

Tchwee's grin—his whole demeanor—suggested barely suppressed mirth. "A fine speech, Prince of Belleger," he declared in tones that made the leather window shades quiver, "and grateful to the ear. No doubt many of your questions will find answers. At the risk of discourtesy, however, I must remind you that you are Master Ungabwey's guest. His curiosity takes precedence."

"As does mine," said the most holy devotee of Flesh, speaking unexpectedly in Belleger's language. "The advantage of soldiers is that they are trained for strength." Her voice was seductive, like a fresh spring in the heart of an oasis. "His stamina must be remarkable."

"Also weapons," put in Suti al-Suri. "Rifles. Lead arrows. Never seen."

Tchwee dismissed these comments with a wave of one hand. "Tell us of your homeland, Prince." His note of authority was unmistakable. "Describe Belleger to us. Where does it lie? How do its people live? And what is *theurgy*?

"Master Ungabwey's curiosity grows. It may be that one day he will elect to alter the route of his train to visit your lands."

Again the caravan master said nothing; or nothing Prince Bifalt could hear.

He found himself wondering who actually commanded the caravan. Despite his bulk, Set Ungabwey acted like nothing more than a figurehead. Unless the interpreter's gift of languages included the ability to read minds—

No. If Tchwee could do that, he would not need to ask questions. He would already know Prince Bifalt's secrets.

Still, the Prince addressed the fat man. "With respect, Master Ungabwey, I disagree. My men and I are lost. You are not. We cannot travel the desert. You can. We are few. You are many. Also, you are familiar with lands beyond our knowledge. I am disadvantaged in your presence. My questions are not meant as insults. They come from need."

"Another fine speech," remarked the reclining carnival owner, "but specious." He, too, knew Prince Bifalt's tongue, although his accent was peculiar. "Master Ungabwey is your host. His courtesies bind you. If you refuse his curiosity, you refuse his welcome as well."

Ponderously, Set Ungabwey turned his head to Tchwee, a movement which looked difficult for him. Tchwee leaned closer, and the two men seemed to confer, although the Prince could not hear them.

When they were done, the interpreter straightened. "Prince," he said, "your straits tug at Master Ungabwey's heart. Be assured that he also speaks with respect. Nevertheless, he insists on precedence. He cannot assess you wisely until he understands your need, its nature and extremity. You were not dropped from the sky in our path. You were driven by hard choices. Have you come in service to your king, or were you sent into exile? Distinctions of that kind have weight. They may affect the whole caravan.

"When you have given an account of yourself, Master Ungabwey will know how to respond."

While Prince Bifalt frowned, scrambling inwardly to decide what he could say and what he should not, Tchwee continued more gently, "Be at ease, Prince. Seat yourself. Set aside your weapons. Take wine. You are not threatened, neither you nor your men. If you are bound by Master Ungabwey's welcome, he is also. Fear nothing. Speak freely."

As if to contradict or enforce the interpreter's assurances, the devotee of Spirit, Amandis, let one hand show beyond her sleeve. For an instant, her small fingers held a throwing knife whetted to a keenness that seemed to cut the light. Then it and her hand were gone.

"Tut, sister," murmured Flamora. "Do not act in haste. It would be sin to mar such flesh as his."

Behind his frown, Prince Bifalt sighed. With an assassin on one side, the chief scout at his back, and two enormous men before him, one of them too strong to be stopped, he did not hesitate. It was both his duty and his nature to accept challenges. Sinking to a pillow, he unshouldered his rifle and ammunition, unfastened his saber, and set them down within easy reach.

When he was seated, one of the young women came to kneel at his side. Taking a nearby ewer from its tray, she filled a goblet with the same ruby wine he had tasted earlier and pressed it into his hands.

At the same time, her sisters served wine to their father, Tchwee, Flamora, and Alleman Dancer. Apparently, they knew the monk and the assassin would not partake, and Suti al-Suri was on guard. The young woman attending Set Ungabwey helped him lift the goblet to his mouth, and lower it again when it was empty. Then the four daughters returned to their places.

Prince Bifalt held up his goblet to his host—a Bellegerin salute—then sipped the wine. It was more pleasant than his memory of it, and he drank more deeply before putting the goblet aside. With a sensation of refreshment tingling on his tongue, he prepared himself to speak.

Holding the caravan master's pinprick gaze, he let iron show in his voice. "Master Ungabwey, I will tell you of Belleger.

"It lies far to the west. We traveled beyond its maps when we entered the desert. It was once a land of plenty, but it has been impoverished by a long war. Our losses cripple us. For generations, the struggle was comparatively equal. Now it has become ruinous. My men and I were sent by King Abbator to answer the riddle of our coming destruction. We were sixteen when we set out. Four I instructed to carry word of our progress to the King. The rest are dead."

"A heavy cost," commented Tchwee. "I begin to grasp your plight. But you say you were once equal to your foe. How was your struggle made ruinous?"

Prince Bifalt clenched his fists, holding tight to his resolve. "When I spoke of 'theurgy,' I could have chosen a different word. It is 'sorcery.' Our foes have sorcery. We do not. Our foes bring terrible forces against us, fires and pestilences, earthquakes and lightnings. We have only rifles. And our rifles are too few. They cannot counter sorcery."

"Strange," put in Alleman Dancer. "Do you say *terrible* forces?" He glanced at the monk. "I did not know the Cult of the Many worships gods whose powers are used to determine the outcome of wars."

The Prince wanted to ask—to demand—*Gods?* Do men worship *sorcerers?* But Tchwee silenced the carnival owner and forestalled Prince Bifalt with a commanding gesture.

Again the interpreter leaned close to Set Ungabwey. Although the caravan master did not turn his head or speak, Tchwee nodded an acknowledgment.

To Prince Bifalt, he said, "Your straits are dire indeed. Who is your foe?"

"It is Amika," answered the Prince bitterly, "a realm on Belleger's northern border. Their attacks have been relentless for so long that their causes have become meaningless. We know the source of their enmity, but we do not know why it endures. We only know that we can no longer withstand it."

"You explain much," offered Flamora. "Your dilemma wrings my heart." Her limpid gaze suggested sincerity. "So many brave men slaughtered. Strong men. Worthy men." Then she frowned delicately. "But you do not explain your presence here. How can an attempt to cross this cruel desert win survival for your people?"

Prince Bifalt allowed himself to sigh aloud. He suspected that answering her would be a mistake; but he saw no alternative. Sweating under the lanterns, he replied as if he were sure of himself.

"Among our people, legends speak of a storehouse of knowledge. Perhaps it is a library. Perhaps it takes some other form. But if it exists—if the legends are not mistaken—it lies among the moun-

---

tains to the east. Now we seek it. There we may learn how to prevent our doom. We have no other hope."

To his surprise, his words seemed to strike his audience like an insult—or a threat. For a long moment, no one spoke. Tchwee appeared to consult with the caravan master again, although Set Ungabwey betrayed no response. The five advisers remained motionless, held by suspense. Prince Bifalt felt he was in the presence of issues and dangers too great for him. He could not gauge them. He hardly dared to breathe.

Then Suti al-Suri said in a tone of disgust, "Lead arrows," and the moment passed. Alleman Dancer shifted one of his pillows. The devotee of Flesh whispered to Amandis in her foreign tongue. A flick of Set Ungabwey's eyes called for more wine. One of the young women rose to fill his goblet and assist him.

While she served the caravan master, the monk surprised Prince Bifalt further by bowing his forehead to the floor. Then he resumed his unassuming posture, head lowered, gaze shrouded.

With a loud rumble, Tchwee cleared his throat. "Prince of Belleger," he declared, "you have answered. Now you will be answered. Ask what you wish."

Prince Bifalt's opportunity had come. He felt its pressure beating in his chest. He wanted to ask where the caravan would take him: a natural question, perhaps an innocent one, but wasted. He would not recognize any name the interpreter might mention. He did not know the world. And he had a more urgent question. It might lead him to the revelations Belleger required.

Enunciating each word with a soldier's precision, he began.

"Master Ungabwey, I hope to understand how you travel with

such ease. You have many scouts. Their numbers tell me that you face dangers, but I cannot imagine what danger threatens you here. Brigands cannot prey in this desert. Hostile war parties cannot. The wasteland itself protects you. Only sorcerers can harm you in this region.

"Yet in Belleger we know scouts are useless against sorcerers, who can strike at any distance and remain hidden." Carefully, he skirted the edges of falsehood. He had learned that other theurgists did not share the limitations of Belleger's former Magisters—or of Amika's. "How, then, is your trek made easy? How is your train kept safe?

"I can think of no explanation, Master Ungabwey, except that your scouts are only needed in other lands. They serve no vital purpose *here*. *Here* you are warded by sorcerers."

The silence that followed was more fraught than the previous moment of tension. Tchwee knelt, completely still, at the caravan master's side. He did not appear to breathe. Flamora's lips shaped prayers. Amandis allowed the Prince to see knives in both hands. The monk startled him by gazing at him directly. Even Set Ungabwey's daughters shifted anxiously on their pillows.

"A man once bitten by a snake," drawled the Wide World Carnival's owner, "sees a snake in every shadow."

Alleman Dancer did not continue. A glance from Tchwee made him close his mouth.

Prince Bifalt heard a weapon unsheathed behind him. Instinctively, he reached for his rifle, then drew back his hand, empty. His muscles tightened, anticipating the stroke of a cutlass. He was not fast enough to stop Suti al-Suri from killing him where he sat.

———

The lanterns seemed to shed an unbearable heat.

Abruptly, Flamora laughed, a chiming sound like the tinkle of a fine bell. "If you are able to find the library of your legends, how will you use the knowledge you seek?"

Without pausing for thought, Prince Bifalt replied, "We will reduce Amika until its people must surrender or *die*."

His words hung in the air as if they had assumed a life of their own. Inwardly, he cursed himself. He had said too much; revealed too much. His anger and fear had outrun his caution.

A moment later, he heard Set Ungabwey speak for the first time. The caravan master's voice was a crooning falsetto, as if he customarily spoke only to soothe small children. Nevertheless, it was distinct; even implacable.

"The knowledge you seek," he pronounced, "is the knowledge of sorcery. You will wield it against Amika. We cannot help you."

He did not speak again.

Shocked beyond bearing, the Prince retorted, "You are their allies! You help *them* against *us*. You want *Belleger* destroyed!"

He expected murder for his accusation. He expected Suti al-Suri's cutlass in his back, the devotee of Spirit's dagger in his eye. But he did not move, despite his yearning to snatch up his rifle. His shock was too great. Sorcerers who intended to use him had sent the caravan to snatch him and his men back from the edge of death. How could he be refused? How could his search fail *now*?

Even an Amikan born and trained might not kill a sitting Bellegerin who did not defend himself.

However, he was not attacked. Instead, strangely, Set Ungabwey's advisers relaxed as if they were content; as if questions

Prince Bifalt did not understand had been answered. Smiling with an air of sadness, the interpreter rose to his feet.

Towering over the caravan master's guest, Tchwee said firmly, "You are mistaken, Prince. We know nothing of Amika. We do not travel there. And we do not join wars. If we cannot aid you, we will not stand in your way. You are welcome among us. Your men are welcome. You will remain, or you will depart, as you choose. Seek the library of your legends if you wish. Remain among us, be our guest, and go where we go—if that is your desire. In either event, no hand will be raised against you.

"This audience is ended. Suti al-Suri?"

At once, the chief scout slapped his cutlass back into its scabbard. "Come, Prince." His tone sounded forced. "Dancing waits. Wine. Maidens. Pleasure. Then sleep." He gestured toward the door. "Come."

Fuming with consternation, Prince Bifalt reclaimed his weapons and stood. What else could he do? *We will reduce Amika—* He should not have said that. It was a mistake. He had revealed too much. But he had no idea how to amend his error. Shamed by his failure, he made no pretense of politeness as he left the carriage.

But he did not return to the bonfire. He was who he was. In the darkness of full night, with the light of high flames on his face, and the noise of instruments, dancers, and carousing onlookers in his ears, he waited for Set Ungabwey's advisers to follow his departure.

As they descended the steps, he did not acknowledge the monk, or the women devoted to Spirit and Flesh, or the carnival owner. He ignored the chief scout's urging to move on. But when Tchwee emerged, Prince Bifalt dared to grasp the huge interpreter's forearm.

Outfacing the grin of a man who could have broken him with one blow, the Prince demanded, "Your gift of tongues. You speak all known languages, and others as well. You even know *mine*. And you appear to know your master's mind. Is that not sorcery? Do you deny you have dealings with sorcerers? Do you deny you are a sorcerer yourself?"

Tchwee frowned. "A man once bitten—" he began. Then his expression cleared, and he laughed. "Yes, Prince," he answered through his amusement, "I deny it. Like the name I have given you, my claim to 'speak all known languages' is a convenience. The truth requires more explanation.

"My gift is for the *study* of languages. I have learned how they are formed, and why. This enables me to acquire new tongues when they are needed. But I cannot shake the earth, or bring down fire, or see from afar. There is no sorcery in me."

Prince Bifalt did not relent. "Yet you are fluent in our tongue. You heard it before Suti al-Suri found us. You must have. He speaks only fragments himself. If you do not know Belleger, you must know Amika. Or you must know merchants who trade with Amika. Belleger has no trade. Otherwise, how can you speak with us?"

He meant, How have you been turned against us?

But his challenge did not touch Tchwee. Laughing again, the interpreter replied, "I know your language, Prince, because I have heard you speak with your men. I learned it from you."

"What of that carnival mountebank?" protested the Prince. "What of Flamora?"

Still chuckling, Tchwee countered, "How can I tell? Perhaps they have encountered traders, as you suggest. Their travels are

177

many. If you persist in this query, you must ask it of them. I have no answer to give you."

Then he turned away, freeing his forearm easily, and leaving the Bellegerin to boil alone.

Prince Bifalt knew no expletive or curse adequate to express his frustration—or his fear that his father would be ashamed of him. Old pain had taught King Abbator patience. Burning to prove worthy of his father's trust, the Prince had not learned the same lesson. When Suti al-Suri urged him toward the bonfire again, he only complied because he did not know what else to do.

He could not imagine when or how the interpreter had overheard his conversations with Elgart and Klamath.

※

On the blanket where he had left them, the Prince found the guardsmen. The plates of food had been taken away: the flagons of wine remained. To Prince Bifalt's bitter eye, it was plain both Klamath and Elgart had drunk too much to remember his implied command. If he had not returned, they might not have thought to look for him for hours.

Although they greeted him with blurred voices, they had not lost interest in the activities around them. The reflections of flames were keen with excitement in Klamath's eyes, and he watched the dancers as if nothing else existed. Elgart's attention was more divided. The bonfire's flames gleamed on his scar as he, too, studied the maidens dancing. He and Klamath had been away from women too long. But he also kept his head cocked to the music, and his hands tapped his knees, repeating the complex rhythms of the dance.

Prince Bifalt swallowed an impulse to reprimand his companions. He had instructed them to act like guests. And not many years ago, he would have done as they did. He understood their fascination. Clad in garments as graceful and enticing as silk, and seen by firelight under the black sky, the young women seemed almost mystically alluring. They whirled and scampered and sprang high as if they were carried along by ecstasy. And their partners, mostly young men bare-chested, moved with the fluid suddenness and strength of deer. They spun the maidens, tossed and received and exchanged them, followed them as avidly as courtship. As for the music: tambourines, cymbals, and hand-thumped drums drove the melodies of strange stringed instruments and shrill flutes, their harmonies both unexpected and urgent, inspiring abandon.

Many of the caravan's travelers shared Klamath's and Elgart's appreciation. Beyond the ring of blankets—most still occupied—a throng of onlookers had gathered, scores or perhaps hundreds of teamsters, drovers, laborers, performers, tradesmen, merchants, families: folk from six or eight or ten distinct lands, some simply pleased to watch, others plainly yearning to join the dance if they could learn the steps or match the rhythms.

Among so many people, the Prince was alone, isolated by the darkness on his spirit. He had failed to learn where he was, or where he was going, or where the library might be. He had failed to win any aid for himself, or for Belleger. Amid the clamor and frenzy, his fear and disgust felt universal. They included the whole caravan and all the doings of the travelers. He did not speak to his comrades as he resumed his seat between them. Finding his flagon full, he drank deeply. Then he propped his elbows on his knees, held his head in his hands, and tried to think.

His plight was impossible. It had been impossible from the start. At every stage along the way, he had misjudged his choices. And here, where he had expected to find hope, Belleger's needs—for help, for knowledge, for sorcery—had been flatly denied. Remain or depart? As he chose? All well and good. A fine speech. But how could he choose? He did not know where the caravan had been, or where it was going. He had no idea where to look for the Repository of the sorcerers—and no way to reach it without food and water, which only the caravan could supply.

And that was not the end of his difficulties. He felt certain now that Set Ungabwey and his counselors treated with sorcerers. The Cult of the Many. Gods. Spirit and Flesh. The caravan master was protected by them, or was in communication with them—or was one of them himself. As were others. Tchwee. The monk. Amandis. Flamora.

Sorcerers wanted him alive. Yet they—or others—did not want him to locate them? None of them would help him save his people?

He drank again.

Nothing made sense.

A maiden spun herself out of the dance to stand before Klamath. She extended her hand. Trembling with eagerness, he accepted it. The musicians played more loudly. She whirled him away. In a moment, the Prince lost sight of him.

———

Well, why not? Prince Bifalt could think of no reason to deny Klamath any pleasure the rifleman craved.

He peered at his flagon. It had been refilled. More sorcery: no one had approached him.

This wine was a different vintage. It had a peculiar aftertaste. He took one swallow. Then he took another. He could ignore the aftertaste.

Abruptly, Elgart reached a decision. He rose to his feet, strode away toward the musicians.

They appeared to understand him without words. One of them handed him a set of drums like small pots overturned and bound together. Seating himself among the players, he held the set between his knees and began to pound the leather drumheads with his palms. Prince Bifalt could not tell whether Elgart kept time with the music, but other drummers nodded their approval.

A fine speech. Your men are welcome. Klamath and Elgart could make places for themselves in the caravan. Unlike Captain Swalish, Camwish, Nowel, and too many others, they would live. Set Ungabwey might allow them to serve as guards. If they did not forget their rifles—or surrender them—

The Prince drank again. *He* had no place here. His father's command, and Belleger's need, and his own nature ruled him. For this one night, he would drink and sleep. In the morning, he would buy or beg supplies, if not from Suti al-Suri, then from one of the many merchants. Then he would head toward the mountains. If sorcerers wanted him alive, they would provide guidance in the same way they had provided the caravan. What else could he do?

A more subtle man might have elected to remain with the caravan for days, if necessary, asking questions until he gleaned something useful, even if the answers he received were only scraps. Flamora might be receptive. And Alleman Dancer might be too self-assured to keep silent. But Prince Bifalt was not that man.

His flagon had been filled again. He continued to drink. The aftertaste was becoming pleasant.

From among the flurry of the dancers, a young woman left her partners and drew near. For a moment, she twirled alone in front of the Prince. As she moved, the blazing of the bonfire outlined her form through the flow and float of her attire, a shape as desirable as sunrise after a bitter battle. Then she stopped. Her breasts rose and fell with every breath. Gazing at him, she extended her hand.

Prince Bifalt avoided her eyes. He did not take her hand.

Frowning uncertainly, she sank to her knees. She was near enough to touch his face, although she did not. Instead, she extended her hand again. Her gaze was moist with invitation. It promised more than dancing.

Rather than accept her clasp, he gripped her wrist and drew her closer. He wanted to grip her hard enough to wring truth from her slender bones. "Tell me," he rasped: the hoarse vehemence of a man who felt intolerably thwarted. "Where are you from? Where are you going? Do you know sorcerers?"

She turned her face away. Her whole body shied from him. She tried to break free.

He tightened his grasp. "Answer me," he demanded. "I need sorcerers. I need their books. Tell me where to find them."

He thought he heard her whimper.

At once, two men came to her sides. They were young and strong. Sweat streamed from their naked chests. Anger glared in their eyes. They showed the Prince their clenched fists.

He released the woman. Holding up his hands, he let the men see that he did not reach for his weapons.

Glowering, they raised her to her feet, escorted her away.

Alone again, Prince Bifalt trembled with anger. He sloshed wine as he drank once more. Then he surged to his feet.

"*Wastrels!*" he howled through the din of dancing feet, the squall of music. "Your lives are *ease*! You have no cares! You feast in lifeless deserts! You guzzle ale and wine where there is no water! You give welcome, but you have no *hearts*!

"*My people will be slaughtered!*"

At that moment, a hand touched Prince Bifalt's shoulder. "Enough, Prince," said Suti al-Suri. "Our wine strong for you." His tone was inexplicably mild. "You sleep."

As if the chief scout's words—or his touch—were an enchantment, the King of Belleger's eldest son slumped into his own darkness.

PART
FOUR

Sleeping, the Prince was not aware of time. He understood only darkness and complete rest in a place far from his doubts and fears. Strong arms of slumber cradled him, comfortable and contented. The fire in his heart had burned itself out, or had been quenched. He had no desire to wake.

Eventually, however, he was touched by the sensation that unnatural quantities of time had slipped away. Hour and hours; perhaps days. At some point, he would need to rouse himself. Of course. He could not avoid it. But while he slept, he craved only sleep.

Nothing except impossible responsibilities waited for him in the conscious world.

Nevertheless, comfort and contentment left him. Without his consent, he began to dream: a formless *something* without shape or meaning. At first, it was nothing more than lurid streaks of color leaping like flames. Then, slowly, he realized that he was dreaming of fire. A fire for cooking? A bonfire? The inferno of heat in the heart of a forge—or in his own heart? He did not care. It was only a dream. It had no significance until he began to believe that he was being roasted alive.

Still, he did not awaken. He fretted where he lay, jerked his head from side to side, batted his hands against a hard surface like the wall of a prison. Grinding his teeth, he groaned. But he remained asleep, dreaming of incineration despite his efforts to escape.

Somehow, he clung to the mirage of himself until a great voice shook his bones. It shouted like thunder; like the breaking of the world.

NOW are you ready?

Burning, he began to break free.

He could not open his eyes. He had been gone too long, and the sun was too bright. But he felt the rough bed where he lay and knew it was stone, rutted and pitted: old stone swept bare of dust and sand and life. He sweated under the fierce weight of heat, and smelled the scent of baked sand, and knew he was in the desert. He heard nothing except the scraping of distant breezes, the subtle spill of grit, and knew he was alone. Without looking, he knew Elgart and Klamath had been taken from him.

Finally, he understood that the caravan was gone. He had been left to die.

So much for promises of welcome. He had been drugged and abandoned because he had revealed his desire to rid Belleger of Amika. He had said too much about sorcerers. He had given Set

Ungabwey reason to consider him dangerous—or the caravan master had received instructions from his own masters—or he and those powers had a standing agreement concerning men like the Prince—

—or he was still being challenged. Still being asked to declare some kind of allegiance to men who wanted to own him.

On cruel stone under the ferocious sun, a terrible clarity came to Prince Bifalt. Were the sorcerers who shouted in his thoughts men of power? Well and good. Let them wield as many Decimates as they had. Let them scorn the obstacles of distance and death. He, too, had power. He could lie where he was and let the sun have him. If his foes had some compelling need for his service, he could make them come to him. And if they did not, he could foil their demands by the simple expedient of refusing to move.

Unfortunately, clarity was indeed terrible. It exposed too much. When he had convinced himself that he could choose his own death, he discovered he was unable or unwilling to take that course. His foes had another power, one they did not need to wield: the power to rescue or destroy his homeland. Belleger's plight was a goad in his mind. It lashed his every thought. And he could easily imagine that his antagonists might give up on him. He was too stubborn. If they wanted a Bellegerin, they could find one more pliable. To claim King Abbator's eldest son, they were willing to exert themselves—but to what extent? Prince Bifalt could not guess. He was sure only that if he exhausted their patience, he would be allowed to die wherever he pleased. Then Belleger would be lost.

The goad was set. He could not turn his back on his father, or on his people. Although the truth galled him utterly, he could not set down his burdens. His own life was a mere feather in the scales, too light to outweigh Belleger's need. He knew too well what sorcerers could do to their victims.

Gritting his teeth, he rubbed his eyes to remove sleep and sand. With a thrust of his leg, he rolled himself onto his side, then onto his chest. When he had worked his arms under him, scraping them painfully on the stone, he pushed his torso upright until he was able to kneel. Finally, he opened his eyes.

He needed a long moment to blink away the blur of dryness and heat. Then he was able to see.

The vista around him was exactly the one he had expected and feared. The shape of the caravan track was not quite as he remembered it: it curved at different angles and different distances. But the stone of the track itself was the same, stripped bare by ancient forces, rutted by the passage of innumerable wagons, chipped and gouged by decades or centuries of iron-shod hooves. The dunes piling high on both sides, east and west, were unchanged, as forbidding as barricades. The breezes playing on their crests brought no relief to the valleys. And the sun— It felt hot enough to forge rifle barrels. The sky was dulled to a grey brown by the haze of heat.

No sign remained to suggest that Set Ungabwey's train had been here. From south to north, every span of the track was bare of refuse, fire-blackened stones, scattered ashes. The caravan had carried away or destroyed even its own waste. No visible watcher regarded Prince Bifalt's kneeling form.

And his weapons had been taken from him. He did not have as much as a dagger. Also his water flask was gone, his satchel, his bedroll. He had been left with nothing to cover his head.

Was he ready now? Oh, yes. He was prepared to make promises that he did not intend to keep. He would not call it dishonorable to break his word. Men who had claimed and abused him so casually were not worthy of honor.

Sickened as much by revulsion as by thirst and weakness, he forced himself to his feet. He did not doubt he would be heard.

At first, his throat was too dry for sound. His tongue and lips were too raw to form words. But he was Prince Bifalt, King Abbator's eldest son. He made himself able to speak.

"I surrender," he confessed. Even to himself, his thin wheeze was barely audible. "I am ready. Tell me why you want me. I will hear you. I will do what I can." For his own sake, he required that much honesty. "I am ready now."

Then he sank back to his knees, bowed his head, and composed himself to wait for prostration or rescue.

✳

He had sprawled on his face without realizing it when he heard Elgart's voice in the distance.

"Highness!" called the guardsman. "They said you live, but I did not believe—"

A heavy slide of sand covered Elgart's words. Then came the hard clop of hooves cantering across the track. Confused by heat and thirst, the Prince could not tell whether they approached from east or west.

Raising his head by an act of will, he saw a blur that may have been a familiar shape on horseback. The rider appeared to lead a second mount by its reins.

"Highness!" repeated the guardsman. In a rush, he dismounted. By main force, he turned the Prince, lifted the Prince's head. Squinting, Prince Bifalt saw a bulging leather flask in front of him. It smelled like water.

With trembling hands, he took the flask. With Elgart's help, he brought it to his mouth and drank sweet life.

While the Prince quenched the misery of his tongue and throat, and sudden sweat beaded on his brow, Elgart flapped a large square of silk, making a brief breeze, then draped the cloth over Prince Bifalt's head. Water and shade blessed the King's son. They were bliss.

Elgart sat in front of his commander, still supporting the flask. "I have food, Highness." He spoke as if he addressed a man to whom simple words might exceed comprehension. "I will bring it when you can sit without help."

After a pause, he added, "Your surrender was heard. They sent me to bring you. To the Last Repository."

The Prince avoided his companion's eyes. He could not endure their probing. Even simple words were not simple enough. He did not know how to interpret them.

The last? he wondered. Then he forgot about it.

Instead, he asked the first attainable question in his head. "Klamath?"

"He rides to the King." Carefully, the scarred rifleman urged Prince Bifalt to sit. "He was given a message. He will tell the King your quest has succeeded. In your name, he will ask the King to do nothing against Amika until you return. Belleger will be protected." Elgart's shrug suggested helplessness. "I do not understand it. But I heard it. I saw Klamath ride away."

"Across this desert?" croaked the Prince.

"He was promised an easy path. He had a map. And he was glad to obey. He trusted what he was told." Sourly, Elgart remarked, "He trusts too easily. It is his nature."

Prince Bifalt nodded. He felt unable to stop nodding. He had agreed to everything. And Klamath had said, *We have too many enemies. And I have killed too many of them. I have seen too many Bellegerins die.* Naturally, the man was glad to carry a message that seemed to imply the war might end.

Now the Prince was able to ask, "You found it? The library?"

Elgart removed his hands, assured himself the Prince was able to remain sitting. Then he rose to his feet. "Food, Highness. You are too weak to ride."

When he left, he seemed to vanish in the heat.

Almost at once, however, he returned. Seated again, he unwrapped a bundle protected in oiled canvas. Squinting, Prince Bifalt saw grapes, apricots, and bread.

The bread smelled fresh-baked. The fruits filled his mouth with juice and flavor when he bit into them. A sensation like singing ran through him. He had believed himself capable of choosing to end his life. He still believed it. Certainly, he had faced death in battle without flinching. But he had never wished to die. He did not wish it now. He wanted his false surrender to shift the balance between Belleger and Amika.

Water and food gave him the strength to move his limbs. His mind began to resume some of its functions. He ate until he judged that he had satisfied his immediate needs. Sipping water now rather than gulping it, he met Elgart's gaze.

———

"You found it?" Speech still required effort. His voice quavered as if he were on the verge of tears. "The library? The Repository?"

In the baking heat, the old scar dividing Elgart's features seemed unnaturally pale. Complex emotions were written there. Relief? Alarm? They filled his gaze, confusing the Prince. Elgart had found him alive. What disturbed the guardsman now?

He shook his head. "No, Highness." He sounded uncharacteristically cautious. "We did not find it. We were taken to it. It was the caravan's destination. If you had not done something to offend the caravan master— Or if you had not interrupted the dancing with your outrage—"

Prince Bifalt remembered. He had accused Set Ungabwey of contributing to Belleger's destruction. He had roared his anger and despair at the dancers around the bonfire. No doubt Master Ungabwey felt justified—

Grimacing, Elgart stopped himself. Instead of continuing, he changed his explanation.

"Klamath and I were drugged. You must have been. So were we. When we awoke, the train had already made camp at the gates of a castle. It looked high as a mountain, built like a mountain until it reached the sky. We—"

"Wait," commanded the Prince. His thoughts were sluggish. They did not move quickly enough to keep up with Elgart. "If you did not see the road, how did you find *me*?"

Elgart looked away. "Like Klamath, I was given a map. An easy path through the dunes. Easy for horses. A ride of a few hours, no more. But too narrow for wagons. The caravan could not have gone that way."

"Wait," repeated Prince Bifalt. He needed to understand what he was hearing. "You saw Klamath ride away? He left before you?" And now Elgart sounded unsure of himself? "Why?"

Apparently, his arrival to rescue the Prince had troubling implications.

Elgart studied the bare roadway. "The dawn after our drugged sleep," he said reluctantly. "After the caravan reached the library. Klamath was sent to the King. He went at once. The caravan left the next day. After that, I was kept in the castle. Treated well enough. Food, ale, wine. Good quarters. And nothing else for two more days. Nothing until I was told to retrieve you."

Abruptly, the guardsman faced Prince Bifalt, exposing his chagrin. His shame.

"Highness, I was frantic. I had failed you. I feared you were dead. Killed while Klamath and I were kept alive. I searched the train before it moved on. Then I made demands of the sorcerers— or of their servants—or of other visitors. I cursed and threatened. I had my rifle. I could have killed some of them. But I was ignored. Treated well, yes. Hells, Highness! They were *kind* to me. All my needs were met. But I was not answered. I could not find you. And I was not allowed outside the castle again. Until this morning.

"Then a man spoke to me. Magister Avail, he called himself. He told me to bring you. He said you were *ready*. That is the word, is it not? *Ready?*" When Prince Bifalt nodded, Elgart continued. "He gave me a map with my path marked.

"I cursed him. I *knew* you were dead. The caravan master betrayed you. He betrayed all of us. No man could survive so long in the desert. But that sorcerer did not appear to understand me.

Highness, he did not appear to *hear* me. He only repeated that you were ready. He told me to bring you.

"A servant gave me food and horses. He gave me your weapons. I rode out from the gates. When I followed the path, I found you."

Again Elgart looked away. "The Magisters have us. There is no escape. We must return to the castle. If we do not, we will die. The map ends here. I have too little water and food to wander among the dunes.

"Highness—" His voice broke for a moment. "They sent me to ensure your surrender. To make you serve them. I did not know what to do, so I obeyed. If you were alive, I had to find you."

Prince Bifalt had nothing to say. No words at all. He had survived, asleep in the desert—for days? For *days*? It was impossible.

Except by sorcery.

Theurgists had heard his surrender. Apparently, they had accepted it. Now he was at their mercy.

He could not pretend that he was surprised.

But he had been at their mercy from the first, a toy for them to play with. He understood Elgart. They were both soldiers. Under the skin, they were brothers. In Elgart's place, he would have done what the guardsman did.

Instead of answering directly, he asked, "Do you know how long you slept?"

Elgart frowned. "Highness?"

"You and Klamath," insisted the Prince. "From the night of dancing to the Repository gates, how many days? Do you know? If your wine was drugged? Do you know how far the train traveled while you were asleep?"

Perplexed, the man shook his head. "I slept. When I woke up, I felt well. I thought it was just a day. How could it be more? But now I am not certain. It could have been one day or a dozen."

Prince Bifalt sighed. "Yet you did not starve while you slept, or die of thirst. The drug did not harm you. Think what that means. If you could not account for your own condition, how could you know mine? It is a great drug, Elgart. Great and terrible. It must have preserved my life until you were sent for me.

"The men who supplied it knew what it could do. You did not."

He meant, What else could you have done? Do not doubt yourself. Blame the sorcerers. They use our lives like counters in a game. We are pawns until we know what they want.

By increments, Elgart's look of dismay became a more familiar sharpness. "I think, Highness," he said slowly, "I begin to understand why you want to rid the world of sorcery. It makes every man who does not have it helpless. And those who have it become careless of other lives."

The Prince nodded to himself. Without sorcery, he thought, we would be dead—and Belleger would be defenseless. If these Magisters are allied with Amika—if they want to harm Belleger—why have they chosen me? Why have they kept me alive?

Nothing that had been done to or for him made any sense. To the Magisters, he was only a game piece. They had no reason to care if he did not understand the game.

He took more water. He returned the flask to his companion. Then he extended his hand.

Elgart's grasp helped him to his feet. When the Prince was able to stand, however, the guardsman hesitated. Awkward again, avoiding his commander's gaze, he asked, "Highness? What will you do? They—the sorcerers—they believe you have surrendered. Will you obey? Will you turn against Belleger? If they demand it?"

Prince Bifalt braced himself on Elgart's shoulder. The veteran was all he had left of his homeland. Even Klamath was gone beyond his reach. He made the same promises he would have made to his father.

"I cannot guess what they want with me. They are a mystery. A curse. I understand nothing except my task. I will search for Marrow's book. If I find it, we will contrive an escape. If I do not, I will learn what they think my surrender means. I will try to gain their trust. Perhaps, then, they will give me the book.

"But I will do nothing to harm Belleger, or our people, or our king. If they judge me forsworn, I will endure the outcome. I do not call it dishonorable to lie to such men."

Elgart studied the terrain to the north. "Then I am yours, Highness," he said grimly. "Among the dunes, I questioned your loathing for sorcery—or for sorcerers. Now I share it. Do what has to be done. I will stand with you."

Prince Bifalt nodded again. He had expected nothing less from a Bellegerin guardsman. Still, Elgart's support vindicated him. It made him stronger.

Klamath would reach King Abbator: Prince Bifalt did not doubt that. The sorcerers would ensure it. And the King would not act against Amika. He would believe Belleger was safe, at least temporarily. He would put his faith in his eldest son, as he had done from the start.

If the Prince could grasp the game the Magisters played, with

the lives of ungifted men for counters— If he could avoid the pit-
falls of a false move—

He was a man who met challenge with challenge. That was how
he knew himself. He did not flinch now.

When his weapons were restored to him—when he felt the
comforting weight of his rifle and ammunition satchel on his shoulders, his saber on his hip, his dagger at his belt—he tried to mount
the horse Elgart had brought for him. With his comrade's help, he
succeeded. Angry and eager, he rode away from the stone track at
Elgart's side to face the men who wanted to harm his homeland:
the culmination of his search.

⁕

He would have said that the dunes were impassable for horses.
Certainly, he could not have crossed them on foot, weakened
as he was. But when Elgart had led him around a loose slope, they
came to a path concealed between the mounded sands. There the
surface had been packed hard, and the mounts had sure footing.
The winds curling and carving among the dunes should have covered the path with drifts of sand, yet it remained as unobstructed
as the caravan track. Although the desert defended the library
against any chance discovery, the sorcerers made sure that they
could be reached easily by their chosen visitors or minions.

And as the path twisted among the dunes, it also ascended.
Through every northward gap, the Prince saw that he was drawing
closer to the mountains. They reared higher by surprising increments, as if they were reaching out for him.

He drank water sparingly while he rode. He ate cautious rations of food. His heat-pummeled body recovered a small measure of vitality.

His comrade guided him in silence. At intervals, Elgart consulted his map, although the trail looked plain enough to the Prince. Prodded by a question, the rifleman explained, "Other paths, Highness. If we need to flee, a choice of ways might confuse pursuit. Several are marked." He muttered a curse. "But they do not go west. And this map ends at the caravan track." Harshly, he concluded, "We will never escape if we cannot survive the desert."

Prince Bifalt gritted his teeth. "Then," he answered, "that is your task. Mine is Marrow's book." And sorcerers. "Yours is a better map."

"I understand, Highness."

The ire in Elgart's tone satisfied the King's son.

✳

The way seemed long to Prince Bifalt; but two or three hours by the sun brought the riders to a wide, windswept plateau at the foot of the mountain where the Repository of the sorcerers had been formed.

The open space was extensive, more than large enough to accommodate Set Ungabwey's long caravan—and perhaps another of the same size as well. Still, it was dwarfed by the high castle cut from the native stone of the mountain. Above the massive wooden gates—the only apparent entrance—were ramparts which could have held a hundred defenders comfortably, although the Prince saw none. And over them loured the huge bulk of the castle or keep that housed the sorcerers and their library.

Instinctively, Prince Bifalt reined his horse to a halt and stared.

The Repository was all of white stone, so white it hurt his eyes in the afternoon sunlight. From the plateau to the ramparts, it was seamless and smooth, clearly carved rather than built. The Decimate of earthquake in the hands of a powerful Magister might not have shaken it: no form of siege known to the Prince would threaten it. Above the ramparts, however, it presented a different aspect. Squinting against the glare, he was able to distinguish sections or levels like prodigious wheels laid flat one atop the next, all white, all perfectly curved—and each set slightly off center from the one below it. To his eye, this staggering looked irregular, unpredictable. It did not lean toward the mountain supporting it. Nor did it tilt away. But the size of the sections or slabs remained constant. The result resembled a stack of coins piled unevenly by a child with clumsy fingers—if the child had been many times a giant, and each coin were as thick as four big men, each standing on the shoulders of the next. The effect was both careless and majestic.

Gaping, Prince Bifalt was only able to ask, "What—?"

Yet Elgart understood him. "I do not know, Highness." His frustration was plain. "While I was kept here, I did not go as high as the ramparts. I wanted to explore. To search— If I accomplished nothing else, I wanted to find someone who would tell me how long I had been there, or where you were, or what they wanted from me. Hells, I would have been glad to see Suti al-Suri. Or one of those drummers.

"But I was *discouraged*." He snarled the word. "Not forbidden, exactly. The servants were too polite to deny me outright. But their refusal was plain. And I did not trust my safety enough to defy them. I learned nothing useful. Not even where they stable their horses."

"Books, perhaps," mused the Prince, staring up at the stacked levels. He was thinking, *Thousands* of them. *Many* thousands. He might have to search for the rest of his life. "Can *all* of them house books? *All* of them?"

Elgart gave him a look of horror mixed with awe. "There cannot," he protested, "be enough books in the *world* to fill that keep."

Prince Bifalt might have said, If there are, this library is another desert. A wasteland of words instead of sand. We will be as lost as we were days ago. But he did not speak.

While his thoughts sucked him dry, like exposure to the sun, horns sounded across the plateau. Mournful as a funeral proclamation, sackbuts tuned to a minor chord cried out at the distant dunes. And when the call faded, the Repository's heavy gates began to open.

Soundless and somehow fatal, like doors in a dream, the gates eased outward. They parted only far enough to let two men pass between them. Then they stopped.

"Now, Highness," breathed Elgart. With one hand, he gripped his rifle, but did not unsling it from his shoulder.

Prince Bifalt wrapped his fingers around the hilt of his saber. Without realizing it, he held his breath.

Still in their saddles, the Bellegerins watched the two men emerge from the gates. Holding hands, the two approached the Prince and the guardsman.

One was plump and placid, of medium height, with an untended chaos of hair on his head and a fleshy smile above his beardless chin. The crinkling at the corners of his eyes, and the lines of his smile, gave him a look of habitual pleasure. In contrast, his companion was a glowering hunchback, dark of visage, bitter of mien. He had the shoulders of a blacksmith and the gnarled arms of an oak. Apparently seething with unrequited rage, he half dragged his milder comrade forward, resisting the plump man's impulse to amble.

Both of them wore the slate-grey robes of sorcerers.

"Magister Avail," whispered Elgart quickly. "The fat one. I do not know the other."

With an effort, Prince Bifalt released his saber. Nodding to his comrade, he swung unsteadily down from his mount.

Visibly reluctant, Elgart let go his rifle, dismounted, and came to stand beside the Prince.

At a distance of five paces, the castle's emissaries stopped. "Prince," said the smiling man in an easy rumble. "I am Magister Avail. My friend is Magister Rummage. Welcome to our library, our Last Repository. We are glad that you have come."

Magister Rummage did not look glad. Neither sorcerer bowed.

Once again, Prince Bifalt wondered, The *last*? But he did not pause to think about it. The theurgists demanded his attention.

Because they did not honor him, he merely nodded. "You know who I am," he replied curtly. "You summoned me. I am here to find out why."

Nothing in Magister Avail's face suggested that he had heard the Prince. However, the hunchback shifted his grip on his companion's hand. Scowling murderously, Magister Rummage tapped Magister Avail's palm with his fingers.

203

"Ah." Magister Avail's sigh indicated understanding. His smile broadened. "Discourtesy is as welcome as respect. It tells me that you do not fear us. I am pleased.

"For my sins, I am stone deaf. I would not hear a cannon if it fired at my side."

"That explains it," breathed Elgart.

"For that reason," continued the pudgy sorcerer, "and because he is infinitely kind, Magister Rummage aids me." He glanced at their joined hands. "Alas, he is entirely mute. He cannot utter a sound. When he wishes to be understood—which is seldom, I confess—I speak for him."

Unwilling to show surprise or doubt, Prince Bifalt replied to the hunchback, "Then, Magister Rummage, please assure Magister Avail I do *not* fear you. I am only impatient. I want to know why I am here."

Magister Rummage grinned like a man who liked the taste of blood and was eager to sample the Prince's. His fingers wrote quickly.

When the message was complete, Magister Avail laughed: a sound as amiable as his smile. "Like my companion, Prince," he said, "you are hasty. You are here for several reasons, all of which will be made clear. Clarity, however, is an effortful task, and you are sadly worn. You have lost valued companions and been betrayed, and your strength is gone. We will not trouble you with our reasons, or your own, until you are recovered." He beamed beatifically. "For the present, impatience and disrespect will not serve you, though both are welcome. Your ire is love by another name."

This rejoinder silenced Prince Bifalt. His ire was love? The idea was insane. These sorcerers had shown an impossible knowledge of far-off events and deeds. Their powers were immeasurable. But if they believed any secret chamber in him held *love* for them, they did not know him. They did not understand him at all.

That thought lifted his heart. Their ignorance gave him an advantage he had not expected.

At the same time, he could not deny that he was exhausted.

Briefly, Magister Avail waited for Prince Bifalt to speak—or for Magister Rummage to tap his hand. Then he continued with unruffled pleasantness, "Will you accept our hospitality, Prince? You will find it less oblique than Set Ungabwey's. He is honest, in his way, but his loyalty is to *us*, not to strangers met by seeming happenstance. You will not be drugged or otherwise mistreated while you reside among us."

This explanation of the caravan master's deeds answered one of Prince Bifalt's many questions. It did not content him, but it was enough in his worn condition. "We will accept," he responded. "You have some use for me. You will not harm us until you have given me a chance to serve you.

"But we will keep our weapons."

For some reason, the hunchback did not relay this assertion. But the smiling sorcerer did not question his companion. Instead, he gestured toward the gates. "Accompany us, Prince. You and your staunch comrade will not regret our welcome"—he chuckled again—"unless you choose to do so."

Together, he and Magister Rummage turned away, still holding hands.

Prince Bifalt and Elgart exchanged a glance. The guardsman's scowl echoed what was in the Prince's heart, but the King's son did what he could to make his features a mask. Leading their mounts, they followed their hosts.

�֎

The gates closed behind the Bellegerins as they entered, sealing them away from the world they knew. The desert was suddenly as unattainable as Belleger. But they were not left in darkness. At once, ranks of large cressets around the walls sprang alight; and the Prince saw that the Magisters had led him into a cavernous hall. It had a polished stone floor, an arched ceiling made dim by distance, many doors of varying heights, widths, and decorations, and several broad stairways leading upward; but it was empty of furnishings—and almost empty of people. The space was large enough to serve as a mustering place for an army. At need, it could have sheltered Set Ungabwey's whole caravan. Only the size and number of the cressets made the full extent of the hall visible. And only their brightness softened Prince Bifalt's impression that he had entered a place more dangerous than grenades or lightnings: as dangerous as the powers which had kept him alive while he was many leagues away.

Several servants awaited the arrival of the Magisters and their guests. With a twinge of surprise, the Prince saw that they were all garbed and groomed like the men whom Tchwee and Suti al-Suri had called *monks*. Men and women alike, they wore dun cassocks cinched with white ropes, and their hair was trimmed and shaved into tonsures, leaving the crowns of their heads bare. *The Cult of the Many*, the interpreter had named them. Many *what*?

Gods, as Alleman Dancer had implied? Hells? Sorcerers? *Books?*
Prince Bifalt had no idea.

Their heads lowered, their eyes downcast, two monks came to
relieve the travelers of their horses. The mounts were led away
toward a set of wide doors. When the doors opened, the Prince
smelled the thick odors of stables: ripe droppings, urine, and beast-
sweat mingled with the subtler scents of leather, water, and grain.

Prince Bifalt and his comrade paused to watch where their
horses were taken. The theurgists did not. Tugging his slower companion, Magister Rummage drew Magister Avail deeper into the
hall. When the Prince felt sure that he would recognize the entrance to the stables again, he and Elgart went after their hosts.

They moved directly toward a stair at the far end of the hall.
Halfway there, however, the sight of a figure descending another
stairway halted the sorcerers. Turning, they faced the woman.
When she reached the foot of the stair, they both bowed, Magister Rummage more deeply than Magister Avail.

She was small: Prince Bifalt could have rested his chin on her
head, her loose hair. Her modest white cloak covered her from neck
to ankle, and her hands clasping each other were wrapped in its
wide sleeves. He caught his breath as he recognized Amandis,
described by Tchwee as a "most holy devotee of Spirit"—and also
an assassin.

She must have joined Set Ungabwey's caravan for the purpose of
visiting the Repository. Therefore, Flamora, the killer's "partner or
antagonist," a most holy devotee of Flesh, was probably here as well.

But Prince Bifalt was not given time to wonder how many of
the caravan's other travelers had ended their journeys in the keep.

Walking with fluid grace, Amandis approached. Ignoring the bows of the Magisters, she faced the Bellegerins. Without preamble, she announced in a low voice harshly accented, "Elgart. You will come with me."

Like Flamora, she knew Belleger's tongue.

The Prince and his scarred comrade froze. While Elgart stared at the woman, Prince Bifalt said stiffly, "Lady, I do not know how to address you. You are not a priestess, yet you are 'most holy.' I mean no disrespect if I neglect an appropriate courtesy.

"Elgart is my guardsman. He stays with me."

Amandis flicked a glance at him, then returned her attention to the lean veteran. Her tone did not change. "It was not a request."

The Prince looked to the theurgists for support, but found none. Magister Avail's smile remained bland, oblivious. Magister Rummage grinned like a wolfhound.

Studying Amandis with fire in his eyes, Prince Bifalt answered, "He is not yours to command. Nor am I."

The devotee of Spirit continued to regard Elgart. She remained as still as stone. "My skills suffice to kill you both where you stand." Her voice held a touch of amusement. "Is that command enough? Must I demonstrate?"

She did not appear to move, yet now she stood at Elgart's side. One slim hand pointed a dagger at the guardsman's throat. The other gripped Elgart's arm to keep him still.

"Highness!" gasped Elgart.

Hells! As fast as he could, Prince Bifalt snatched his rifle from his shoulder.

But before he drew back the bolt, the dagger disappeared into the assassin's sleeve. With her hands open, showing their emptiness, Amandis withdrew a step.

"A demonstration," she told the Prince, still amused, "nothing more. You did much the same for Suti al-Suri. Your purpose then may also have been much the same. No harm will come to your companion. It is forbidden here."

Holding the Prince's glare, she added, "I require him. That is command enough for him, and for you."

Prince Bifalt's pulse beat in his throat. It leapt like flame.

At the edge of his vision, he saw Magister Rummage tapping on Magister Avail's hand.

At once, the portly sorcerer cleared his throat. "I assure you, Prince," he rumbled. "Any devotee of Spirit is bound by her word. He will not be harmed. And your reasons for coming here do not depend on his attendance. Also, he has reasons of his own, which do not depend on your authority or presence."

The Prince wanted to roar. He wanted to throw the bolt of his rifle and open fire. The Magisters knew why Amandis wanted Elgart: that was obvious. Her secrets were hidden only from him and his comrade.

While Prince Bifalt controlled himself, however, Elgart said sharply, "Highness, be wary. We are guests. Do not offend them. There is too much we do not understand." He drew a deep breath, held it, then added in a burst, "I will go with her. I may get what we need."

A better map.

Trembling, Prince Bifalt strove for calm. He had to remember his purpose. Belleger's desperation. His father's pain. His realm's peril was not diminished by the message Klamath carried. It was only suspended. Everything still hinged on the Prince's actions here.

Shouldering his rifle roughly so that Amandis and the Magisters would not see his hands shake, he nodded his consent. "Go, then," he rasped. "Risk nothing. We will speak of this later."

The corners of Amandis' mouth tightened, restraining a smile. Still without acknowledging the sorcerers, she turned away. Gliding or floating, she went back the way she had come.

Elgart met the Prince's glower. Grimacing, he confessed, "Curiosity. What use can anyone here have for me?" Then he followed the devotee of Spirit.

Cursing to himself, Prince Bifalt joined his hosts again. With Magister Avail's smile and Magister Rummage's scowl fixed in his mind, he accompanied them toward the far end of the hall. Whatever happened, he meant to show the fat one's complacence and the hunchback's bitterness that he was more than they had expected when they chose him. But his own "demonstration"—if he could manage it—would have to wait. The assassin's secret intentions did not alter his quest. His mission demanded more from him than determination and anger. It also required him to emulate King Abbator's patience.

Emulate or feign.

⚜

From the head of the broad stair, the theurgists led the Prince through a bewildering series of corridors and doorways, down a second stair, up a third that was longer and narrower. Along the way, they passed a few servants—none of whom acknowledged the

Magisters or their guest—but encountered no other people. His hosts, Prince Bifalt assumed, were taking him into an isolated region of their domain. They intended to sequester him. They did not want him to find his own way, or to speak with anyone, or to rely on someone else for guidance.

When they reached the quarters they had prepared for him, however, several monks awaited him, three women and two men. One opened the door. The others preceded him into a spacious chamber comfortably furnished, with rugs to soften the floor and a cheery fire in the hearth to warm the chill of the Last Repository's thick stone. Heads bowed, eyes lowered, the monks showed him the bed with its elaborately woven coverlet, the desk with a supply of paper and pens, the shelves laden with books in strange languages, the bathing room and privy, the tub filled with steaming water. A low table near the desk held a flagon of wine as well as a ready repast covered by a dome of silver. This deep in the castle, there were no windows. Instead, the walls displayed a variety of tapestries, all depicting scenes or images that meant nothing to the Prince.

The sorcerers did not enter. Magister Rummage left at once. Magister Avail stood in the doorway until the serving monks were gone. Then he said, "Be at ease, Prince. Here your needs will be met while you regain your strength. There will be servants outside your door, but they will not intrude. Ask for whatever you require. Give them your soiled garments. They will be cleaned. Others in the same style will be made for you. More wine, food, firewood, hot water, all will be brought to you. Your only task is recovery.

"When your vigor has returned, and your thoughts are clear, inform the servants. At that time, we will begin to unravel your confusion."

Prince Bifalt did not waste himself on a reply Magister Avail would not hear. He stood scowling until the sorcerer left, and the door was closed. Then he went to the door and discovered to his relief that it could be bolted. No one would take him by surprise while he was here.

When he had sealed the door, he surrendered to his hunger and thirst.

✳

For the remainder of that day, and all the next, Prince Bifalt rested. His fatigue was more profound than he had allowed himself to recognize. It had the effect of patience. And the comforts of his quarters soothed him. His bed made sleep welcome. The discreet attendance of the library's servants pleased him. He expected to fret incessantly, but he found that he could not. Through Klamath, the sorcerers had promised to protect Belleger. While their promise held, he could afford to lose a little time. He could afford to enjoy the utter silence of his surroundings and regain his strength.

He ate and drank often, bathed often, slept long. He welcomed the feel of clean clothes on his clean skin. When he was not sleeping, he tended his weapons. And he did not entirely neglect his quest. Twice he opened his door and told a servant he wanted to speak with Elgart. If the guardsman could not come to him, he wished to be taken to his comrade.

The servant—a woman on one occasion, a man on another—bowed without speaking, and left at once, presumably to convey Prince Bifalt's desires. But he received no reply. The guardsman did not come. And the monk he had sent with his message did not return. A different servant took the woman's place at his door, or the man's.

This lack of response—clearly a refusal—vexed him, but the effect was brief. Irritated, he ate again, drank more wine, and surprised himself by tumbling into bed and sleep.

Toward the end of the second day, however, he grew restless. At intervals, he caught himself wishing for a mirror. He wanted to study his face; wanted to see if he shared the lines that loss and hopelessness had cut into his father's flesh. He imagined that he had earned them. But there was no glass—or any other reflective surface—in his chambers.

Then he started to pace, remembering in every detail his last moments with King Abbator. He remembered every word as if he and his father were saying their final farewells.

Your quest is surely implausible. Nevertheless, I entrust it to you. What else can we do?

For you, Father, I will do what I can. For Belleger, I will do all I can. Perhaps it will be enough. It is our only chance.

Prince Bifalt considered it intolerable that he might fail such a man: his father, his king—and so deeply wounded.

During the evening, he reached a decision. When he felt his bed whispering his name, he went instead to the door, unbolted it, and addressed the monk outside.

"Tell Magister Avail," he said, speaking with less authority than he intended, "I will be ready in the morning."

To the servant's bow, he replied by closing the door, bolting it, and composing himself for sleep.

⁜

Again, he slept easily. For the first time in this chamber, however, he was aware of dreaming. In his dream, he rode with the former Magister Slack, who had lost the use of his gift, and had betrayed Belleger. He asked questions which Slack answered. With a precision, a specificity—or perhaps a threat—found only in dreams, the man pronounced, *A man is not a man at all if he cannot enter and enjoy every chamber of himself.*

Dreaming, Prince Bifalt judged the sentiment dishonest. It was contradictory. *Every* chamber? Did none of those chambers contain devotion to Belleger, or loyalty to King Abbator? Was Slack incapable of valuing the lives of the men with whom he traveled, or those of the starving children he used to bait his trap? He had confessed that his teacher was Amikan. He must have been Amikan himself, a lifelong spy. But if so, as a pretended Bellegerin, he had lost his gift—which he professed to treasure—through Amika's use of the seventh Decimate. Did no chamber in him hold resentment for what his homeland had done?

When the Prince awoke, he felt as clear as flame. He had strength again, and determination, and a readiness to take risks.

Washed and dressed, he opened his door to accept his breakfast from one of the servants. But the woman waiting there did not hold a tray. To his stare, she bowed, showing him the shaved crown of her head. In a low voice, she said, "If it pleases you, Prince, I will guide you to the refectory. There you may break your fast among the other guests. When you have eaten, Magister Avail will come to you."

Prince Bifalt swallowed a sudden lump of surprise, eagerness, alarm. *Other guests* would include Amandis. They would include Elgart. And they might include people at least somewhat familiar from Set Ungabwey's caravan; people less daunting to approach than Amandis herself. Perhaps Flamora, the most holy devotee of Flesh? Or if not them, then some talkative scholar?

Without hesitation, he collected his weapons and told the woman to lead him. Other inducements aside, the prospect of a chance to speak with Elgart drew him. He wanted to feel less alone with his burdens. Elgart's curiosity and quick thinking would steady him.

The scarred veteran had vowed to stand with him.

He did not try to learn the route his guide took. He was confident that the sorcerers would not permit him to wander the keep's passages alone. He would be attended wherever he went. Otherwise, he might stumble on one of the Last Repository's secrets.

For that reason, his thoughts were elsewhere as the serving-monk led him along unfamiliar corridors, up and down several short and one long stairway, through chambers furnished like council chambers, and—abruptly—into a hall full of noise: boots and sandals on stone, plates and utensils clattering on trays, voices murmuring in quiet conversation or raised in vigorous discussion.

By the measure of the Repository's cavernous mouth, the space was small—but only by that measure. Under a ceiling high enough to accommodate men on horseback with other men on their shoulders, trestle tables stretched in long ranks from wall to wall, each lined on both sides with an abundance of chairs, each lit by shaded lamps. High cressets illuminated the hall itself; and from a wide opening in the far wall came a blaze of light and the incessant clamor of a busy kitchen.

His guide gestured Prince Bifalt toward a table laden with plates, utensils, mugs, and trays. Clearly, he was supposed to ready a tray and carry it into the kitchen to get food, then return to the hall, take a chair, and eat. But he ignored her instructions. Standing silent in the din of eating and voices, he studied the people.

The hall was not full: it could have held twice as many guests without crowding. Still, he guessed he was looking at close to a hundred men and women. And virtually all of them were as unprecedented in his experience as Suti al-Suri had been, or Set Ungabwey, or the folk of Alleman Dancer's Wide World Carnival. Some were wrapped in elegant cloaks and had their hair styled in spikes. Others huddled in barbarous furs like people for whom the refectory was unpleasantly cold. A few clanked in heavy armor. Fewer still were naked, apart from the loincloths around their hips and the twigs and beads knotted into their hair. Some carried longswords on their backs: others were festooned with short spears. Black, brown, and yellow skins mingled with white; but some were so white that they looked albino, and others—primarily women—were either born or painted entirely blue. Several groups had tattoos or scarifications in unlikely places.

At a distant table, Magister Rummage sat alone, gulping his food like a beast. Prince Bifalt grimaced at the sight, then ignored the hunchback.

During his first survey, he did not see Elgart anywhere. Or Amandis. He recognized only the row of monks seated at a nearby table. In attire, tonsure, and posture, they were indistinguishable from the library's servants. But their faces were familiar from his short time with the caravan. And one was unmistakably the monk of the Cult of the Many who had been among Set Ungabwey's counselors.

As he scanned the hall a second time, his eyes moved more slowly, searching out individual faces among the crowd. He still hoped to locate Elgart. If Amandis was present, he hoped to keep his distance. After a few moments, however, his attention was riveted by a man sitting alone four tables away near the far wall.

In an instant, Prince Bifalt's anger became a bonfire.

The man had the sallow skin of his people, the sharp features. His face wore the waxed goatee and moustache favored by soldiers of his kind. Around his brow was knotted a bright orange head-band, the chosen color of his monarch, useful for recognizing comrades in the confusion and bloodshed of battle. And from his belt hung a leather scabbard dyed the same orange hue. It contained a long blade slightly curved, almost a scimitar.

He was Amikan.

A red haze bloodied the Prince's vision. Through it, he saw Slack fleeing amid the shots and arrows of combat. He saw Vinsid blown apart, Camwish killed by an arrow in his throat, Captain Swalish pierced to the heart, Bartin shredded by his own gun. He saw Hught's throat gaping. So enraged that he could not breathe and did not need to, he saw the bloom and smoke of grenades—

The man was not a Magister. *He* had not singled out Prince Bifalt to commit treason. But he was *Amikan*. His people had used the seventh Decimate against Belleger. And the Prince needed *some* outlet for his thwarted yearning, his interminable frustration and outrage, his promise to his father; for his dread of what the Repository's sorcerers might do to him and his people. He *needed*—

Then he was running, his saber in his hand. As fast as he could, he rounded the end of the fourth line of tables, raced between the rows of chairs. He wanted and did not want his enemy to see him coming. He would not strike a seated foe from behind, but he blazed to take the Amikan by surprise.

His natural enemy. Not a sorcerer who could dispatch him with a word: a soldier like himself. A man he could kill.

Ten paces from his target, he found an empty chair. Without breaking stride, he sprang from the chair to the tabletop. Swift among the scattered plates and lamps, the startled guests, he gripped his saber with both hands and raised it. In every straining muscle, he felt primed with strength and justice; with outrage earned by generations of blood and pain—

—and with doubt. Any Amikan death could be justified. Anywhere but here. *Here* there were Magisters who wanted to use Prince Bifalt against Belleger. *Here* there were degrees of power and levels of treachery he could not measure. He had not even *begun* to measure them. Amikan blood spilled *here* might end his quest before he learned to understand it. Before he knew what the real stakes were.

The pound of moccasins on the table caused the Amikan to jerk up his head. Prince Bifalt wanted that to be the last movement of the man's life. As soon as the Amikan drew his sword, every doubt would become meaningless.

Ready for killing, the Prince stamped to a halt in front of his foe.

The Amikan flinched back in his chair. Lamps and cressets

caught fear and fury in his eyes. The muscles at the corners of his jaw bunched like fists. But he did not reach for his blade. Deliberately, he crossed his arms on his chest.

Defying death.

Prince Bifalt remembered Camwish and Nowel, Captain Swalish and Bartin. Oh, yes, he remembered them. But more than those lost comrades, he remembered Slack. He remembered starving children.

And he remembered his father. How often had King Abbator instructed him, *Think before you speak*? How often had his king said, *Speak before you act*? How often had he been called, with love and pain, *My son*?

The Amikan refused to defend himself.

King Abbator would be ashamed of his son now.

Knowing that he could not cut down a foe who refused to defend himself made Prince Bifalt wild. "Draw your *sword*!" he roared: a yell that tore his throat. "Fight and *die*!"

The man's chin jutted. Malice shone in his eyes. "Kill me," he snarled, baring his teeth. "Show these people the truth. Bellegerins are butchers. Only butchers would devise a weapon as cruel as that"—for an instant, he was too angry to find words—"that *gun*."

"*We* are butchers?" howled the Prince. *"You kill your own wounded!"*

"Only," retorted the Amikan, "so Belleger will not take and torture them."

It was too much. If Prince Bifalt struck now, he would fail his quest, his king, his people. But he could not swallow lies from his enemy. He *could* not. He was who he was.

Belleger did not torture wounded Amikans. None were ever captured.

219

Deliberately, he feigned a cut at the Amikan's neck. The man was a soldier, a fighter. If he could be provoked or startled into pulling his sword, the Prince would be able to vindicate himself to himself. Perhaps even to his father.

But his foe did not react. His eyes flicked away—

—and before Prince Bifalt could check his swing, his hands and his blade stopped as if he had slammed them against a wall. The wrenching impact flung him away from his target: it seemed to break his wrists. He lost his saber as he landed on his back against the far edge of the table.

He should have tumbled off the table onto the laps of other guests, knocked them backward. But his wrists were caught in a grip of stone. Another wrench prevented him from plunging farther.

The force of his fall stunned his chest. He did not feel pain yet. The shock left him numb, breathless. Dizzy with rage and lack of air, he could not see the figure standing over him, except as a vague blur.

Then he drew a whooping breath and recognized Magister Rummage.

The hunchback stood on the table, still holding the Prince's wrists in one heavy hand. He must have snagged them from behind. The sorcerer's grip was too strong to be broken. The malevolence of his glower resembled hatred. It resembled madness.

Dimly through the confusion and indignation around him, Prince Bifalt noticed Magister Avail's approach.

Now the pain in his wrists reached him. And in his back. His landing on the table-edge must have damaged his ribs or spine.

The Amikan stood across the table from him. He expected to see his foe's sword flashing. But the man's hands were empty. He gave the Prince one infuriated glance. Then he turned to the sorcerers with a look of betrayal on his face.

Trying to shout, Prince Bifalt gasped, "He is *Amikan*!"

The Amikan's yell filled the air. "And he is *Bellegerin*! *I* did not threaten *him*!" Grinding the words between his teeth, he added, "I saw him enter, but I did not *touch* my sword! Even when he challenged me, I did *not*."

Magister Rummage nodded, perhaps to the Amikan, perhaps to the Prince.

In an apparent flurry, Magister Avail arrived. "Oh, my," he panted, gazing down at Prince Bifalt. His hair was a storm on his head, and his smile was gone. "Did I fail to explain that we will not tolerate violence among our guests?" Amandis had said, *It is forbidden here.* "The fault is mine. We are all friends in the Repository, whatever our inclinations may be.

"Magister Rummage does not respond gently when the principles of our hospitality are ignored."

"I did *not* touch my sword," repeated the Amikan. "Is this your hospitality? I trusted it. I have *respected* it. This Bellegerin does not."

With his free hand, the hunchback clasped Magister Avail's arm and began to tap a message.

The portly theurgist attempted reassurance. "Calm yourself, Commander. Fear nothing. I have said that the fault is mine. When the Prince accepted our invitation, I imagined that I had no clear cause to doubt his readiness. I neglected to caution him.

"But if there is no fault in him, there is certainly none in you.

You are our guest, as he is. Magister Rummage will permit no harm between you."

Without warning, Magister Rummage released Prince Bifalt's wrists. The tearing pain as the Prince's limp hands fell to the table forced a cry between his teeth.

"Come, Prince," continued Magister Avail. "I will see you mended."

Prince Bifalt attempted to roll off the table, get his legs under him. But his limbs refused to obey him. Through a veil of pain, he watched the Amikan commander resume his seat.

After a moment, the familiar monk, Set Ungabwey's adviser, took the Amikan's place among the crowded spectators.

"If you will permit it, Magisters," murmured the monk. Head lowered, he regarded the tabletop rather than the sorcerers or the Prince. "I will stand surety for him. His back is hurt. His wrists will not heal themselves. And he is known to me, in a small way. I will escort him to the physicians."

Magister Rummage tapped rapidly on his deaf comrade's arm. In a moment, Magister Avail recovered his smile.

"Thank you," he replied to the monk. "Your offer is gracious. His ire may be eased if he speaks with a man who can both hear and answer."

Bowing, the monk of the Cult of the Many moved around the end of the table to reach Prince Bifalt. As the monk drew near, the hunchback gripped the Prince's shoulders, lifted him bodily, and set him on his feet. At once, the monk clasped his arm so that he would not lose his balance.

Prince Bifalt's hands hung at his sides. They felt like lumps of iron dragging on the savaged bones of his wrists. In his back, every rib seemed dislocated. He had mind enough to know that he needed a physician. Even the best surgeon in Belleger would probably leave him crippled. Still, he refused to move, despite the monk's gentle pressure, until Magister Rummage, gnashing his teeth, snatched up the Prince's saber and slammed it into its scabbard at his belt. Then he allowed himself to be led away.

Using the last force of his will, he avoided any glance at the Amikan.

He could not imagine why his enemy was here. The man was not the first Amikan to visit the library. Someone before him had read and mastered Marrow's *Seventh Decimate*. What more did Amika need to satisfy its hunger for Belleger's destruction?

But Prince Bifalt was in too much pain to think. He did not notice where the monk took him when they left the refectory, or what corridors they traveled. He did not hear the monk murmur, "Soon, Prince. Soon." Unable to suffer the hurt of his wrists, he concentrated instead on trying to shuffle his feet in a way that might loosen his back.

What did *stand surety* mean? The words told him nothing.

✳

Their passage through the Last Repository may have been short. To Prince Bifalt, it felt intolerable. By the time the monk reached his destination, the Prince was staggering. He needed all the support the monk could give him.

The monk had not said a word during the confrontation in Set Ungabwey's wagon.

223

The library's infirmary was spacious and well lit, but it was not clean. Dirt, feathers, beads, and strange powders were scattered across the floor. There were only two cots, both soiled with sweat, blood, and other fluids. The room had no surgeon's table, no array of knives, probes, or bone-saws, no recognizable supply of balms, unguents, or obvious medicines. Instead, the walls were lined with shelves holding piles of small bones and large feathers, dirty pouches of beads or powders, an assortment of rattles, and strips of cloth which appeared to have been used to bind many seeping wounds without ever being washed.

The cots were empty. A single individual occupied the chamber. He was one of the naked men. Like them, he wore only a loincloth. Like them, he had a number of beads and feathers woven into his hair. However, he was distinguished by tattoos on his arms, torso, and legs. Each of them depicted some form of mangled flesh.

Instinctively, Prince Bifalt recoiled. The man was a savage.

The savage gave his patient a contemptuous glance. More respectfully, he regarded the monk, although the monk did not lift his gaze from the floor. Then the man turned away to study his shelves.

Hardly able to form words, the Prince managed to ask, "Who *is* he?" He meant, *What* is he?

"Amika is a small place," answered the monk, speaking softly, "but Belleger is smaller. The world is large. This healer undertook a year's journey and crossed an ocean to study among the Magisters and their tomes. Now he repays the opportunity, which he considers a debt.

"In the language of his people, he is a shaman. His gift is sorcery by another name. But it is not a Decimate. It cannot be used for harm.

"Any Decimate has two uses. One is beneficial. The other wreaks damage and death. But sorcery is greater than you know. Decimates are a lesser portion of the knowledge gathered here."

During his quest, Prince Bifalt had learned that sorcery exceeded his conception of it. The voice in his mind, and the saving of his life, had told him as much. And in Set Ungabwey's caravan, he had discovered that the world itself was far larger than he could have realized. Now, wounded and bitter, he found that he could not accept further expansion. If the world were too large to be understood, it made Belleger too small to be valued. Of necessity, he closed his mind to the implications. Rather than struggle to imagine realms a year and oceans distant, he clung to his purpose.

Through his pain, he demanded, "The sorcerers *keep* this knowledge?" He meant, Keep it for *themselves*?

"They *preserve* it," amended the monk. "They share it freely with any who will not misuse it."

There Prince Bifalt stood on surer ground. "You are mistaken." If his perception of the world's scale—and Belleger's—had shifted, one truth did not. "They shared the seventh Decimate with Amika. Amika has used it to ensure Belleger's ruin."

During this exchange, the savage or healer selected a pouch and two rattles from his collection. Before the monk could reply, the man approached the Prince, opened his pouch, and tossed a foul powder at the Prince's face.

Prince Bifalt tried to flinch away, but he could not stop himself from inhaling.

At once, a fit of coughing took him: a spasm of revulsion so fierce it seemed to rip the muscles of his chest.

Fortunately, the fit was brief. And when it passed, the pain in his back had vanished. His chest ached for a breath or two. Then that discomfort faded as well.

Sneering, the savage or healer turned away again. Shaking his rattles, he began to stamp his feet in a small circle, around and around. Deep in his throat, he made a guttural sound. It had the cadences of chanting.

Prince Bifalt gaped. He could not stop himself. He was transfixed. At every turn, he saw that the shaman's eyes had rolled back in his head. They showed only a moist glare of white.

Compelled by chanting, or by the irregular beat of rattles, the Prince's mind made circles like the shaman's. It spun around and around until it was gone.

✳

When he returned to himself an hour or two later, awakened by the rank odor of old stains, he was lying on one of the filthy cots. To escape the smell, he swung his legs off the cot, rolled to sit upright. Blinking away the residue of sleep, he regarded the infirmary.

The tattooed savage was absent. The monk of the Cult of the Many sat on the other cot with his eyes closed like a man deep in meditation.

After a moment, the Prince realized that sitting up did not hurt his back. Cautiously, he moved his fingers. Wincing in anticipation, he turned his wrists. They were not swollen. The bones did not grind against each other. There was no pain. His hands and fore-arms felt as strong as ever.

—*sorcery by another name.* He had no other explanation. That shaman was a better physician than anyone in Belleger.

A disquieting thought. It confirmed Belleger's littleness. Worse, it suggested that Magister Rummage could unleash violence when-ever he wished. There would be no lasting consequences. As long as he did not kill his victim outright—

Prince Bifalt tested his neck. He tested his wrists again. He made sure he still had his weapons. They lay on the floor nearby. Then he shifted his attention to the monk.

The man seemed to feel the Prince's gaze. He opened his eyes, took and released a deep breath. But he did not look at his com-panion. Softly, always softly, he asked, "Are you satisfied, Prince?"

Satisfied? wondered Prince Bifalt. Satisfied how? That he had been healed? Yes. That the shaman's sorcery could not do harm? No. That he could trust the Last Repository's hospitality? Never.

That the Amikan he had wanted to kill was here for some in-nocent purpose? Absolutely not.

Clearing remembered pain from his throat, the Prince said the first words that came to him.

"The shaman healed me." He rolled his wrists to demonstrate their wholeness, flexed his fingers. "But he holds me in contempt. I saw it in his eyes. He did not heal me because I was broken. He did it to pay his debt.

"I am a prince of Belleger, King Abbator's eldest son. My quest is honorable. It is also vital. How does he imagine I have earned his scorn?"

He meant, How does he dare despise me? Is this what the sorcerers teach, men who have more power than kings and princes?

The monk may have shrugged under his robe. "His gift is the healing of wounds. He knows only that you provoked Magister Rummage. In his mind, such folly merits scorn. He does not see *you*." After a pause, the monk added, "That gift is mine."

Prince Bifalt started to ask how the savage could have known that the hunchback had broken his wrists. But then he realized what the answer would be. Magister Rummage enforced the sorcerers' prohibition against violence. Only he had the authority—or the inclination—to harm anyone who violated that principle.

Shaking his head, the Prince asked a different question.

"What do you see? What does your gift tell you?"

Without hesitation, the monk replied, "I see your confusion, Prince. You are at war with yourself. Your struggle is not with Amika. It is within you. But you do not know it."

This unexpected response startled harsh laughter from Prince Bifalt. "Absurd," he retorted. "If *that* is what you see, your gift is an illusion. I serve my king and my people. I serve Belleger's survival. Amika will not rest until we are destroyed or enslaved. My war is there."

The monk made a low musing sound. Without raising his eyes, he asked, "How will they destroy you?"

The Prince saw no reason to hold back. This was not an occasion for diplomacy. He did not need caution with the Cult of the Many. Whatever the monks might be elsewhere, here some of them were mere servants.

"They have already done it," he answered. "They have worked

the seventh Decimate against us. They have rid us of sorcery. Now we have only our rifles, and they are not enough."

"Dire straits indeed," admitted the monk, nodding. "But they do not explain your presence. Why have you come so far, when you are needed to defend your homeland?"

"We have our rifles," insisted the King's son. "Amikan armies will not overcome us easily or quickly. Still, their sorcery will slaughter us eventually. I have been sent to acquire the seventh Decimate for Belleger. If our enemies also are deprived of sorcery, we can stand against them for a time."

"Ah," reflected the monk. "The *Seventh Decimate*. One of Hexin Marrow's books. And, of course, Amika does not have rifles.

"What will you do, Prince, when you have balanced the scales?"

Prince Bifalt knew his answers. He had them ready. "They will not be balanced. Our rifles are too few. Without the Decimate of fire, they are difficult to forge." He meant impossible. "And Amika's supply of men seems endless. There are always more. But *our* population has been shredded. Generation after generation, we put fewer men in the field.

"Our enemies do not need sorcery to overrun us. They will sweep us from the earth when they realize we do not have enough rifles."

The monk appeared to consider Belleger's plight. After a moment, he remarked, "Yet you imagine the seventh Decimate can save you. Your quest serves no purpose otherwise."

"I think it *can*," asserted the Prince. "As I have said, it will end Amika's use of sorcery. But I think it will also restore *our* Magisters." He had no other explanation for the desperation of the ambush that had killed more than half of his men. "Then the atrocity of our losses will be avenged."

Briefly, the monk raised his eyes to Prince Bifalt. However, the Prince saw nothing in them. They regarded him as if they were unaware of his presence.

Returning his gaze to the floor, the monk asked, "Will such a victory be honorable? You suffer in a conflict that is unequal in Amika's favor. Will you be vindicated when the conflict is unequal in yours?"

"It will be *just*," countered the Prince. Then honesty forced him to confess, "But I understand you. I have considered your question. Perhaps you will understand me.

"An unequal victory will not be honorable, if it is gained by sorcery. There can be no honor in the world while sorcery exists. There can be no honor while one man can kill another, or use him, without hazard to himself because his victim is defenseless. The gifts of Magisters are given unequally. Those who are not gifted are helpless through no fault or failing of theirs.

"Monk, I loathe sorcery. I despise its arrogance. I hate its power to corrupt those who have it. It is dishonorable. If I could, I would rid the world of it."

"But not," suggested the monk mildly, "until Belleger has defeated Amika."

"Yes!" snapped the King's son. "I will not sacrifice my people to soothe my conscience. *I* am not so arrogant. Amika must be broken. It must be made to surrender."

Gathering his cassock, the monk rose to his feet. His gaze

considered the shaman's shelves, the walls of the chamber. Slowly, he moved to leave the infirmary.

Near the entryway, however, he turned to the Prince once more. His gaze regarded the floor.

"Then, Prince Bifalt," he said gently, "eldest son of Belleger's King, I stand by what I have seen. You profess to loathe sorcery, but you mislead yourself. If you did not covet it, you would not consent to Amika's ruin. An equal contest would content you. You would not choose to dishonor yourself. You would not choose dishonor for your people."

Prince Bifalt swallowed a spike of anger. "Again you are absurd," he retorted. "Belleger's struggle is not only a matter of honor. Its cost in lives is high. Bellegerin lives, yes—but also Amikan.

"Have you *seen* how Amika abuses its own people? Do you know Amikans kill their wounded after every battle? Have you watched them starve their own children in order to sacrifice them as *bait*?"

The monk bowed his head. "I have not. It must be terrible."

"Then," avowed the Prince, "you judge what you do not understand. I admit that the means I strive to acquire are not honorable. I accept the dishonor. The ends I want to achieve are just. They are *necessary*.

"*That* will satisfy me."

The monk sighed. "I do not judge, Prince. The Cult of the Many does not. I merely inquire. If your cause is just, why does serving it enrage you? Do you need anger to stifle your judgment of yourself? Are you not already corrupted?"

For an instant, Prince Bifalt stared. Then he burst out laughing.

Does he accuse me—*me!*—of judging myself? Of hiding my judgment behind a screen of anger? He does not know me.

The Prince had made mistakes. He understood them all. But his wrath was not one of them. It was more than honest: it was reasonable. His interminable frustration and Belleger's helplessness explained it. Only a madman would not feel as he did, believe as he did.

Prince Bifalt's laughter sent the monk out of the infirmary.

Mirth relieved him for the moment. It vindicated him to himself. But it did not answer any of his needs. When it subsided, he wrapped his resolve around him, retrieved his weapons, and stood. If he could find a servant who would guide him, he meant to seek for some sorcerer who might tell him what he had to know. Failing that, he wanted to return to the refectory. He had not broken his fast; and perhaps Elgart would be there. He would force himself to ignore the Amikan.

In one way, however, he did not know his own mind. At unexpected moments, he remembered what Slack had told him.

A man is not a man at all if he cannot enter and enjoy every chamber of himself.

Why was he haunted by the words of a man who had betrayed him and Belleger?

※

Aservant waiting in the passage outside the infirmary led him back to the refectory. Although he told her plainly that he wished to speak with someone of importance in the Repository—with any personage who was not deaf or mute—she did not reply.

When they reached the entrance to the refectory, she gestured him inward, but did not accompany him.

Prince Bifalt found the hall almost empty. He saw no more than a dozen men and women seated at widely scattered tables, and none of them were Elgart, or Amandis, or anyone he knew. If any of them noticed him, they did not show it. Only the sounds of bustle from the kitchen assured him that he would still be fed.

When he had filled a tray amid the noise and steam of the kitchen, he took a chair at a far table and composed himself to eat. Since he had no obvious alternative, he concentrated on continuing to rebuild his strength.

—*not a man at all*—

Hells! That traitorous sorcerer had cursed him.

✳

He ate quickly, like a soldier before a battle. But he was not done when his enemy entered the refectory. At once, the Amikan strode past the ends of the tables toward him.

Prince Bifalt's nerves sprang taut. He gripped the hilt of his saber, loosened it in its scabbard; confirmed that his rifle hung free on his shoulder. Then, by an act of will, he placed both hands flat on the table where they were clearly visible. Poised in every muscle, he watched his foe's approach.

Passing between the chairs, the Amikan came to stand across the table from him. The man's face was rigidly blank as he folded his arms behind him. With a disturbing lack of inflection, he said, "Bellegerin."

Feigning ease, the Prince leaned back in his chair. While he held his enemy's gaze, he watched the man's arms obliquely, alert to sudden movements. In an insolent drawl, he demanded, "Why do you come to me, Amikan?"

The man's shrug sent a quiver of expectation through the Prince. But the Amikan did not shift his arms. His reply betrayed only a hint of sarcasm. "Apparently, I am expected to do penance for your attack on me. Among sorcerers, absurdity passes for reason. But I am their guest. I cannot refuse. I must show as much willingness as I am able to stomach. It is not much, but I do what I can.

"They have asked me to take you to—" He faltered for an instant, then shrugged again. "I consider him the Repository's over-lord. He is the librarian."

Prince Bifalt scowled to conceal the leaping of his heart. With his hands still flat on the table, he rose from his chair. "Magister Rummage," he said distinctly, "is insane. I do not want more broken bones. Like you, I will stomach what I can. I accept your offer."

The Amikan raised an eyebrow. He appeared surprised by the Prince's manner. Perhaps he had expected Prince Bifalt to refuse. Perhaps he wanted that. A harsh "No" would have spared him another moment in the presence of a Bellegerin. It would certainly have spared him the pretense of courtesy. But then he shrugged; nodded. Turning his back—a tempting target—he moved away.

The Prince allowed himself a feral grin as he followed. The librarian, he thought. The keeper of the books. He will answer me.

From that moment on, Prince Bifalt paid close attention to his route through the keep. He foresaw a need to find his own way to and from the librarian—and then to the great entry hall and the stables. At the same time, however, he remained acutely conscious of the Amikan a step ahead of him. There was too much he did not understand. After two turnings and a stair apparently high enough to reach the level of the outer ramparts, a sudden thought occurred to him: a way to learn more about where he stood in the Last Repository.

Hoping to startle an honest reply from his guide, he asked, "Were you summoned?"

His enemy paused on the stair, looked back at him over his shoulder. "Summoned? No. Sent. Who would summon me? King Smegin commanded me to this duty." His lack of inflection had a tinge of fatality. "If I had known I would be forced to contend with a Bellegerin butcher, I would have refused the task."

Provoked by that word, *butcher*, Prince Bifalt almost cried out, *Why?* Why did King Smegin send his man here when the seventh Decimate had already ensured Belleger's destruction? And why did the Amikan call Bellegerins *butchers*? The butchery was all on Amika's side. King Smegin's men killed their own wounded. They used their own children to bait an ambush. They tried to hamstring oxen. And King Fastule had savaged Queen Malorie with the Decimate of pestilence when she wed Fastule's brother.

But the Prince bit back everything that was in his heart. He refused to reveal so much of himself to his foe. This challenge was one of taunts, not of truth.

Heavy with sarcasm, he retorted, "You enjoy calling *us* butchers. I am surprised you can justify yourself so easily."

Finally, anger flashed in the Amikan's eyes. Baring his teeth, he came down a step, although he kept his arms locked behind him. "I call you butchers," he snarled, "because that is what you are. You have rifles, but they are not enough for you. You have come here seeking some more crushing advantage. Naturally, my people call you butchers."

Then he regained his self-possession. More softly, he sneered, "When our children misbehave, their parents warn them that they will be taken by Bellegerins. The children prefer beatings. *Bellegerin* is the worst threat they know.

"We fight only to defend ourselves. We were prosperous before Belleger tried to take what is ours. We will be prosperous again when Belleger no longer exists."

A shout rose in Prince Bifalt, but he stopped it between his teeth. *This* accusation had the sound of truth, and it shocked him. Did Amika fight only to defend itself? *That* was a lie. But the idea that Amikan parents used the name of their enemy to frighten their children—! The Prince had not expected so *much* honesty. He was not prepared for it.

And he had no answer.

Biting the inside of his cheek, he kept silent. His hands he clasped across his chest to demonstrate that he did not reach for his weapons. What else could he do? To frighten their children? He wanted to kill the Amikan at once. Or try to. If he were fast enough, he might succeed before Magister Rummage broke him. But then his quest would end in blood and folly. All hope for his people would be gone.

His foe did not deign to glance at him again. Turning away, the man resumed leading King Abbator's son up the stairs and across the halls of the castle. Their passage gave Prince Bifalt time to calm his breathing and steady his mind—to set aside the impact of what the Amikan had said—before they reached their destination.

Abruptly, they came to an entryway without doors or attendants. Beyond the threshold lay a chamber twice the size of the Prince's quarters. It was brightly lit, but not by cressets or lamps. Across the angled ceiling, a row of clerestory windows filled the space with midmorning sunlight; and along one wall, more windows with their shutters open provided a view of the keep's ramparts. After days in its closed depths, the effect of so much sunshine blurred Prince Bifalt's vision.

Blinking, he studied the chamber.

Its only furnishings were a long trestle table like those in the refectory, more than a dozen tall stools scattered between him and the table, and opposite them—behind the table—a massive armchair that looked too heavy to shift. Irregular piles of books and scrolls covered the table, some ten or more volumes high, others spilled here and there as if they had been tossed aside. In no apparent order, sheaves of papers bound together by strings joined tomes with elegantly tooled leather bindings. Books the size of a man's hand were mixed with folios that could not have been opened by anyone with short arms.

In the armchair, only his head and shoulders visible over the disarray of texts, sat an old man with long, flowing hair and a heavy beard, both as white as the opaque film that filled his eyes. He was as blind as blank paper.

"Bellegerin," announced the Amikan flatly, "here is the librarian of the Last Repository. He is Magister Marrow."

Without another word, the man turned and left the chamber.

Staring, Prince Bifalt forgot his enemy. He forgot courtesy. Diplomacy was gone from his head. "Marrow?" he demanded unsteadily. "*Hexin* Marrow?"

"Prince Bifalt." The blind man faced his visitor as if he knew exactly where the Prince stood. "You are here at last. And very welcome." His voice held a complex mixture of timbres, some amiable and soothing, others irascible, ready for anger. His blindness and the beard hiding his mouth made his expression unreadable. "Hexin Marrow was my grandfather six generations removed. And no librarian. Too busy researching and writing. I am *Sirjane* Marrow. I tend his legacy. Among other tasks.

"Take a stool. Rest your nerves. I can feel your fears from here. Your legs will start to tremble soon."

The sorcerer was right. Every muscle in Prince Bifalt's body was stretched tight. Sirjane Marrow was the keeper of the books: the door to Belleger's future, for good or evil. Scrambling to recover his scattered wits, the Prince seated himself. Fortunately, the stool was tall enough to let him keep his gaze fixed on the librarian. He could not stop staring.

No inhabitant of the castle had called him by his name.

Nodding at the Prince's compliance, Magister Marrow said in a neutral tone, "You wanted to speak with me."

Prince Bifalt took hold of his confusion. Caution, he reminded himself. Reticence. He was facing a man who could erase him from life with a word. A man who had kept him alive in order to manipulate him. A man who did not merit trust. The Prince needed a counselor's skills here, not a soldier's. He did not want to repeat the mistake he had made in Set Ungabwey's carriage.

But he had little subterfuge in his nature. He could only be who he was.

Doing his best, he replied, "I believed, Magister, *you* wanted to speak with *me*."

He meant, *Tell* me, old man. What do you want?

"Oh, I do, I do," said the librarian, flapping a hand dismissively. "But we have plenty of time. You could have refused. We gave you opportunities. Why did you come?"

Remembering the voice he had heard only in his mind, Prince Bifalt mustered an illusion of calm. "Your summons was urgent."

Magister Marrow nodded. "It was. It is. As is your purpose. We can wait."

His manner suggested that he was not prepared to wait much longer.

The Prince glared. "King Abbator of Belleger, my father, gave me a quest. I strive to complete it."

"As you should." The sorcerer managed to sound simultaneously relaxed and impatient. "It is your duty.

"What is it?"

The King's son tried again. "I could explain more clearly if I knew why you summoned me."

And why *me*? Why not some other Bellegerin? A former Magister with a trained mind? A counselor with more subtlety?

Again, Magister Marrow flapped a hand. "Nonsense. You are our guest. We have a reputation for hospitality. Your needs take precedence. We will try to satisfy you. Later, we will decide whether you can satisfy us."

That was a challenge Prince Bifalt could not refuse. Taking his courage in both hands, he answered bluntly, "Hexin Marrow's *Seventh Decimate*. I need it. If I can, I need to use it."

Although Magister Marrow raised his eyebrows, he did not sound surprised. "A trivial request. I expected something greater. Something to change the world, a man as indignant as you are.

"I will show you the book, of course. Nothing could be simpler. Why do you need it?"

The Prince felt that he was taking a great risk. "Belleger will die without it."

"Is *that* all?" The theurgist's tone suggested disappointment. "I should have guessed." Then he said more briskly, "But of course, of course. Come with me, Prince. Until now, you have been immured. You have not seen the library."

Without difficulty, he slid his chair aside and rose to his feet.

He was taller than Prince Bifalt had supposed, at least a head taller than the Prince himself. In outward appearance, only his beard and blindness distinguished him from Magister Avail and Magister Rummage: his raiment and sandals were the same as theirs. Where the plump sorcerer took his ease, however, and the hunchback was goaded by haste or violence, Magister Marrow emanated authority.

Weaving his way between the stools, he strode from the chamber.

Prince Bifalt hurried to follow. The troubled thudding of his heart insisted that the librarian had acceded too readily. Magister

Marrow had motives other than hospitality. Did he trust his guest's—his victim's—surrender? The Prince did not believe it.

Later, we will decide whether you can satisfy us. That implied a test of some kind. Yet another challenge.

Had the monk who had taken him to the infirmary betrayed him? Had Elgart revealed too much to Amandis? Did the Magisters here know he loathed sorcery? Did they know he yearned for Amika's absolute defeat?

As he pursued the librarian through several passages to a wide flight of stairs reaching high into the keep, Prince Bifalt's resolve hardened. Was he being tested? He could devise tests of his own. Even in battle, he was not a man who outwitted his opponents. But he had learned how to probe them—and to take advantage of what he discovered.

For the first time, he wondered whether the seventh Decimate could be used to deprive the Repository's Magisters themselves of sorcery.

An exciting prospect. The perfect punishment for what had been done to him; for what theurgy and arrogance had done to his world. Nevertheless, he pushed it out of his mind. It was a mirage. Despite Magister Marrow's assurances, he doubted that he would be given the book. Sorcerers did not teach their secrets to the ungifted. Men like the librarian treasured their superiority. And if the Prince held *Seventh Decimate* in his hands, he might not be able to read it. The peoples of the world spoke too many incomprehensible languages. Marrow's text might be written in a foreign tongue.

And even if he could read the book, he might not be able to use it. He had no gift for sorcery.

His mission required patience.

Ahead of him, the librarian ascended the stair with an ease that belied his age. The Prince trotted upward until he climbed at the blind man's side. Then he attempted a test.

Abruptly, he stated, "One of your guests is Amikan."

He meant, At least one. And he is not the first.

"Ah, yes." Magister Marrow sounded unaccountably cheerful. "Commander Forguile. He leads the Amikan monarch's honor guard.

"His conduct is better than yours."

Prince Bifalt missed a step. Swearing to himself, he recovered. "Why is he here?"

"Ask him," returned the sorcerer.

"He will not tell me." Of that, the Prince was certain. Commander Forguile had already answered the question without revealing anything.

The librarian did not pause in his ascent. "Would *you* tell *him*? If he asked you?"

Hells, the Prince thought. "No. He is my enemy."

"Then," concluded Magister Marrow, "you have no cause for complaint."

Prince Bifalt stared. Vexation hissed between his teeth. "Who complained? *I* did not. I asked *you* why he is here. I *did* ask him. He gave me no real answer." *We will be prosperous again when Belleger no longer exists.* "If you will not tell me, I will put my question another way.

"How many of his kind have come before me?"

Magister Marrow seemed to chuckle privately, playing a game he enjoyed. "Ask him."

The Prince gripped the hilt of his saber with one hand. With the other, he clasped the shoulder strap of his rifle. The librarian was mocking him. He knew that; but he had no answer for it. Frustrated again—*endlessly* frustrated—he concentrated on the stairs.

Only the book, he told himself. Only the book matters. When he had it—when he had taken it to Belleger—he would have time to think about ways to repay the affront of his summons.

Finally, he and his guide reached the head of the stair. The air at this level seemed thin: he had difficulty drawing enough into his lungs. Sweat moistened his brow. In contrast, the old sorcerer breathed easily, and all his movements were strong, as if he had limitless stamina.

Sure of his way despite his blindness, Magister Marrow led the Prince around a curved wall to a formal entryway with obscure symbols engraved above its arch. Following the librarian, Prince Bifalt entered the library itself.

They stood on the floor of one of the immense circles or wheels he had studied as he and Elgart had approached the Repository. The floor was round and open, a sheet of stone polished smooth by centuries of use, and so wide that it surely occupied much of its wheel. Still, there was room near the walls for at least twenty of the castle's familiar trestle tables, all supplied with a number of chairs, and some occupied by men and women. Either alone or in small groups, these people pored over books. Taken together, they were a motley collection of the diverse races and styles Prince Bifalt had seen in the refectory. Among them were a few monks, and fewer savages like the shaman. Most of the rest were more elegantly or elaborately clad. However, they included several men and women wearing the plain robes of sorcerers.

A handful of the students or scholars raised their heads when Magister Marrow and the Prince entered. The others remained bent over their interests.

The volumes they studied must have come from the bookcases circling the walls: dozens of bookcases of various sizes, some so tall that their higher shelves could only be reached with ladders, some deep and broad to accommodate scrolls. A few showed empty spaces where tomes had been removed. Most were full. Prince Bifalt had never seen so many books in one place. Hells, he had never seen so many book*cases*—

Yet this was only the first of the library's many stacked levels or wheels. And he could count them all. The clear space where he and the librarian stood had been cut out from the floors above him, leaving those levels open, slab upon slab, until they reached the Repository's vaulted ceiling. Each opening was guarded by a high railing that suggested a balcony: a balcony wide enough to hold more trestle tables, more chairs; many more bookcases.

Squinting upward had a vertiginous effect on Prince Bifalt, as if he were peering down into a fatal pit instead of up at the ceiling. He had to bow his head and plant his feet in order to stop the spinning of the world.

When he looked upward again, the effect diminished slowly.

Now he was able to see how the huge space was lit. The distant ceiling held an array of heavily glassed windows to admit as much illumination as the day offered. And set into the edges of each opening below the balcony railings were a multitude of lamps, all shining with a brightness that seemed unnatural—and none smoking. They burned some oil that did not fume; or their light was made by sorcery.

After further scrutiny, he understood why the levels of the library were offset from each other rather than stacked evenly. Their irregularity allowed each to be reached by wooden spiral staircases from those immediately above and below it. But why the sorcerers had elected to construct stairs within the enormous cavity rather than through its walls baffled him. The makers of the Repository could have designed it however they wished. Apparently, they wanted to preserve the thickness and solidity of the walls for some reason.

To protect the books from assault?

Prince Bifalt knew the world was larger than his capacity to imagine it. That disturbing, undesired recognition had been imposed on him against his will. Still, he could conceive of no force anywhere mighty enough to take by siege—or even to harm—the Repository of the sorcerers. The *Last* Repository.

Nevertheless, thinking that the library had enemies comforted him. If the Magisters here felt a need to ward their treasure of knowledge from attack, they were not immune to fear; not secure in their superiority. Despite the power of their inhuman gifts, they were natural men to this extent: they could be made afraid.

Prince Bifalt did not want to meet any strength terrible enough to threaten the library. He did not want to know what it might be. He had already encountered too much that surpassed him. But he was comforted to suppose that such a force might exist.

Any man who could be made afraid could be beaten.

While the Prince gnawed on elusive possibilities, Magister Marrow interrupted him. "There," said the librarian, pointing upward. "All of my ancestor's books. They are on the seventeenth round. The one you want is there.

"Come."

Without waiting for a reply, the sorcerer headed unerringly for the nearest spiral staircase.

The theurgists of the Repository could be made afraid. Magister *Rummage* could be made afraid.

Sudden eagerness sent Prince Bifalt after his host.

However, eagerness did not carry him far. The climb was more strenuous than he expected. He had eaten well, rested thoroughly. Still, his lungs and muscles had not regained their familiar stamina, their trained endurance. And the librarian set a brisk pace. Before long, the Prince began to pant. Later, only a strict effort of will kept him from gasping audibly. In spite of his determination, his steps slowed.

The sorcerer's did not. The blind old man was a floor above his guest when he halted at last. Without obvious impatience, he called down, "Soon, Prince. Take the time you need. There is no hurry."

Mocking the King of Belleger's eldest son—

Hells.

To measure his progress, Prince Bifalt glanced down—and nearly cried out. The floor seemed impossibly far away. The distance had increased more than he had climbed, or the thinness of the air had unmoored his mind. The lower levels wheeled below him: the steps where he stood tilted. The library itself mocked him. Without the railing of the staircase to protect him, he might have pitched headfirst to his death.

There were too many *books*—

The Last Repository was as arrogant as its Magisters. It held unnatural quantities of power of impossible kinds; immeasurable resources. Because they could do anything, its keepers believed they had the right to do everything. They could determine the life and death of realms, and did not fault themselves for doing so.

Gasping for air—for balance—Prince Bifalt fought to recover his resolve. He began to withstand the library's endless circles and spirals, its chaos of written words. For a moment, he seated himself heavily on the stairs, held his head in his hands, and breathed. When he resumed his ascent, he left dizziness and falling behind.

"Here you are," said the librarian as the Prince joined him at last. If he smiled, his beard concealed it. "Where we stand is higher than any point in Belleger. Much higher. The air is indeed thin. You are not accustomed to it."

He was offering Prince Bifalt an excuse; but the Prince had no use for it. Through his panting, he answered only, "The book."

"Of course." Magister Marrow nodded. "The book. Hexin Marrow's *Seventh Decimate*." His tone expressed exasperation and amusement equally. "It is here."

Gesturing behind him, he turned and strode away around the balcony.

As the Prince had guessed, the balcony was wide enough to accommodate a number of tables and many more chairs without crowding them against the uninterrupted wall of bookcases. Here two women clad as Magisters were the only other people present. They sat with their books several tables away from each other, and did not raise their heads as the librarian and then Prince Bifalt passed. Indeed, they were motionless in their concentration, so rapt and still that they resembled effigies. Neither of them appeared to breathe. If he had not seen one of them turn a page, the Prince might have suspected that they had died in their chairs unnoticed. With no sound or memory for guidance, the blind librarian might not be aware of them.

At his destination, Magister Marrow stopped. Facing the bookcases, he spread his arms. "Here," he announced. "The complete writings of Hexin Marrow. All of them. He lived a long time and wrote everything down. *Everything*. Mountains of paper. Shelf after shelf of notes. Most of it disjointed. Much of it useless."

While the librarian talked, Prince Bifalt peered at the shelves, trying to read titles or recognize names. But he was still laboring for air, and his eyes refused to focus clearly.

"Fortunately," continued the sorcerer, "it is not *all* useless. Whenever his researches led him to an important conclusion, he troubled himself to organize his thoughts and compose a tome. All the *Decimates* are here. All so lucidly written that only an illiterate fool could fail to understand them."

As if the question implied no offense, he asked, "Are *you* illiterate, Prince?"

Without pausing for a reply, he pounced at the shelves. "And *here*," he announced, "is my ancestor's *Seventh Decimate*."

Snatching a volume from the bookcase, he thrust it toward his guest.

With trembling hands, Prince Bifalt took the book, turned it to examine its cover.

It was bound in leather as heavy as a form of armor: it could have stopped a bullet. Its author and title were deeply inset, the lettering gilded until it seemed to glow. He could not fail to read it, or be mistaken.

Sounding stupid, even to himself, he muttered, "This is not the book."

Another test. A trick.

A betrayal.

"Not?" cried the librarian. "Preposterous! It *must* be."

Vehemently, he tore the book from the Prince. With his hands, his fingers, he examined it front and back. Then he held it at arm's length, squinting as if he sought to see through his blindness.

"Absurd!" he exclaimed. "Impossible. I *know* this book. I know them *all*. It is Sylan Estervault's work. *A Treatise on the Fabrication of Cannon Using Primitive Means*. It belongs on the fourth round." Suddenly clasping the book to his chest, he added in a changed voice, "Though it might interest you."

Swallowing every word he wanted to spit at Magister Marrow, Prince Bifalt ventured, "A mistake—"

Of *course* the book interested him. Without sorcery, Belleger would need every possible form of gun. But guns were not what he had been sent to find.

"Mistake?" snapped the librarian, instantly irate. "What do you mean?"

"It was put here by mistake." The Prince shrugged stiffly. "Some servant—"

"Impossible!" repeated the sorcerer. "Absurd. You mock me, Prince. Every book taken from the shelves is returned to *me*. It is not *put back*. It is delivered to my *chamber*. *I* restore it to its proper place. How else can I know where every scroll and paper and volume in the library *is*?"

Now Prince Bifalt felt sure that some trick was being played on him. He abandoned caution. "*I* do not mock you," he retorted. "*You* mock *me*. There was no mistake. You are toying with me. You knew from the first that the book was not here."

"Nonsense." Magister Marrow rasped an obscure curse. Scowling like thunder, he faced the bookcase again. "There!" He pointed at a book beside the space left by *A Treatise on the Fabrication of Cannon Using Primitive Means*. "Marrow's *Sixth Decimate*."

Prince Bifalt read the book's title on its spine. *Sixth Decimate*. He read its author's name. Hexin Marrow.

"And *there*," continued the librarian. "*Fifth Decimate*. And *there*." He pointed past the gap. "*Eighth Decimate*. Then *Final Decimate*." He recited the titles as if the clear letters on the spines proved his honesty.

Despite his fuming, the Prince read the spines. An *eighth* Decimate? A *final* one? If the seventh blocked the very possibility of sorcery, how much harm remained? What could be worse?

A man is not a man at all—

"*Seventh Decimate*," insisted the librarian, "should be with its companions. It is *always* here. I brought you because I believed it would be here."

To Prince Bifalt, the reason for the book's absence was obvious. Clenching his fists, he suggested harshly, "Then Amika has it."

"What?" The old man wheeled on the Prince. He sounded more than surprised: his tone suggested chagrin. "How would *Amika* have it?"

Not *why*. *How*. As if the *why* were trivial. As if only the *how* had import.

Without flinching, Prince Bifalt held the Magister's opaque glare. He bit the inside of his cheek to prevent himself from saying what was in his mind.

These sorcerers had conspired with Amika to arrange Belleger's destruction. The librarian was surprised by the accuracy of Prince Bifalt's insight. He was chagrined by the prospect of exposure.

But Magister Marrow recovered his poise in an instant. Suddenly calm, he admitted, "A mistake, yes. A mistake of *mine*. There is no other explanation. You have seen my chamber, the piles on my desk. Those texts were brought to me so that I could put them in their proper places. *Seventh Decimate* must be there.

"I have been too much distracted. I have forgotten—"

The sorcerer spread his hands: a gesture of placation. "I offer my apologies, Prince. The book you want is surely there. It has not been removed from the Last Repository. No. I would have felt its departure. A sting like a wound here." He patted his chest. "When I find it, I will send it to your quarters."

Then he added almost humbly, "The study of sorcery teaches strange sources of amusement. It is not my intent to mock you."

The Prince snorted to himself. Clenching his teeth, he kept silent. He had never loathed sorcery and sorcerers more than he did now.

✳

Although his sharpest wish at that moment was to be free of Magister Marrow's company, Prince Bifalt followed the blind man down through the rounds of the library toward the inhabited levels of the keep. As he spiraled lower, however, his determination gathered force. He had suffered more indignities than he was prepared to endure. His willingness to attempt the misdirections of diplomacy was at an end. He only held his tongue because he wanted a chance to speak without being overheard.

When he and his guide finally left the imponderable mass of books behind, he seemed to feel their weight lift from his shoulders: the weight, perhaps, of his own ignorance. Beyond question, he was no match for men who knew so much; men who felt such scorn for ordinary people whose only failing was an accident of birth. On this level of the keep, however, he could breathe. He squared his shoulders and lifted his head, stopped watching where he put his feet. Trusting himself on stairs that did not circle, on floors that did not need railings, he spoke as soon as he and the Magister were alone.

"I will ask one question," he announced abruptly. "One answer will satisfy me until I have the book in my hands."

Pausing, the old man cocked an eyebrow.

"When," demanded Prince Bifalt, "will you tell the truth?"

Magister Marrow sighed. "When you do, Prince. When you do."

Then he waved his hand. At once, a servant appeared from a side passage. "This monk," said the sorcerer, "will escort you to your quarters. I have had enough of you for one day.

"Do not return to the refectory. Food will be brought to you when you request it. I am not inclined to risk another of your outbreaks. Magister Rummage will not be so gentle a second time."

Turning his back, the librarian walked away.

Not inclined? Prince Bifalt was not inclined to restrain himself.

"When we speak again," he called after the librarian, "I will ask why you are afraid."

Magister Marrow did not reply. He did not appear to have heard.

Cursing viciously, the Prince allowed himself to be led back to his isolated quarters.

※

At his door, however, he stopped. "Hear me well, monk," he said to his guide. "Inform the Magisters I must speak with my comrade, Elgart. He must be brought to me. If he is not, I will force Magister Rummage to cripple me. I will force him to cripple me *repeatedly* until I am killed, or Elgart is brought here."

He needed to speak with the only man in the castle who understood his dilemma and shared his purpose.

He needed to be sure Elgart had not been harmed. Or swayed.

And he wanted a map. If the librarian kept his word, the Prince intended to escape from the Last Repository. Somehow. If he could.

Promising nothing, the servant bowed dutifully.

When he was gone, Prince Bifalt entered his rooms, slammed the door, bolted it. Then he grabbed a flask of wine and drank until its acidic aftertaste threatened to choke him.

—I will send it to your quarters.

He did not believe anything that Magister Marrow had told him. *Seventh Decimate* would not be delivered to him. It was in Amika's possession already. Or Commander Forguile had it. The librarian had lied. He would not stop lying. Slack had taught Prince Bifalt that the gift of sorcery was also the gift of lies. And if he had failed to learn his lesson from Slack, he had been given fresh lessons in Set Ungabwey's carriage.

Briefly, he considered drinking himself into unconsciousness. Then he set the impulse aside. In spite of every frustration, he still hoped to speak with Elgart; and if his last comrade were brought to him, he would need a clear mind. He was Prince Bifalt, the King of Belleger's eldest son. He could wait to dull the distress of his thwarted heart.

PART FIVE

Nonetheless, his helplessness ate at him. It gnawed on his bones like a feasting predator. When he heard a knock at his door at last, he staggered to answer it as if he had suffered a convulsion.

Throwing the bolt, Prince Bifalt wrenched the door open—and found himself confronting the small, slim figure of Amandis, the devotee of Spirit. Clad in her modest cloak, with her clasped hands hidden in her sleeves, and her hair flowing loose, she regarded him gravely, without a word.

Made stupid by surprise, Prince Bifalt stared. He was barely able to find words. "Where is Elgart?"

She did not answer. Instead, she advanced on him until he felt compelled to retreat. As he withdrew, she entered his quarters and closed the door.

He tried to ask again, Where is Elgart? Her manner stopped

him. *My skills suffice to kill*— He was relieved when she did not advance farther.

In her harsh accent, she began, "You have uttered a threat against the Magisters. They will not suffer it." She watched his face like a woman who wanted to see his expression as she drove in her dagger. "At their request, I have come to demand it recanted. Their purposes and yours will both fail if you insist on provoking Magister Rummage."

Like her arrival, her words made Prince Bifalt's wits spin. Even here, he was caught in the library's circles. Striving for balance, he clutched at the first response he could find.

"What do you know of my purposes?"

"Your man Elgart is in our care." For the second time, the Prince heard a hint of amusement in the assassin's harsh accent. "I command what I desire. Flamora's method is persuasion. Together, we learn what we wish. However, we do not speak of it to others. It is not ours to reveal.

"She offered to come in my place. But I perceive that your self-righteousness rules you. You would repulse her. You will not refuse to hear me."

Her assertions were offensive. Challenging. For that reason, they steadied him. Tightening his hold on himself, Prince Bifalt regained a measure of self-control. With more of his familiar assurance, his habit of authority, he countered, "What do you want with Elgart? He is no threat to you. Neither of us threaten you. And he is loyal to me. More than that, he is loyal to Belleger. What use do you have for him?"

He meant, How have you tricked or seduced him to expose my intentions?

Amandis did not reply to that question. Instead, she said, "We are speaking of your threat against the Magisters, Prince. I will have your word that you will not act on it."

The nature of her regard seemed to promise that she would not hesitate to exact his word with blood and pain.

"And I will have answers," he retorted. "I have many questions. I will not ask them all. But you will answer some. That is the price of my word."

Still holding his gaze, Amandis took her hands from her sleeves to show him her daggers. For a moment, she twirled them in and through her fingers like a juggler practicing her skill. Then she hid them again.

"Ask," she commanded. "Some I will answer—if my answers will not betray the Magisters. Flamora and I have not betrayed you—or Elgart. The Magisters deserve the same respect. Their secrets are not ours to reveal."

"Good." Wary of her blades, the Prince retreated another step. Then he broke her grip on his eyes to locate a chair. Deliberately, he seated himself, trying to convey the impression that he did not feel threatened. "Tell me *your* purposes. What do you want with Elgart?"

Amandis frowned slightly, perhaps to mask a smirk. She said nothing.

An instinctive grimace twisted his features. He did what he could to smooth it away.

"Has he done what I require of him?"

Again, she did not speak.

"If you command him, why did you not bring him with you?"

That question she took more seriously. "We have too little time." Her tone made her accent sound like an axe on wood. "He is an apt student, but he has much to learn. When he does not train with me—"

"Much to learn?" interrupted the Prince. "He is a veteran. He has ridden through hell. He has drenched himself in blood and killing. I doubt you can say the same. What can you teach him that he does not already know?"

The devotee of Spirit ignored him. "—he profits from his hours with Flamora," she finished.

"Indeed?" Prince Bifalt snorted. "What does *she* teach?"

"What I cannot," replied Amandis.

"No doubt." He resisted an impulse to clench his fists. Instead, he folded his arms. "You share your skills. She shares her bed. But you explain nothing."

The assassin's eyes flashed. "You *understand* nothing. I teach him to choose. She teaches him to love his life. Together, we teach him that only a man who loves his life can choose an honorable death."

The King's son dismissed her statement as devout nonsense. "*Still*, you do not explain."

He meant, Why do you imagine he needs your lessons?

She shrugged. "Ask a worthy question. Perhaps you will receive a worthy answer."

Abruptly, he slapped his thighs with his palms. "I will." Then he stood so that he could glare down on Amandis. "What do these Magisters *fear*? They pretend to fear me, but I am no threat to them. Elgart is not. *Belleger* is not. Belleger and Amika together could not scratch the walls of this keep. No siege can weaken it. No force of arms can harm it. Yet the library is a fortress. It is impregnable. An earthquake would not shake its walls. If the mountain behind it crumbled, it would remain standing.

"You are an assassin. You understand me. This Repository was made by men who are afraid. Tell me what they fear."

To his surprise, she allowed herself a smile: an expression so uncharacteristic that it made her look almost girlish. "Can you not guess, Prince?" Her harshness now resembled a form of teasing. "The library is called the Last Repository. Is the truth not obvious? There is no secret in it."

Then she resumed her severe manner. Without waiting for a response, she continued.

"The Magisters here do not rule the world you know. Their influence is great. It extends the length and breadth of this continent. But they do not *rule*.

"And there are other continents. On those continents are realms and kingdoms and principalities and confederations without number. Some are content as they are. Some indulge in petty wars. Others have become empires. In some, monks and devotees are revered. In others, we are condemned as heretics—tortured and killed. And in all those lands, distant and near, large and small, cruel and kind, live men and women gifted in sorcery.

"The Magisters of the Last Repository worship knowledge. The library is their temple. For its sake, they crave peace. Knowledge can only flourish in times of peace. With peace, caravans such as Master Ungabwey's bring books. They bring tales and scholars and strangers. Other travelers find their way. They feed the library's hunger for knowledge, or their own.

"It is otherwise in times of war. Then knowledge is lost. Its temples are laid waste. Books are destroyed. Secrets are forbidden or forgotten. For that reason—to preserve its treasure of knowledge—the Repository is also a fortress.

"Other sorcerers in other lands hold different desires. They serve different convictions. Some desire power for its own sake, or for their own glorification. Others favor tyranny, seeking to be tyrants themselves. Still others dread any knowledge they do not possess. They fear that their ignorance exposes them to defeat—to conquest, slavery, or death.

"Such men are not uncommon." The assassin's tone became sharper. "They seek an end to what they fear, or they desire to hold it for themselves alone. They, too, have fortresses. And some are mighty. The day will come again, as it has come before across the millennia, when they will lay siege to the Repository. And they will not assail it with any mere force of arms. As they have done before, they will challenge it with every possible power until it has been torn down. Until it is utterly destroyed.

"This Repository is the Last because the Magisters who care for it cannot flee again. They are not warriors. They cannot defeat their enemies. In centuries past, they have escaped secretly when the strength arrayed against them was too great. But now there is no safer place where they can house their treasure of knowledge.

No other place is as remote, or has this desert and these mountains to defend it.

"Do you understand, Prince?" asked Amandis. Her bitterness was unmistakable. "The Magisters do not fear *you*. Your war does not threaten them. They fear your weakness. Belleger does not guard their borders. You are a road their enemies can take to come against them."

Prince Bifalt listened until she was done; but he was not entirely present. Not for the first time, he seemed to feel the foundations on which he stood shifting. The scale of the world she described affected him like a tearing sensation in his mind, a rip as acute as physical pain. Boundaries were shredded: implications wavered like hallucinations. He did not know who to be when mighty sorcerers on distant continents could cross wide oceans to wage war. Who *could* he be, a minor prince in a small realm with only rifles to defend itself and him?

But then he took hold of himself. Regardless of his stature, his significance or meaninglessness, he had to be who he was. He had no other choice. The scale of the world did not change what he had to do, or why he cared about it. His only concerns were those he could understand. Grimly, he told himself that distant continents and the animosity of unknowable sorcerers had nothing to do with him. *His* problems were *here*. Belleger was weak because Amika had invoked Marrow's seventh Decimate—and *that* was not the Prince's doing, or his father's, or his people's. The blame belonged to the Magisters Amandis defended.

When he could speak again, he countered, "Is that their justification for dishonesty and false dealings?" His voice rose. "For holding in contempt men and women who were not born gifted?" He wanted to shout, but no mere shout would satisfy him. He needed words that would cut more deeply than blades. "For imposing their will on people who do not consent? They are tyrants themselves. They pretend that they do not rule to conceal the extent of their tyranny."

The devotee of Spirit studied him for a moment. Her eyes, her expression, her posture: none of them betrayed her reaction. Only her tone revealed it.

"Is that your answer?" she inquired coldly. "Then I will advise the Magisters to expel you. You are useless to them. You are useless to Belleger. You have no place here."

Prince Bifalt had endured enough. He did not choose to suffer more. He was King Abbator's eldest son. He would not *allow* himself to be made weak by shifting boundaries; by attempts to confuse his allegiance. The Magisters had sent Amandis here to test him. To test him *again*. He responded in kind.

In one tearing motion, he swept his saber from its scabbard and swung it at the assassin's neck.

As he expected, his blade did not touch her. He had seen her quickness before. With untroubled ease, she stepped aside.

But she did not return his attack. Her daggers remained hidden. She did nothing to threaten him.

"Is *that* your answer?" she insisted. Her calm covered her like her cloak.

Satisfied for the moment, he returned his saber to its scabbard. His gaze did not release hers. "No." He scowled to disguise his admiration. Her inaction told him what he needed to know. "It was a test. I have been tested myself, repeatedly, for no honest reason. You came to test me again. I know you are able to kill me. Your skills suffice. Now you know I am not afraid to take the risk. You know I do not fear you." And, he did not add aloud, I have learned that these Magisters fear to lose me. They need me to believe their enemy is great. "Also," he concluded, "I wanted you to earn my answer."

That she had done. Her composure—like her skill and her restraint—was flawless.

"You have my word," he assured the assassin. "I will not act on my threat. I will do nothing to incur Magister Rummage's wrath." Deep in his chest, he shook violently; but he kept his voice firm. "I will abide by the rules of these tyrants. I will find some other means to obtain what you do not give."

When will you tell the truth?

When you do, Prince.

His father might disapprove of his son's actions—but he would understand them.

For an instant, the cast of Amandis' eyes suggested surprise. But the look was brief: Prince Bifalt could not be sure that he had seen it. Her only reply was a nod as she turned to the door.

There, however, she paused. "Trust Elgart to us," she said in parting. "He is in no danger, unless it is of your making."

Without another word, she left.

He stared after her when she was gone. A long time seemed to pass before he thought to bolt his door.

He knew a threat when he heard it—a threat or a warning—but he could not imagine what it meant.

———

❋

Some hours passed before another knock summoned him to his door.

During the interval, he had convinced himself to expect only lies and deception. Before his exchange with the devotee of Spirit, he could have believed that she would not stoop to falsehood. Now he knew better. Her claim that Magister Marrow and his fellow theurgists feared Belleger's weakness was plainly dishonest. They had *caused* it: they had provided Amika with the seventh Decimate. For some reason Prince Bifalt could not fathom, they desired Belleger's defeat. And if they could persuade, command, or lure a woman like Amandis to lie for them, they had no truth in them.

Did they enjoy *strange sources of amusement*? No doubt they laughed among themselves at lesser men, ungifted men—men like the Prince—who were so easily misled.

That, surely, was the point of the assassin's indirect threat.

His conclusions were infuriating, yet they had the effect of calm. They enabled him to rid his heart of illusions; to remember the hard man he had always tried to be, despite his mistakes. He no longer galled himself wondering whether Hexin Marrow's book would be delivered. The librarian's word was meaningless. The book would not arrive.

Meanwhile, Prince Bifalt set his anger aside. He would find a better use for it when his opportunity presented itself.

Answering this new knock at his door, he expected to face a servant who had come with food.

But there was no servant. Deaf Magister Avail stood in the corridor alone. With both hands, he clutched a heavy volume to his prominent belly. The hair on his head resembled wreckage. And he had forgotten or misplaced his customary smile. Its absence suggested distress.

A sign of honesty? No. The sorcerer was here to offer a deeper lie, one that troubled even him.

Holding the door so that Magister Avail would not enter, Prince Bifalt returned a blank stare.

After a moment's hesitation, the plump man extended his hands, presenting the book.

The Prince accepted it without a glance. Deliberately, he held the Magister's gaze.

Magister Avail cleared his throat. "Prince," he began uncomfortably. "No librarian has ever allowed a book to leave the Last Repository, but this is now yours. Do with it what you will. If you do not understand yet why it is given to you, perhaps you will in time. And perhaps one day you will see fit to return it."

Prince Bifalt did not reply. Magister Avail could not hear him, and he saw no reason to waste a response on empty air. Instead, he dismissed the plump sorcerer with a wave of his arm. Then, making no attempt to soften his rudeness, he closed and bolted his door.

Finally, he looked at the book.

He felt no surprise at all when he saw that it was not Hexin Marrow's *Seventh Decimate*. It was Sylan Estervault's *A Treatise on the Fabrication of Cannon Using Primitive Means*.

Of course. Another test.

Yet this evidence of further duplicity did not enrage him. He did not pace the floor, or seethe, or drink—or waste regret on his various misjudgments. He was satisfied to know where he stood.

And he remembered what Slack had told him. *A man is not a man at all if he cannot enter and enjoy every chamber of himself.*

He had a soldier's interest in cannon. If nothing else, such guns might serve to protect Belleger's Fist, if they could not preserve the Open Hand. Seating himself in the nearest chair, he opened Estervault's book and began to read.

⁂

By the time he went to bed, he knew what Sylan Estervault meant by "primitive means." He meant that cannon could be made without the Decimate of fire—or any other form of sorcery. Not without the book, unfortunately. The instructions were too complex, and there were too many diagrams: Prince Bifalt could not pretend to retain them. But he understood enough of the process to recognize that it was *possible*. It would require skilled blacksmiths and iron-wrights, alchemists and perhaps even jewelers. But it could be done.

Of course, the knowledge was useless. It would not save Belleger. He could not leave the Last Repository until he had been told why the sorcerers wanted him; until he had met or refused their demands. Until he had obtained Marrow's *Seventh Decimate*. But under other circumstances— Certainly, possession of Estervault's *Treatise* could have turned any battle he had fought against Amika. Cannon could augment Belleger's use of sorcery. They might even break the Amikan lines, allowing Belleger to hold some of its men in reserve. For that reason, his studies served to concentrate his mind until he was ready for sleep. In effect, they enabled him to conserve his resolve and anger for whatever awaited him.

When he was awakened the next morning by a woman bearing a tray of food to break his fast, Prince Bifalt informed her that he wished to speak with Magister Marrow. For the sake of politeness, he added, At the Magister's convenience. To her bow of acknowledgment, and her small flicker of surprise, he replied with thanks.

There. Confident that he had done what he could to ensure that the librarian would summon him promptly, he ate with a good appetite, drank water rather than wine, bathed himself. Clad in new garments made for him by the castle's servants, he cleaned his rifle, giving particular care to the mechanism that ejected spent casings from the breech and received fresh bullets. While he worked, he wondered idly whether such a mechanism could be adapted for cannon. Eventually, he concluded that it could not. The weapon Estervault described would already be *heavy*—as would its version of bullets. An added mechanism might make the gun too heavy to move, or even to aim.

Engaged in his task and his thoughts, he was not conscious of impatience until a new knock called him to his door. Then, however, he sprang to his feet with his heart pounding. His hands shook as he checked his dagger, secured his saber at his hip, slung his satchel of ammunition over one shoulder, hung his rifle by its strap on the other. He had to hold his breath in order to unbolt the door and open it without flinching at the prospect of another disappointment, another frustration.

Fortunately, the woman outside his quarters was the same monk who had carried his request. Keeping her head lowered, she said the librarian was ready for him.

Prince Bifalt's heartbeat seemed to fill his throat as he followed her. Fire licked along his nerves. Now, he thought at every stride. Now.

When will you tell the truth?

When you do, Prince.

Now he would learn whether Magister Marrow had any honesty in him. The arrogant old man might not even be *capable* of it. Despite the many subjects on which the Prince remained ignorant, he believed he had learned enough to distinguish truth from falsehood in the Last Repository. Certainly, he had learned not to credit any statement that implied a *promise*.

This time, his passage through the inhabited levels of the keep felt interminable. He recognized none of it, apart from an occasional stairway. Eventually, however, he found himself near a familiar threshold, the entrance without doors or attendants that would admit him to the librarian's workroom. There the monk bowed herself away, leaving him to announce himself.

Prince Bifalt took a deep breath, let it out. Reflexively, he checked his weapons. Then he entered the sorcerer's presence.

Three paces from the laden trestle table, he halted. Confident that the old man was aware of his approach, he said coldly, "I am ready. Let us test each other."

"Ah." Seated in his armchair behind the table, Magister Marrow shifted a few books. Despite his blindness, he made a show of peering over his stacked tomes. "The Bellegerin prince. The *belligerent* prince.

"How will we test each other?"

"I have not lied to you," stated Prince Bifalt. He spoke like a man whose intentions never shifted. "However," he then admitted, "I have not answered fully. I will tell you my purpose. That will test me. Your reply will test you."

The Magister sat back in his chair. "Ah," he breathed again. "You begin to interest me.

"Answer one question first. Why did you not speak of this earlier?"

The Prince did not hesitate. "I do not know what you want with me. How could I trust you?"

The librarian considered for a moment, then conceded, "A fair point. *I* do not trust *you*.

"What will you tell me now?"

The King's son had prepared himself. He was ready.

"I need Hexin Marrow's book. You are aware that Amika has used it to deprive Belleger of sorcery. I want it to restore my people. But I want more. I want to deprive Amika in turn. I want to drive them and break them until they can do nothing except surrender. I want to extinguish Amika as a separate realm. If I fail, they will surely do the same to us.

"In addition"—he swallowed an unexpected impulse to hold back—"I hope to repay the disrespect of your summons. You did not ask for my consent. I did not give it."

"*Extinguish* Amika?" retorted Magister Marrow. "Repay *us*? You astonish me." He did not sound especially surprised. "Your desires are reprehensible. You covet bloodshed.

"But your wishes are wasted," he added at once. "You cannot

satisfy them. Still, I will not reproach you. Clearly, your wits are too slow for your needs. You suffer under a misapprehension that misleads you. Have you not spoken with Commander Forguile?"

"*When?*" snapped the Prince. Given the chance, he would not have approached the Amikan. But he had a practical excuse. "You forbade me. When we parted yesterday, you instructed me to remain in my quarters."

The librarian stared sightlessly. In an altered tone, he confessed, "So I did. I apologize. I was hasty."

Rearranging more books, apparently seeking to distract himself from contrition, he answered a question Prince Bifalt had asked the day before. "The commander has been with us for a season or more. He speaks respectfully. He listens with attention. But he is relentless. His petitions never end. And when he is not repeating them, he devotes his hours to the library.

"The first ten rounds are open to all, but only the fourth interests him. That is where we keep our volumes on the many arts of warfare. His appetite for them is insatiable. He studies the uses of trenches and redoubts. He devours treatises on the strategies and tactics of sieges. He pursues expertise concerning siege engines. He compares running battles with direct conflicts. He has consumed every text on edged and piercing weapons. Yet the knowledge he desires most eludes him."

Abruptly, the librarian focused his full attention on the Bellegerin. "Above all others, Prince, Commander Forguile hungers for the book I have given you. He wants Sylan Estervault's *A Treatise on the Fabrication of Cannon Using Primitive Means*. I hid it among Hexin Marrow's *Decimates* to prevent him from finding it."

Prince Bifalt stared. "Why?" He meant more questions than he could express quickly. He chose the simplest one. "What does he want with so much knowledge? He does not need it. Amika has enough men to overrun us, more than enough. Our rifles cannot withstand sorcery. They are too few to withstand an army. He cannot need—"

"He does," asserted the sorcerer. Then he corrected himself. "He believes he does. His people lack the secret of making rifles. They have failed often. He believes they must have some defense against the carnage of Belleger's guns."

"Why?" repeated the Prince, too confused for any other query.

Magister Marrow sighed. "Here is your misapprehension. Truth for truth, Prince. Amika did not deprive you of sorcery. No Amikan has seen *Seventh Decimate*. Commander Forguile certainly has not. And Amika itself has been denied its use of sorcery. Like Belleger, Amika cannot wield any of the Decimates.

"That is *our* doing. *We* deprived both realms. Amika is blameless for your loss."

We—? Prince Bifalt's world reeled yet again. The very stone under him seemed to stagger. It became a threat. Shocked out of his composure, he protested, "You *lie!*"

The librarian shrugged. "When I have reason to lie, I do not hesitate." If he took offense, he did not show it. "But since our purpose is to test each other, lies will not serve me. Here is the book." He picked up a tome from a nearby pile. "It has not left my possession."

He held the volume so that the Prince could see its cover. The lettering was distinct.

Hexin Marrow.

Seventh Decimate.

It was the reason for everything Prince Bifalt had endured, everyone he had lost, every suffering inflicted on his people.

Indirectly, it was also the secret with which Slack had taunted him before dying. Slack had known that Amika had no theurgy.

The librarian did not surrender the book.

While Prince Bifalt gaped in dismay and mounting rage, Sirjane Marrow continued. "Amika has known for some time that Belleger's loss matches theirs. They are a more subtle people. Their spies are more effective than yours." As he spoke, his tone became severe. "But they also know your animosity matches theirs. If it did not, they would have conquered you long ago. And now you have rifles. That is why Commander Forguile searches for Estervault's *Treatise*. He believes—with some justice—that men are not enough. His people have suffered as much as yours. As many soldiers have spent their lives. As many children starve. You imagine you are weaker than your foes. They think otherwise, for better reasons. They have no rifles. They suspect that you are unable to make more, but they do not know how many you have set aside to destroy them."

He paused briefly to emphasize his next words. "Without cannon, Amika cannot save itself from Belleger. Now that knowledge is yours. Do you want to break your foes? You have the means."

Prince Bifalt hardly heard the sorcerer. His shock was too great: he was deaf with fury. "It is *you*. From the first, *you* have been our true enemy. *You* made us weak." Acid spat and steamed in his veins. *"Why?"*

He meant, How *dare* you? You have not earned so much arrogance.

***

"I would like to think," replied his host, "our purpose is obvious."

"It is not *obvious*. It is *wrong*."

Now Magister Marrow appeared surprised. He cocked an eyebrow. "How so?"

Prince Bifalt gathered himself. If he could not cut the old man down, or shoot him outright, he could hammer at him with honest abhorrence.

"Do you call it *right* that one man has talent and another does not? That one can kill another in perfect safety? That you determine life and death for a people you have never *met*? Does an accident of birth supply you with *virtue*?"

The Magister shrugged again. "It is not right or wrong. It is a fact. The world will not change itself to comfort your desire for justice."

"Yet," raged the Prince, "you call it *right* to interfere in the fates of realms—to choose who will endure and who will perish—to impose your will on all the world. *You*, who are nothing more than a man with a talent others lack."

A man is not a man at all—

"The right is mine," retorted the librarian sternly, "because the *power* is mine."

But then his tone softened. "You refuse to understand. Misapprehensions still rule you. I see that I must tell you the truth you do not grasp.

"My power is sorcery. It extends to sorcery—and therefore to those with the gift for sorcery. But it does *not* extend to the wills of men. Not even to those whose talents I efface or strengthen. I cannot make their choices for them. I cannot make *yours*. I can only encourage you to a choice I desire. I cannot prevent your defiance. Your mind—every mind—is closed to me. I cannot see it, or alter it. I cannot impose acceptance when you choose rejection."

—if he cannot enter and enjoy every chamber of himself.

Magister Marrow sounded honest. He was making an effort to sound honest. Certainly, the Prince could have chosen to die alone in the desert. But that was the *only* choice he had been allowed. Serve us or die.

His outrage carried him past the sorcerer's obfuscations.

"And *that* is your truth? It is not enough. It does not excuse you. You say I am able to choose, but you do not say what you want me to choose. You keep *that* truth to yourself."

What would rejection cost him, except death? What would acceptance gain him, apart from servitude?

"Why am I here? Why have you summoned me? And do not tell me I am here for Estervault's book. Do not say you wish victory for Belleger. That will be a lie. I will not believe it."

In response, the sorcerer scowled darkly. His tone became adamant. "Very well. You demand an answer. It is this.

"We want you as Belleger's emissary to Amika. We want you to negotiate terms with Amika. We want you to forge *peace*.

"You are your father's eldest son. Amika will heed you. Your father himself will heed you. But he will not choose peace if you do not persuade him. Amika will not."

Prince Bifalt gaped like a fish. "Peace with *Amika*?" The librarian's audacity stunned him. Sirjane Marrow's arrogance had no limits. "You expect me to grovel for *peace*?"

The librarian snorted. "If that is how you choose to think of Belleger's survival."

"*No,*" snapped the Prince instantly. "Tell the *whole* truth." Shock fed his anger. It was fire. "Have you urged Commander Forguile to beg *Belleger* for peace?"

"I have," answered the Magister. "He refused. And I could not fault his reasons. Why do you suppose that most of your spies and all of your emissaries for generations did not return? They were killed. The Amikan kings have no interest in peace. They covet only victory. And now you have rifles. Amika does not. The advantage is yours. King Smegin might well execute the commander if he suggested peace."

Prince Bifalt dismissed that assertion. It was a distraction. It was surely accurate; but it was not honest. Belleger was nearly destitute: Amika had more men. Rifles were not the whole truth. They did not justify how he had been used, or what had been done to his people.

Through his teeth, he retorted, "Yet you treat my *enemy* as an honored guest while you maneuver to compel *me*. I am done with your ploys and half-truths. Answer plainly.

"What will you do if I refuse? If I accept, how will I be anything more than your *tool*?"

He himself would not be a man if he could not *enter and enjoy* his own chambers.

Magister Marrow spread his hands. He seemed to consider himself irrefutable. "If you consent, you will do so because you have chosen that path. The initiative will be yours. The terms will be those you negotiate.

"Peace will preserve Belleger. War will not. Why would you refuse? Peace will not make you a tool. It will make you the savior of your people."

"No," repeated the Prince. He did not shout. Words could not contain his vehemence. Instead, he uttered them like splashes of blood from the cut of a blade. "I will not allow Belleger's fate to be determined by men who have not risked their lives in its defense. You have no stake in our war. You do not care what becomes of us. You do not seek peace for our sake. You want a defensible border, nothing more. You want *vassals* for your own war. When it comes, we will be your western buffer. You will sacrifice us against sorcerers who hunger for your destruction.

"I will not be your servant. I will not seek peace on your terms. I will not impose them on my people. They are dishonest. There is no honor in them."

Again the librarian cocked an eyebrow. "You have spoken with Amandis," he observed. "No doubt she was eloquent. But she is a devotee of Spirit, an assassin. Her world is skill and killing. It is war. *Our* world is knowledge. It requires peace. We strive to surround ourselves with peace so that there will *be* no war between sorcerers.

"Our motives are not yours. How could they be? But they do not diminish the worth of your consent—or the dishonor of your refusal."

Now, thought the King's son. Now I will finally have truth.

"Yet I *have* refused," he replied, steady as stone. "We will earn whatever becomes of us. It will not be chosen for us."

"You will sacrifice your people?" The old man sounded baffled; thwarted. "You *prefer* war? You can accept Belleger's ruin?"

"*I* do not sacrifice them," snarled Prince Bifalt. "*You* do. The power is *yours*. To you, I am nothing more than a pawn. You cannot fault your pawns when they fail you.

"You have tested me. Now *you* are tested. What will you do to me?"

Abruptly, Magister Marrow slapped his table with both hands. Braced on them, he rose from his chair and leaned closer to the Prince. His blind eyes searched the Bellegerin.

Prince Bifalt held the sightless glare without flinching. At the same time, however, he realized that he and the librarian were no longer alone. Indistinct at the edges of his vision, Magister Avail and Magister Rummage stood a few steps behind him, one on either side.

He ignored them. Did Magister Marrow want witnesses? Did he need defenders? Would they use their theurgies against him? Let them try. Their presence made no difference.

Earlier, the old sorcerer had been severe. He had been stern and censorious. Now he matched the Prince's anger with his own.

"*Do* to you? Nothing. You are a fool. We will not trouble ourselves to harm you.

"But we will not accept your refusal. You understand only animosity and conflict. So be it. I propose a compromise you can comprehend. A bargain. A way to *earn* what becomes of you.

"Our disagreement will be resolved by mortal combat. You will fight to the death against a champion of my choosing. If you prevail, I will give you Marrow's *Seventh Decimate*, to use or abuse as you see fit. I will give you both the book and the ability to act upon its secrets.

279

"If my champion kills you, I will continue as I am. My failure with Belleger will not stop me. I will turn my efforts to Amika.

"But know *this*, Prince," he warned. "I am not concerned with fairness or equality or justice. I do not promise you hope."

Then he straightened to his full height, glowering down at the man who defied him. "The choice is yours. Earn your fate. Consent or fight. Approach Amika and argue for peace, or hazard your life to gain what you desire. One or the other. But choose *now*. I have no more patience for you.

"Your alternative," he concluded, "if you believe you have one, is to saddle a horse and leave. Take Estervault's book. You have the means to destroy Amika, but it will not serve you. You will not live to reach your homeland. We will let you wander in the desert until the sun consumes your bones."

Prince Bifalt understood the Magister. —*turn my efforts to Amika*. The sorcerer meant that he would help Amika defeat Belleger. The Prince's death would deliver Estervault's treatise to Commander Forguile.

Still, King Abbator's son did not hesitate. He had never felt less inclined to falter. He had no other thought in his head. Why else had he been born? Why else had he sworn not to fail his father, or his people, or Belleger?

Facing Sirjane Marrow's opaque gaze, he replied, "I will fight." Then he turned away.

As he passed between the other sorcerers, he saw sorrow on Magister Avail's face, moisture in the portly man's eyes. The hunchback's grin flashed a vicious vindication. To both men, he nodded without expression, masking the surge of his heart.

Outside the chamber, however, he allowed himself the exultation of a man who had achieved a difficult victory. With every stride, the fury in his veins felt more and more like music. It was the calling of trumpets.

At last—at *last*—he had found his way. He had seen the sorcerers for what they were. And he had won his chance to humble them.

✳

His eagerness lingered until a servant had guided him back to his quarters. When his door was closed and bolted, however, and he had spent a time pacing out his gladness from wall to wall, his thoughts turned to the challenge ahead of him; and his mood changed.

He did not know who the Magisters would choose to be their champion. He only knew that the contest would be unfair, unequal, unjust.

But unfair *how*? Unjust *how*? For a time, the thrust of Sirjane Marrow's warning eluded him. To his mind, any form of single combat would be unequal in his favor. Against the Amikan, he would not deign to use his rifle. But against some more formidable opponent—Magister Rummage, perhaps, or a stranger from an alien land, or even Amandis—he would not hesitate to shoot. With a bullet ready in the chamber, he could kill as suddenly as any sorcerer. And one hit would be enough to defeat his challenger. If his shot did not end the fight instantly, the wound would give him time to recock his gun.

Did the librarian have some other champion ready? Whoever it was would suffer the same fate.

281

Why, then, had Magister Marrow *warned* him?

Long moments and long strides passed before an entirely different interpretation of the librarian's attitude, the librarian's threat, occurred to him. Its jolt stopped him where he stood.

He could have saved Belleger without the risk of mortal combat. He had been given Estervault's book. He already possessed the means to destroy Amika. His foes had no sorcery. All Belleger needed was enough time to *fabricate* cannon.

Then—

Prince Bifalt sat down heavily in the nearest chair. Even seated, he felt that he was losing his balance.

He had no reason to risk mortal combat. He did not need the seventh Decimate. Even without Marrow's book, Belleger's victory had been made certain. The librarian had said as much. The King's son could have saved his people with a simple lie.

A simple *Yes*. I will be Belleger's emissary. I will grovel for peace.

The Magisters would not have known his promise was false. They were able to speak in his mind, but they had no gift to hear his thoughts. Magister Marrow had admitted it. If they knew what was in his heart, they would not have needed to summon him. They would not have needed to test or trick him; lie to him themselves.

No doubt they would have questioned his acquiescence. But they would have accepted it eventually. What else could they have done? The truth would be hidden from them until he returned to Belleger and began to prepare his people.

A simple lie. A lie he had never considered telling.

Why had he not said *Yes*? Was he *now* too honorable to stomach falsehood? *Now*, when he had intended his submission in the desert, his "readiness," dishonestly? When he had confessed more than once that he wanted the power of theurgy—a power he professed to loathe—so that he could overcome Amika?

Asking such questions, he felt an emotion with which he was altogether unfamiliar. He called it an impulse to cringe. It may have been shame.

But he had an answer ready. The sorcerers had lied themselves often enough. They could do so again. They might withhold Hexin Marrow's book when he had killed their champion. And the same reasoning applied if he had answered falsely; if he had agreed to sue for peace. The Magisters might then reclaim Estervault's *Treatise*. They might pretend that they did so in good faith. He had found no honor in them. What had they done to deserve honor from him?

Even as he debated with himself, however, he knew that his argument was specious. It avoided the most important truth: the truth about *him*, Prince Bifalt himself.

And *that* truth was that he was sick of dishonor. Sick of the dishonor of his own intentions. Sick of hoping to defeat Amika by dishonoring his own people. *You are at war with yourself.* Sick of lies and manipulations and tests. *Are you not already corrupted?* Sick of bowing to the purposes of other men.

He had chosen mortal combat instead of falsehood because he wanted to live like an honorable man if he could—and die like one if he could not. *That* was the truth.

The monk of the Cult of the Many had tried to tell him—

If he failed against his *unjust* opponent, the cost would be high. But if he succeeded, the cost would still be high. And either way, he would remain himself. The dishonor would belong to the Magisters, not to him.

He had chosen to be a hard man. Belleger needed that from him. His father needed it. But he had not imagined that he would be asked to choose between a future for his people and honor for himself—or that the choice would be as cruel as this.

He had no curses fierce enough to express what he felt. The world was too big. He was too small to accommodate its demands.

And now, at last, he was able to understand that the Magisters did not truly care who won Belleger's war with Amika. For their purposes—a defensible border—one united realm ruled by either Belleger or Amika would serve as well as two lands at peace. If they urged peace, they urged it only so that the eventual defense of their western border would be stronger.

At present, however, they had nothing to lose in the Prince's fight with their champion. If he died, Amika would conquer Belleger—or the Magisters would defeat Belleger by other means. If he killed his opponent, Belleger would conquer Amika. That contest, like his refusal to be an emissary, and his missed opportunity to lie—like every possible outcome of his quest for Hexin Marrow's *Seventh Decimate*—would give these sorcerers what they desired.

Wincing, Prince Bifalt saw no escape from the trap they had set for him. *The right is mine because the* power *is mine.* Were there any chambers left in him that he had not entered, to his cost and diminishment? He did not believe so. He would have to fight the librarian's champion. There was no other hope for his father, or his people. If he died, his quest would be proven futile. If he lived, he would soon learn how many more of their promises these theurgists were willing to break.

None, he imagined bleakly. They would send him on his way with both books, Sylan Estervault's and Hexin Marrow's. They would rather sacrifice Amika than let the war continue. Any outcome that prolonged the fighting would weaken the west further.

And, of course, they would consider themselves blameless, whatever happened. Amika's ruin—or Belleger's—would be on Prince Bifalt's head, not theirs. *He* had chosen his course: *they* had not.

That thought was as bitter to him as his impulse to cringe.

✳

Later, he began to wonder when he would be called to fight. He was not ready. He felt drained to the bone, as if he had spent days contending with Sirjane Marrow. Yawning, he ate a light repast, drank a little wine, and went to his bed. Within moments, he was asleep.

In his dreams, Slack said endlessly, A man is not a man at *all*. A man is not a *man* at all. A man is *not* a man at all. But the Prince had no idea what the former sorcerer was trying to tell him.

Eventually, the words became a knocking in his head, which in turn became a knocking at his door. Too groggy for alarm, he blundered out of bed and went to answer the summons.

At his door, he found the monk who had studied him in Set Ungabwey's wagon, the nameless monk of the Cult of the Many. On a tray, the man carried a soldier's meal, the kind of food Prince Bifalt would have chosen to eat before a battle.

Vaguely glad that he would have time to wake up while he ate, the Prince gestured the monk into his quarters.

In silence, the monk entered. When he had set down the tray, he adjusted his cassock and seated himself in a nearby chair. There he waited, head lowered, while the Prince sat down as well, poured and drank a flagon of cold mountain water, then turned his attention to eating.

By degrees, Prince Bifalt shed the effects of sleep and dreams. Feeling more alert, he asked simply, "When?"

The monk folded his hands together in his lap. "When you are ready." After a moment, he added without raising his eyes, "Magister Marrow finds the occasion distasteful. He is impatient to see it concluded. But I stand surety for you, Prince. There is no need for haste."

The King's son had no intention of hurrying. He chewed another mouthful and drank more water before he spoke again.

"You offered to 'stand surety' for me. No doubt I have cause to be grateful, but I do not know what you mean."

The monk's bowed head did not hide his smile entirely. "Outside Master Ungabwey's carriage," he replied, "Tchwee informed you that the monks of the Cult of the Many do not use names. That is strictly true. At times, however, even we find terms of reference necessary. For convenience, as Tchwee says, you may call me Father. The monks who serve here are my sons and daughters in the Cult. If you would prefer some more specific title, I am Third Father."

Third Father? Prince Bifalt wanted to ask what a title like that indicated; but the monk had not paused.

"Offering to stand surety for you," he explained, "I made myself responsible for your conduct."

The Prince frowned. "What do these sorcerers fear from my conduct?"

Third Father met the Prince's gaze for an instant, then lowered his eyes again. "At the time," he said mildly, "they were protective of Commander Forguile. Now they have new concerns.

"You will soon engage in mortal combat. You have both a rifle and a saber. Suppose that you raise your rifle and fire, not at your opponent, but at some bystander. Commander Forguile? Magister Rummage? A stranger? Will it be an accidental discharge? A distraction for your foe? Who knows? Or suppose that in the flurry of combat, your saber cuts someone other than your opponent. An unfortunate coincidence, surely.

"In such cases, however, the fault will be mine, not yours. I am culpable for your actions. I will bear any reprisal or punishment in your place."

Shocked out of his composure, Prince Bifalt snapped, "Hells! This is intolerable! My actions are *mine*. Their consequences are *mine* to bear. You—!"

He could not find words for his umbrage.

The monk nodded. "My offer inhibits you," he said placidly. "It requires you to think of me as well as your anger."

"No." Restraining himself, the Prince snorted a harsh laugh. "It *frees* me." The idea was ludicrous. "Now I can kill anyone I want."

He meant, If you think so little of me, you are as blind as the librarian.

Third Father shrugged. "Perhaps. Perhaps not. I have seen the war within you. I am content to hazard myself on its outcome.

"When you struck at Commander Forguile, my first thought

was to ward you from yourself. You knew too little, and dared too much. But now—" He spread his hands. "Your circumstances are altered. *You* are altered. I stand surety for you because I hope you will come to terms with yourself. I hope to encourage the end of your war."

"The risk is nothing to me."

"It *is* nothing," agreed Prince Bifalt. "Your suppositions are chaff. Your inhibition does not affect me. I have chosen my path. The Magisters did not compel me. Their lies and half-truths did not. Other paths were open, but I did not see them, or they offended me. Clearly, I am a fool. Still, I am not fool enough to fight dishonorably while I am watched by men who have the power to destroy Belleger."

The monk nodded again, apparently to himself. "Then perhaps there are other matters of which you wish to speak."

This change of direction confused the Prince. "Other matters?"

Third Father studied the floor. "You face death," he said gently. "Perhaps it will be Belleger's death. Perhaps not. Your own is enough. At such times, some men open their hearts. They name their sins, or their regrets, and ask forgiveness. They seek solace. Or they have sentiments they wish expressed to those who will mourn their passing.

"I am a monk of the Cult of the Many. Say whatever gives you ease. It will be sacred to me. No other soul will know of it, unless you ask me to convey it on your behalf."

The thought snatched Prince Bifalt to his feet: a sudden inspiration; possibilities he had not imagined before. He had no secrets he had not already confessed—and no desire to repeat himself. Forgiveness did not interest him. Nor did solace. Yet there *was* something a man like Third Father might be able to do for him.

It will be sacred—

"Be clear, monk." He did not intend to speak harshly; but his pulse pounded in his throat. He had to force his voice past the obstruction. "Are you able to convey a message to my father the King? Convey it *privately*?"

No other soul—

The monk nodded. "Perhaps not directly. Nevertheless, there is no place on this continent where my sons and daughters cannot wander. Your words will reach your father. They will be sacred to any monk who carries them."

"And if my message is not words?" pursued the Prince. "If it is an object? Will my father receive it? Without the Magisters' knowledge? Without their interference?"

Third Father frowned at Prince Bifalt's boots. "An object that is also a message? I do not know how to answer. Certainly, no one will learn of it from us. But an *object*—?"

For a moment, Prince Bifalt glared down at the nameless man, gauging the monk's uncertainty rather than his own. Then he strode to the desk.

When he returned, he held Sylan Estervault's *Treatise*.

"A *book*?" For an instant, surprise overcame the monk. He forgot himself so completely that he faced Prince Bifalt. "It belongs to the Last Repository!"

"It does not," retorted the Prince. "Magister Avail *gave* it to me.

He said it is mine. 'Do with it what you will.' Those were his words."
If you do not understand yet— "The Magisters cannot protest at the use I make of it.

"It is my message. Will the Cult of the Many deliver it to King Abbator my father?"

At once, Third Father resumed his bowed posture. He seemed to huddle into himself as he murmured, "They will know of its absence. It was false pride to say that my life is nothing. You have made it too great. The Cult of the Many has served the Last Repository since its founding. *I* have served the library whenever service was asked of me. But now, of my own volition, I have offered to stand surety. If the Magisters see fault in what you seek—if they see *crime*—you will be held blameless. The blame will be mine. The cost of their disapproval, or of their outrage, will be mine to bear. It may fall upon all the Cult.

"They did not give me leave to meddle in your war with Amika."

"That is an excuse." Now Prince Bifalt chose harshness. His anger was tinder: it caught fire at any spark. "It is not an answer.

"I cannot command you. I have no claim on you. I only ask because you inquired. Because you *offered*, Father."

The monk did not raise his head, but his distress was plain in the hunching of his shoulders and the twisting of his features. A low sound like a moan escaped him as he wrestled with himself. "My vows," he breathed. "I have made too many vows. How can I choose between them?"

Yet his struggle was brief. With his hands braced on his knees, he rose from his seat. Avoiding Prince Bifalt's stare, he said unsteadily, "As you say, Prince. I offered. In turn, you offer me a lesson in humility—a lesson I was too proud to know that I needed.

"Give me the book. I will not involve my sons and daughters. If I live, I will deliver it to your father with my own hands."

Wordless with astonishment, or perhaps with triumph, Prince Bifalt entrusted the means of Amika's defeat to the monk. He had done what he could to preserve his homeland if Magister Marrow's champion killed him.

And he felt a moment of pride. He could say truthfully that he had not expected so much from himself, from the man he had become: a man who had found an impulse to cringe lurking in one of his chambers, and had turned away from the comparative safety of falsehood.

Tucking Estervault's book under his arm, Third Father went to the door, opened it, and beckoned the Prince to accompany him. They had kept the blind librarian waiting long enough.

Prince Bifalt followed without hesitation.

�֍

A soldier by character as well as training, he readied his weapons while he followed the monk. When he had checked the condition of his saber and dagger, he took a full clip from his satchel, slapped it into place on his rifle, and worked the bolt to load the chamber. Then he swung his arms and flexed his torso to loosen his muscles.

Routine movements like these were a form of meditation. They prepared his concentration, settled his mind for battle. He would need the full fire of his anger. But he could not allow it to overrule his skills—or his choices.

After some distance, he realized that Third Father was guiding him toward the keep's refectory.

He did not know why the Magisters had chosen that hall, but he approved. A large space would provide him with room to evade their champion. And if he needed obstructions to protect him, he might be able to use the long tables. Anything that delayed his opponent's attacks would give him time to fire his rifle and work the bolt.

As he and the monk approached their destination, he heard a growing murmur of voices. Apparently, the sorcerers wanted an audience. That, also, he approved. Witnesses to his good conduct would protect Third Father. Then, if the monk were not held culpable in the contest, he might be able—or be permitted—to leave the Last Repository.

The swelling confusion of voices told the Prince his audience would be large.

Still, he was not prepared for the size of the gathering. As he and Third Father neared the open entryway, he saw that the crowd numbered more than dozens of the castle's inhabitants, visitors, and servants; perhaps more than hundreds. Under the high ceiling lit by its blazing cressets, the hall seemed bigger than it had on earlier occasions. All the chairs and trestle tables had been cleared away, making room for multitudes around the walls while leaving an open space like an arena in the center. So many people speaking together in so many different tongues—and raising their voices to be heard—created a din like a reminder of hell. The only sounds missing from the tumult were the battle cries, the screams of fallen men and horses, the iron clang of weapons.

Third Father stopped at the threshold. With a gesture, he halted Prince Bifalt a step behind him. Many heads and shoulders hindered the Prince's view; but in the crowd he was able to identify a knot of savages like the Repository's physician, clusters of men wrapped in barbaric furs, and a large number of soldiers wearing plate armor. He also made out several dozen men and women with elegant cloaks hanging from their shoulders and oiled hair styled in strange shapes adorning their heads. Servants and other monks—Third Father's sons and daughters—were everywhere, as were edged weapons of every description, and races of every hue ranging from black and brown to stark white and an unnatural blue.

In the clear space, the arena, Magister Marrow stood alone. He was motionless with his head bowed, speaking to no one, reacting to nothing. In spite of his stillness, however, his posture steamed with impatience. His back was toward the monk and Prince Bifalt. He may have been unaware of their arrival.

In the rush of the Prince's first survey, individual faces were unrecognizable. But then his attention was drawn as if by a lodestone to the sallow skin, the characteristic goatee and moustache, and the orange headband of Commander Forguile.

Like many of the people around him, the Amikan was armed. Unlike them, he held his curved sword unsheathed in his fist. The light of the cressets glared like flames on the polished iron of his blade.

If *he* were the librarian's champion, thought Prince Bifalt, this contest could be fought honestly by men who were already enemies.

For a moment, he considered the prospect eagerly. Then he forced himself to dismiss it. The librarian had promised him unfairness, inequality. And he had been misled too often. He expected betrayal. He would not be allowed to confront his natural foe. Instead of fixing his ire on the Amikan, he studied the gathering with more care.

After a moment, he spotted Magister Avail and Magister Rummage. The plump man and the hunchback stood shoulder to shoulder, urging or restraining each other. Once again, they were holding hands.

Almost immediately, Magister Rummage seemed to feel Prince Bifalt's gaze. He turned his glare and his grin toward the Prince. The movement of his hand suggested that he was communicating with his companion. Wincing, Magister Avail also looked at the Prince.

Their notice served as a signal. At a nod from the hunchback, Magister Avail said, **Now,** in a voice the Prince heard only in his mind: the same voice that had summoned him. It did not reach his ears. **Belleger's best is among us. Or its worst.** The words made no sound at all. **Prince Bifalt is ready.**

Instantly, the hall was stilled. Every conversation and comment was cut off. The librarian jerked up his head. As one, every cresset flickered. The plump Magister must have spoken directly into the thoughts of everyone present. He had that much power—

Prince Bifalt felt the sudden silence like a punch to his chest. Light and dimness flashed in his eyes. For an instant, his heart seemed to stop. Then it began to beat rapidly, hurrying to catch up with itself. His impulse to cringe returned as Magister Marrow turned in his direction. He had to force himself to stand straight, with his shoulders back and his head held high.

What was *happening* to him?

He knew too well. When he had missed his chance to save Belleger with a simple lie, he had sealed his own fate without realizing it. Somehow, he had opened a door in himself that he could not close.

Belleger's best—or its worst.

There Prince Bifalt came close to despair. Now he understood that the library's champion would be his final test. But in that fight, he would not be tested by the Magisters: he would be testing himself.

Proving who he was.

Despite the librarian's sightlessness, Sirjane Marrow appeared to study Third Father and the Prince. However, nothing in his stance or visage betrayed what he discerned. When he was content with the silence, he nodded to Magister Avail.

In the same voice—a voice heard by every mind, although it was silent and held only sadness—the deaf sorcerer announced, **We do not approve of violence, but we have been reduced to it. You have been called here to witness mortal combat. Prince Bifalt will hazard his life to win power for his people. Our champion will fight for our hope of peace.**

Then he continued aloud, a change that made what he said sound more human. Almost bearable. "We have no ceremonies to sanctify such an event. We have never been driven to this extreme before. But we do insist on an honorable contest. For that reason, we require surety."

Gazing around the audience rather than at Third Father and the Prince, Magister Avail asked, "Who stands surety for Prince Bifalt?"

The monk sighed. Pressing his palm to the Prince's chest, Third Father instructed him to remain where he was. Then the monk made his way through the crowd until he reached the boundary of the arena. There he halted.

Still tucked under his arm, Estervault's tome was plainly visible.

Magister Marrow must have been able to feel the book's presence. His surprise was written on his face. "You?" he demanded. "Why do *you* have—?" Abruptly, however, he closed his mouth. With a threatening scowl, he nodded to Magister Avail again.

"Who stands surety," asked the deaf sorcerer, still sadly, "for the Last Repository's champion?"

From the far side of the hall, a stirring of movement passed through the throng. A moment later, Amandis entered the clearing.

As ever, she was wrapped in the demure white silk of her cloak, with her hands clasped in her sleeves.

When Commander Forguile saw her, he grinned like a man who now believed that he would be granted the outcome he desired. With practiced ease, he slid his sword back into its scabbard.

In contrast, Prince Bifalt let out a slow breath of relief. She was not his opponent. He trusted his rifle against her, but he had no wish to kill her. He would prefer to fight Magister Rummage, despite the hunchback's terrible sorceries.

But the devotee of Spirit was not alone. She was accompanied by Flamora, the devotee of Flesh. The Prince had not seen her since they were together in Set Ungabwey's wagon.

Her arrival drew exhalations like sighs from many of the men. A number of women shifted uncomfortably or looked away. The physician's kinsmen or tribe—the savages—made obscure warding gestures with their hands, then covered their eyes.

Once again, Flamora was arrayed provocatively, displaying a sleek expanse of breast and thigh: an invitation to desire. The gaze and the smile she fixed on Prince Bifalt were also invitations.

At the sight, his throat tightened, but not with lust. Instead, he felt alarm. Perhaps he should have been grateful that *she* was not Magister Marrow's champion. A contest with her would have been absolutely unfair, unequal, unjust—and not in his favor. An assassin he could fight: Amandis was more than able to defend herself. In contrast, Flamora's only weapons were her bright eyes and teasing smile, her scanty apparel, her ready womanliness. If the Prince harmed her, he would carry the shame to his grave.

Nevertheless, he was *not* grateful. For the first time, he thought he knew who the library's champion would be.

The notion gnawed in his guts like a rat feeding on nausea.

Opposite Third Father, the two devotees stopped at the border of the arena. Together, they acknowledged the monk, Amandis with a solemn bow, Flamora with a playful curtsy. Keeping his head bent and his gaze lowered, Third Father gave the women a bow as grave as the assassin's.

Seeming to tower in the center of the clear floor, the blind sorcerer waited until the onlookers had mastered their various reactions. When the silence in the hall was complete again, he nodded to Magister Avail a third time.

Still speaking aloud rather than in the minds of his audience, the deaf man commanded, "Prince Bifalt of Belleger, come forward."

Cursing himself because he was not able to breathe steadily, or to control his trembling hands, the King's son made his way into the hall. He wanted obstacles; wanted to shove men and women bodily aside. With rough handling, he could have summoned his anger. But the onlookers seemed to melt from his path. He reached Third Father's side with nothing except alarm beating in his chest.

The rage that had sustained him for days—no, for *years*—was gone. If he was right—if he had guessed his opponent's identity—

Without the bare acknowledgment of a glance, the monk nudged him to continue out into the center of the clearing.

Prince Bifalt obeyed. He had chosen this path, or accepted it. Like all his choices, it was probably a mistake. He should have known better, or thought more clearly, or been more cautious. Perhaps he deserved its outcome. But he was who he was. More than that, he *needed* to be who he was, without the obfuscations of lies and secret intentions.

Grimly, he avoided looking at anyone. He hardly glanced at Magister Marrow. He did not want to see the librarian's scowl of disapproval, or Commander Forguile's eager anticipation, or the open contempt of the physician's people. Striding dull-eyed, he advanced until he gauged that he was ten paces from the blind sorcerer. There, he took his stand.

Once again, Magister Avail spoke. "Champion of the Last Repository, come forward."

Sickened by his own lack of surprise, Prince Bifalt watched Elgart advance through the crowd and enter the arena.

<hr>

With that one ploy, the Magisters unmanned King Abbator's eldest son. Unjust, unfair, unequal. Accepting their challenge, he had done something worse than make a mistake. He had condoned a crime, a betrayal.

As Elgart passed between the devotees, Flamora touched his arm briefly; kissed his cheek. Amandis gave him a stern command, then waved him onward. But the Prince could not hear her. The silence was too loud. It was the drumbeat in his veins. The knell—

Silence or the audience took all the air in the hall. Prince Bifalt had to fight for breath. He watched, flinching inwardly, as the guardsman approached until he, too, stood ten paces from the librarian.

Elgart was dressed like the Prince in garments made for him by the keep's servants. His weapons were the same as his commander's: a saber and dagger at his waist, a rifle slung over one shoulder, a satchel of ammunition on the other. While he waited opposite his opponent, he kept his eyes lowered. Although Prince Bifalt searched for it, he saw nothing in his former comrade's face except determination.

Magister Marrow let the Bellegerins stand there for a moment. Then, his voice raw with vexation, he commanded, "To the death. Realms depend on it. *Honor* depends on it."

Whirling his robe, he strode from the arena to join Magister Avail and Magister Rummage.

Elgart's fingers twitched, but he did not reach for his weapons.

Prince Bifalt hunted for some spark in himself that he could fan into flames. He needed anger. He had never needed it more. He imagined asking Elgart, demanding, Is *this* the truth at last?

Did you intend to betray me from the first? To side with these sorcerers?

Elgart had promised—

But while the Prince struggled to find some accusation that his former comrade might deserve, Elgart raised his head. Their eyes met.

In Elgart's gaze, the Prince saw anguish. He saw resolve and daring. And he knew Elgart's courage. The guardsman had proven himself too often to be doubted.

The scar on his face gave him the look of a spirit torn apart.

The sight cost Prince Bifalt of Belleger his last hope. Elgart's distress and conviction—oh, yes, *conviction*, it was as plain as his distress—forced the Prince to confront his own despair. He could not fight one of his own men, a man who had stood with him and watched his back. He could not fight *any* Bellegerin, and Elgart was much more than a mere subject of his king. He was a *comrade*. At Prince Bifalt's side, he had faced arrows and grenades, bloodshed in darkness and the cruelty of the desert.

Nor could the Prince allow such a man to kill him. That burden Elgart would bear until its weight broke him. It would be Belleger's death as well.

—not a man at all—

Trembling in every muscle, Prince Bifalt drew his saber and tossed it, ringing, to the floor. His dagger he discarded. With his rifle in his hands, he removed the clip, worked the bolt to eject the chambered bullet, then set the gun and clip by his feet. His satchel he simply dropped.

Defenseless, and shaking like a coward, he walked toward Elgart until he was close enough to put his hands on his comrade's shoulders.

Elgart regarded him with consternation, even with horror; but the veteran did not flinch. He had ridden through hells and earned his courage.

They were cocooned in stillness. They seemed to be alone in the high hall. The cressets shed no light between them, except on Elgart's scar. That pale streak gleamed as if it were the place where his divided nature had been fused. Prince Bifalt needed all his strength to ask hoarsely, "You consented to this?"

"I did, Highness." Elgart sounded as hard as granite, and as brittle as shale. "I have more in common with Klamath than I knew. I have learned so many things! *Precious* things, Highness. *Life* has become precious. I want an end to war and killing.

"I came with you to stand at your side. You are my commander. My prince. I gave you my word. I do not wish to fight you. But I will break my promise if I must." Pleading, he added, "For *Belleger's* sake, Highness."

"Are you blind, Elgart?" countered the Prince. "My death may *destroy* Belleger."

"Perhaps," replied the guardsman. "*My* death may destroy Amika. One way or the other, we will certainly end the war. And when the war ends, the killing will stop." With an air of desperation, he insisted, "It *must* stop. If it does not, the struggle itself will destroy us.

"I do not call death preferable to Amika."

Time passed while the King's son warred with himself. It felt interminable. He had no unopened chambers left. He was sure he would be able to persuade his father. With Elgart's help, yes. King Abbator would understand that peace with Amika was better than death. But Elgart did not know the truth about the library's Magisters. They did not care who won Belleger's war. They desired peace for *themselves*. They had summoned the Prince, misled him, lied to him, because they wanted a defensible border against their own enemies. Peace between Belleger and Amika would not end the killing. It would only change who did the killing.

Nevertheless, Prince Bifalt could not try to kill Elgart. He *could not*. And he could not let Elgart try to kill *him*.

If Belleger and Amika were allies, they might stand a better chance of survival.

There was no other way out. The Prince would have to make promises that he meant to keep.

And then—

Then *what*? He did not know.

While his life lasted, he would question all of his actions. That was the truth about him. He would have to live with it. And he would have to face the consequences of what he did, although he did not know what they would be.

During the silence, Elgart's look of anguish slowly became confusion. When it began to resemble curiosity, Prince Bifalt made his decision. Without releasing his comrade's shoulders or his comrade's gaze, he confessed, "Then I have failed. I am not the man my father trusted."

That admission seemed to take the last of his strength. His legs threatened to fold under him. He had to cling to the guardsman for support as he turned to address the Magisters.

Hoarse with strain and despair, he vowed, "I will do what you ask. I will be Belleger's emissary to Amika. I will argue for peace."

For a moment, the silence around him intensified. He might have been as alone as he felt, as friendless and bereft. Even his father the King might repudiate him now.

Then someone somewhere started to clap. A few people joined in. In an instant, the whole audience erupted. Applause filled the hall like thunder, like an earthquake, like the shaking of the world.

While it continued, Magister Rummage's glower softened, and his deaf companion beamed. The librarian only nodded; but his posture relaxed, and his shoulders sagged.

The effect on Prince Bifalt was bitter. That so many people cheered his defeat tasted like gall—and yet he was not done. He needed to abase himself further.

He tried to go on, but he could not be heard until Magister Avail intervened. **Please**, urged the plump sorcerer to every mind. **There is more**.

The audience took a few moments to comply. Then quiet was restored.

"I will do it," insisted the Prince, "but it is hopeless." He spoke in a snarl. "They will not treat with me. They kill every Bellegerin who enters their lands. They will kill me before I can speak."

Magister Marrow shook his head. Softly, as if he wanted only Prince Bifalt to hear him, he countered, "You have the means to persuade them."

The Prince understood. He had been given Estervault's book. Belleger could make cannon.

His bitterness was not relieved.

Raising his voice, the blind sorcerer continued, "Commander Forguile. You have heard Prince Bifalt. How does Amika answer?"

The Amikan's response was rage. Savagery bloomed in his eyes like an ignited grenade. Snatching out his sword, he held it ready, prepared to vouch for himself with sharp iron. In a whetted voice as keen as his blade, he retorted, "This Bellegerin tried to kill me without provocation. I did not touch my sword, and still he tried. Amika *will not* treat with him. If he comes to us, we will not let him live. We have no use for peace."

Magister Marrow made no reply. No one said anything.

Prince Bifalt sighed; but he did not falter. He had fallen too far to reverse his plummet now.

His foe's sword he ignored. Facing only the Magisters, he said over his shoulder, "Third Father, you hold Estervault's *A Treatise on the Fabrication of Cannon Using Primitive Means.*" He needed to lean more heavily on Elgart; but the guardsman took his weight with ease. "I asked you to deliver it to King Abbator," who might not forgive his son. "Now I ask you to give it to Commander Forguile. He has been searching for it."

Surprise rustled through the throng, a hiss of quick inhalations and startled movements, but it was not loud enough to muffle the whisper of the monk's steps as he entered the clearing.

Half-involuntarily, Prince Bifalt turned to watch.

His own surprise did not resemble that of the onlookers. They had not expected his request, or the monk's possession of the book. The Prince had other reasons. He was taken aback by the sight of Third Father walking with his head high and his eyes bright—and by the monk's broad smile.

Crossing the arena, Third Father approached Commander Forguile. With a formal bow, the monk extended both hands, offering Estervault's book. He sounded vindicated, almost proud, as he said, "I believe you covet this knowledge. It is now yours, Commander, if you want it."

The Amikan's confusion was vivid in every line of his visage. A moment ago, he had been filled to bursting with fury. Now his own world reeled. He brandished his sword as if he meant to ward himself from Prince Bifalt's gift; from any placating gesture made by Belleger. But now everyone in the hall was watching him with the same disapproving suspense they had fixed on the Prince earlier. By degrees, Commander Forguile seemed to recognize the impossibility of his position. Thwarted curses clogged his throat. His king surely had not sent him to the Last Repository to make new enemies. Why else had he comported himself so respectfully? So obediently? His outrage would win him no allies here. A simple, imponderable gesture had defeated him.

And he could not ignore the Prince's offer. He *wanted* cannon—

Fumbling awkwardly, he sheathed his sword. With a visible effort, he unclenched his fists to accept the book.

Belatedly, he returned Third Father's bow.

Elgart wrapped both arms around Prince Bifalt to keep him on his feet. Everyone in the hall waited for the Amikan's reply.

Staring at Estervault's tome, Commander Forguile turned it over and over to assure himself that it was indeed the volume he desired. Then he found a measure of composure. Scowling bitterly, he lifted his gaze.

To the Magisters rather than to the Prince, he said gruffly, "I can promise little. I do not speak for my sovereign." After a brief struggle, he added, "But I promise this. If Prince Bifalt comes to Amika, he will not be harmed." Swallowing hard, the commander concluded, "I will stand surety for his safety."

Again the gathering broke into applause. The Prince heard a smattering of good-natured laughter, a few whistles, a shouted gibe or two; but they meant nothing to him. Without Elgart's support, he would have slumped to the floor. His fall had not reached bottom.

This time, Magister Avail did not quiet the hall. Prince Bifalt could not complete his surrender until the audience subsided at its own pace.

When he was finally able to speak through the fading clamor, he finished his quest.

"If Belleger and Amika achieve peace, I will return for Hexin Marrow's *Seventh Decimate*." His people would need at least that much control over their own straits. And if Belleger had such power, Amika would require it as well. In the name of honor—"Perhaps Commander Forguile will accompany me."

Then he was done.

Others were not. Elgart hugged him, whispering surprise, thanks, intense relief. People he did not recognize from races he did not know clapped his back to congratulate him. The Repository's physician came to stand in front of him. The savage nodded his approval, rested his palm on his heart for a moment, then withdrew. With his own hands, Third Father brought a flagon of ale which Prince Bifalt lacked the strength to lift.

After the first rush of well-wishers, the devotees of Spirit and

Flesh approached. The smile that twisted the assassin's mouth seemed to say, You are fortunate to be alive. Flamora kissed his lips: a brief, scented touch that somehow enabled him to raise the flagon and swallow a little ale. Then he drank more. Eventually, he could stand without Elgart's help.

When he looked toward the Magisters, Prince Bifalt saw the librarian grinning through his beard, his blind eyes shining with triumph. The Prince could almost hear Sirjane Marrow's thoughts.

Now we will have a buffer in the west. At last.

The sight reminded King Abbator's eldest son that he had other promises to keep as well. Someday, somehow, he intended to humble these sorcerers.

It would not happen soon: that was obvious. But he was not going to forget. Perhaps when Belleger had recovered its strength, he would find some way to repay the arrogance of the Last Repository's summons.